DiRTY
SPiRiTS

WRITTEN STUFF BY SAWNEY HATTON

Dead Size (A Dark Comedy Novel)
Uglyville (A Noir Novella)
Everyone Is a Moon (A Dark Fiction Collection)
The Devil's Delinquents (An Occult Novella)
Dirty Spirits (A Paranormal Novel)

EDITED STUFF BY SAWNEY HATTON

What Has Two Heads, Ten Eyes, and
Terrifying Table Manners?
(A Sci-Fi/Horror Anthology)

The Flesh Over Their Hearts

Deacon Codswell turned and walked toward the cabinet be-hind him. He opened it and collected an assortment of items from its dark shelves. He returned to the table and set the items down in front of Liam and Michelle. She tried to focus on each piece, her brain struggling to identify what they were. A purple cloth… A small, corked, black jar (or maybe its contents were black)… A silver blade with a slender hilt. A scalpel?

"Liam, Michelle, now I shall mark the flesh over your hearts, using ink anointed with both your bloods. These holy sigils will bond your spirits, each strengthening the other into mystically forged armor, so that when you venture into life as wedlocked partners, it will be infused with an indomitable energy, repelling the evils and excesses which commonly plague Man. It is written that when Aldrich Bukani received his first divine vision…"

Michelle swayed in her seat. Codswell's voice sounded farther and farther away, growing more and more distorted, as if she were underwater. Her eyes drifted to the portrait of Bukani on the wall. It rippled like hot asphalt, his stoic face stretching and swirling, mesmerizing her. Her mind hardly comprehended the pricking of her index finger, the tip being bled into the inkwell. Hands then stripped off her blouse and bra. There were other voices now, all around her. People watching her. Doing things to her.

She did not care.

She felt good.

DiRTY SPiRiTS

A Novel

Sawney Hatton

Cover design by
Lunnyander

Published by Dark Park Publishing
First Print Edition: March 2024
ISBN: 978-0-9886444-7-2

To Emily, for walking this path with me.

To L., for pointing the way.

INTRODUCTION

The first section of Chapter One is (mostly) true.

While I've never placed too much stock in ghosts—I neither believe nor disbelieve in them—I can't dismiss what happened that one time either. Many of the details of that encounter were changed for this book (e.g., it was a tin barn star that fell from the wall rather than a starburst clock), but the broad strokes are pretty much a blow-by-blow account of the only supernatural-seeming episode I've personally experienced in my life thus far.

So of course, being an author, I used it as inspiration to write this novel. People love ghost stories. So do I. And I hope I put a bit of a fresh spin on the genre.

But that's not the only reason I wrote *Dirty Spirits*.

Being emotionally—in my case romantically—involved with someone with a substance abuse problem was freakier/scarier than any of the otherworldly occurrences I've conjured up in the following pages. Although I had been forewarned about what I could expect should she relapse, I wasn't at all prepared for it, and while I tried my best to be supportive, ultimately I let my "Michelle" down. I failed her, both as a boyfriend and as a friend who could've—should've—done more for her.

Or maybe it would've been a lost cause no matter how steadfastly I stood at her side. Maybe the outcome would have been the same no matter what I did. Maybe none of it was my fault.

Still, it hurts.

This is a story where addiction plays an integral part. I consider *Dirty Spirits* more an Al-Anon story than an Alcoholics

Anonymous one. That said, you typically can't tell an Al-Anon story without relating an AA one. It was important for me to portray Michelle's experiences with addiction as accurately as possible (from a non-addict's perspective, at least) so as not to trivialize or misrepresent the ruinous effects addiction has on the addict. And on a relationship.

Some sinking ships you cannot save, no matter how much water you bail from it or how many holes you patch up. And it's hard—brutally, heartbreakingly hard—to watch someone you care about drown.

My "Michelle" found her way back to recovery, to sobriety, to a healthier life. And I moved away, got married, and adopted a cat. She and I both float on, but not together.

I hope the reader will enjoy the creepy, crazy episodes in this book. I had fun writing them. But along with that fun came something profoundly bleak and melancholic shadowing every sentence I wrote.

For me, the more terrifying true story has nothing to do with an angry phantom knocking down wall ornaments, but rather the darkness that haunts those affected by addiction, be they the addict or the ones who love them.

For those who are still battling addiction, I hope you prevail. For those who care about someone suffering from addiction, I hope you have the strength to stick by them and get them they help they desperately need.

I didn't, and I'm sorry.

-Sawney Hatton

"Of all ghosts the ghosts of our old loves are the worst."

–Sir Arthur Conan Doyle

A. BUKANI PERISHES
IN SHIP BLAZE

Renowned Phyſician and profeſſed Necromancer Aldrich Bukani met a fiery fate this Thurſday laſt when he periſhed in a conflagration whilſt aboard his veſſel anchored in the harbor off Baniſters Wharf.

He had fought, it was ſaid, and argued with another patron, in a manner deſcribed as violent, at the White Horſe Tavern in the late evening, nearing ten o'clock. A rouſed mob then purſued Bukani to the docks, where he attempted to ſhelter on his perſonal ſchooner, The Night Queen.

A perſon unknown, whilſt Bukani hid below, did throw a torch or lantern upon its foredeck. The modeſt ſailing craft was ſoon engulfed in flames and ſwiftly reduced to cinders down to the hull. None of its contents, compriſed primarily of books, furniſhings, and foodſtuffs, were ſalvageable.

Bukani, originally of North Wales, has in recent weeks fallen out of favor among the morally upſtanding Public when he was accuſed of practicing the Dark Arts, an allegation he not only declined to deny, but advocated for with profane ardor.

The remains of Aldrich Bukani will be inhumed in an undiſcloſed location outſide the City.

Newport Sentinel
Newport, Rhode Island
June 21, 1786

ONE

"Liam's dead."

Michelle learns about her ex when checking her Facebook feed on her brand-new iPhone 4.

She stayed over Doug's place last night, something she's been doing at least four or five times a week for the past few months. (Doug's thinking about asking her to just move in with him already.) They re-watched two and a half episodes of *Law & Order: SVU*, cuddling on the secondhand La-Z-Boy sofa before falling asleep in each other's arms. In the morning, both still clad in their matching flannel pajamas they'd bought together at the Hollister store in the mall, Doug brewed them a fresh pot of French roast while Michelle started making them breakfast, one hand laying strips of bacon into a hot cast-iron skillet while the other scrolled through her social media.

"He died yesterday... no, Friday," she continues, monotone, emotionless. Her reaction isn't unusual in these circumstances—what is it now, the third or fourth time somebody she knew from one of her AA groups has died? Though Doug would have expected this instance to be an exception to the usual.

"I'm sorry," he says.

The bacon is burning.

Doug turns off the gas burner on the stove.

Up until now, all Doug really knows about Michelle's ex-boyfriend—her fiancé, actually, but that had only been for a few weeks—is that they'd shared life-threatening amounts of drugs and alcohol while briefly living together in New York City, an arrangement that had been, in her words, a "shitshow." Michelle blamed Liam for losing her job at Morgan Stanley, for losing most of her friends, for losing her dog. She blamed him for a lot of things she lost. She fucking hated him. How could she not?

Michelle browses Liam's Facebook page for a while before crawling onto Doug's queen bed. She lies on her back, her long blonde hair bunched beneath her head in a halo. She stares up at the ceiling, quiet, inert, hands clasped over her belly. *Like a corpse in a coffin*, Doug momentarily thinks before banishing this mental image.

"Can I get you anything?" he asks.

She shakes her head. He lies down beside her on the bed and waits.

"You okay?" he asks after a few minutes pass.

She nods.

He waits some more. *I'll wait here all day if I have to—*

Then she rolls over and kisses him hard on the lips. Pleads for him to touch her. She needs to be close to someone, she says. To him, she adds. So Doug gets close to her, as close as a man and woman can get. Makes her feel him as deep as he can go.

The bed creaks and thumps. Wintry cool air swirls around them. Doug's dog growls and barks. The starburst clock on the wall falls to the floor with a resounding clang.

—

Doug ignores all of this.

He stops when Michelle starts crying.

"What's wrong?" he asks, though he already knows.

She just shakes her head. Coughs.

Doug rises, slips his candy-striped boxers back on, and goes to fetch her a glass of water. Beneath his IKEA computer desk, Rocket, his brown-and-white Jack Russell terrier, watches him, trembling.

Doug kneels and pats the dog's head. "You're okay, buddy." Rocket whimpers, licks his knuckles. "It was just a loud noise."

The dog stays under the desk as Doug stands up and crosses the room.

He picks up the silver wall clock from the floor, inspecting it for damage. He doesn't see anything, save for one slightly bent radiating spoke that may just as well have been like that before it dropped. He finds it odd that the clock was knocked off its spot, clear across the room from where he and Michelle were having sex. He supposes it could happen, though. Vibrations ripple, like an earthquake.

And I did just rock her world, he thinks. He starts to laugh at himself before remembering Michelle just got a blast from her past that's a shock to her system.

Doug tries rehanging the clock, but the screw is missing. He scans the floor, finding tufts of dog fur, a small paperclip, and a red Skittle, but no screw.

He examines the remaining hole in the plaster. It's ragged, roughly the size of his thumbnail. He speculates maybe the screw somehow got pushed into the hole, in which case it'll probably never be seen again.

Doug peers into the opening, seeing only blackness within the wall cavity. But he could've sworn—no, he wouldn't swear to it, because it was impossible—that he had glimpsed a flash of something… a flicker of some *thing*… a milky eye squinting back at him, sharp and angry.

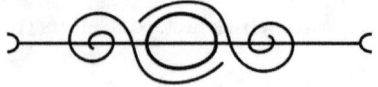

"That was Liam," Michelle says, dabbing her eyes with a tissue. Wadded scraps of Kleenex clutter the nightstand beside her.

"What was?" Doug says as he gives her a glass of water.

"The clock. He made it fall. To show he's not happy."

"With us?"

Michelle nods.

"So he's speaking to us from the beyond by messing with my wall decorations?" Doug smirks. "Think he could do something more productive, like maybe Swiffer my floor instead?"

"Fuck you. I'm serious."

Doug knows she's serious, but he doesn't want to humor her. He figures she must already be in a bad headspace, and validating her in even the slightest way might send her spinning out more. And to be honest, he isn't inclined to entertain the prospect of a ghost. For one thing, he doesn't believe in ghosts (his cousin Fran believed those floating balls of light in photos were in actuality spirits, and he always thought her a crackpot); for another, he has to sleep here and doesn't want to even imagine a phantom could be watching him, plotting some spectral smackdown on him.

All the same, Michelle's having a bad morning and doesn't need him pooh-poohing what she believes. "Sorry," he says. "I was only trying to, y'know… cheer you up."

Michelle gets up from the bed and, telling Doug she's calling Liam's mother in Philadelphia, leaves the room.

Doug initially finds her detachedness unsettling, but then re-assesses his point of view. While his love for Michelle is absolute, and he trusts hers to be the same for him, her ex-fiancé has just died. Of course that would affect her, trouble her. It's reasonable for her to feel this way, if feelings can be counted on for reason-ability.

Though she didn't ask for it, Doug gives Michelle her privacy while she makes the call. He feels strange about this, too. They keep nothing from each other, from sharing one another's kinky fetishes—he indulged her fondness for being tickled with feathers while bound and blindfolded, she his penchant for pervy priest/naughty nun roleplay—to divulging their innermost vulnerabilities. For the past ten months, their lives have become inextricably intertwined, almost symbiotic, so much so that Doug can no longer imagine his life without her.

"I love you," Doug says. Michelle is still in the kitchen, out of earshot. He loves her, and he knows she loves him. Yet the sentiment has thus far remained unexpressed, as if speaking the words to each other represents a nonrefundable declaration, an unbreakable oath, a point of no return.

Doug will gladly step over that threshold whenever Michelle is ready to. For now, though, he may as well vocalize those three little words in a vacuum.

Michelle comes back to the bedroom fifteen minutes later and relays what she learned from Liam's mom. His AA sponsor found him dead in his Brooklyn apartment after nobody had heard from him for a couple of days. The autopsy determined he suffered a massive cardiac arrest. Liam was trying to get clean, swearing off booze cold turkey. This, Michelle explains, is the worst way to sober up. It was too much for his heart.

"I'm sorry," Doug says again.

"It's just… pretty fucked up."

"Are you surprised it happened to him?"

"No," she sighs. "It could've been both of us… if I'd stayed."

"But you didn't stay. You chose to get out. To get better."

"So did he. And he died because of it."

Doug and Michelle go to lunch at Lula's Mediterranean Café. It's not too crowded. The hostess seats them by the mural of an old village street populated by a lone dachshund curled up in a doorway. They order from a pimply teenaged boy in a red vest. With Michelle's attention returned to her iPhone, they barely speak while they wait for their meals. When their food arrives a few minutes later, Doug digs into his chicken and waffles; Michelle deconstructs her Greek omelet with a fork as she again opens up to him.

"After I found out my dad was getting his operation, the first thing I did was buy a plane ticket home. Next thing I did, I popped some OCs, then had a drink. And another. And another."

Doug has heard this story from her before but doesn't interrupt her. She needs to talk about Liam, about her time with him, the good and the bad and the ugly. Maybe she would say more now. It always sounded to him like she was leaving something out.

"I woke up two hours before my flight took off to Chicago. I packed a bag the day before, so I was ready to go. But I was still pretty loaded. And I'm sure after I got up, I had more of whatever we had lying around our place. I remember Liam passed out on the couch, still holding an empty bottle of something or other. He quit his job the month before and hardly ever stopped drinking since then. He drank so much he smelled like nail polish remover. I woke him up and made him drive me to the airport. I should've called a taxi, but I wasn't thinking straight right then. Just needed to get to the airport ASAP and Liam was my ride. I don't even remember getting there. He might've hit something… a stop sign, maybe?… and then I was on the plane. That was our last day together."

"Damn," Doug says. "He smelled like nail polish remover because he drank so much?" She has never shared this detail with him before.

She nods. "He, like, sweated it out."

"That's pretty, uh…" He shakes his head.

"Messed up," Michelle finishes his sentence. She takes a bite of a lump of feta, makes a face as if it tastes nasty. Her omelet now resembles some dissected sea creature.

"When's the funeral?" Doug asks.

"Next Sunday, I think. Or Saturday. I have to check."

"So you're going?"

She looks Doug in the eyes. "Guess I shouldn't…" Then she looks away, toward the mural on the wall. "But I should. Liam's mom, she really liked me. And I liked her. She thought we would get married one day. She said that I would save him." Michelle snorts and shudders. Tears stream down her cheek and fill the tiny scar on her chin from when she fell off her bike as a kid.

Doug reaches across the table and takes her hand. "This is not your fault. You know that, right?"

"I know." Her sobs wane to sniffles. "I know, I know, I… I just don't know what to do."

"Whatever you decide to do, I'll support you. In any way you need me to."

Michelle looks him in the eyes again and clenches his hand tighter.

After lunch, Michelle wants to go to a meeting, and Doug thinks that it's a good idea. She asks him if he would come with her. He agrees.

Usually Doug attends an Al-Anon meeting while Michelle goes to the Alcoholics Anonymous one, both of which are conveniently held at the same time in the same old limestone church downtown, with her meeting upstairs, his in the basement. This time, however, he sticks with her, telling her she's going to be OK whenever she starts choking up again.

Truth be told, Doug prefers the AA meetings. Addicts are a lot more upbeat and fun than their family and friends, who in general share their personal experiences of heartbreak, helplessness, and glimmers of hopefulness convincing to nobody. Michelle's AA brethren crack jokes, hug one another, congratulate those hitting sobriety milestones. In Doug's Al-Anon group, one middle-aged man never smiles, one young woman always cries, and another rambles on about her chronic elbow pain. To top it off, AA meetings serve refreshments: coffee, juice, pretzels, and cookies. Al-Anon has access to the water fountain out in the hall.

Michelle doesn't speak at the meeting, doesn't share what had happened to Liam. It's a packed house tonight—at least three dozen people, from every walk of life—so Doug figures she may be too nervous. Or maybe too traumatized, the event too fresh, too raw to air out in public, even if these are the very people who could best understand, who would most empathize. Still, with all those eyes and ears on you, Doug imagines it's enough to give anybody a legit case of stage fright.

Afterwards, as usual, they go hang out at the Green Door Taphouse with Michelle's sponsor. Michelle was introduced—assigned, actually—to Kimmy at the first AA meeting she went to upon moving back to Chicago. A matronly woman in her mid-fifties with a silver pixie cut, Kimmy says she currently has three jobs: wedding planner, recovering alcoholic, and Michelle's buttkicker when she needs it. Accompanying Kimmy is her longtime girlfriend Lisa, a mousy (though quite mouthy when irked) hairdresser who dresses in premium outlet chic. Doug always thought them an odd pair, like if an ostrich hooked up with a swan. They obviously make it work though, having been together almost ten years, most of them spent cohabitating in a nice but narrow townhome in Andersonville.

"Sorry to hear about your friend, dear," Kimmy says when Michelle finishes telling them about Liam. "It never gets easier, does it?"

Michelle shrugs and sips her ginger ale.

Lisa raises her hand to get their waiter's attention. She does not succeed.

"I swear that's the third time he's passed by our table without even glancing at us."

"He's just really busy, Lis," Kimmy tells her. "You can see how crowded it is."

"It's his fucking job to multitask. He has a section he presides over. He needs to be equally attentive to every customer." Lisa's expression is a tart mixture of *duh* and *dick*. "I just want a goddamn refill of my Diet Coke."

"He'll come around again."

"And probably walk right by us again."

Kimmy sighs, half smirking. This is a fairly typical exchange for them on a Saturday night at the Green Door. The place had once been a speakeasy during Prohibition, a fact it markets to the hilt with not one but two life-size Al Capone statues on the premises. It's a small establishment, often mobbed with drunk and rowdy young professional douchebags. The four of them could have gone elsewhere, but Lisa loves their Spicy Hawaiian pizza, and the ambience is appealing, all buffed dark woods and brass fixtures and Edison light bulbs.

Doug thinks it borderline masochistic for recovering alkies to patronize a spot that boasts a thirty-page cocktail and beer menu, but he's never commented on it.

While Lisa continues sneering and scowling at their harried waiter, Kimmy returns her focus to Michelle.

"Are you going to Philly?"

Michelle casts a glance at Doug, as if hoping he will answer for her. He says nothing.

"I'm... not sure yet."

"You were pretty close to Liam's mom, weren't you?"

Michelle nods, wiping the condensation from her glass with her index finger.

"Do you think she'd want you there?"

"I know she does. I spoke to her."

"Then you should go." Kimmy says this like a judge issuing a ruling.

"It's just..." Michelle dries her wet finger on her linen napkin. "Hard."

"Take it from me, it'll be harder if you don't go."

"Why?"

Kimmy pauses a moment, considering what she wants to say. "Saying a proper goodbye to someone you cared about, even if it all went to blazes at the end, is important for closure—"

"Motherfucker!" Lisa blurts. "He just blew past us again. This is such bullshit!"

Kimmy regards her reproachfully. "Lisa, please."

"Fine. I'll just chew on my ice." She crunches down on the cube she's been sucking on.

"My first girlfriend OD'd on heroin during my sophomore year at college," Kimmy continues. "We had been dating for nine months—long enough to fall in love before I really understood what the heck love was. I was too distraught to go to her memorial service. Most of our mutual friends did. Instead, I mourned her by getting wasted by myself and passing out in my dorm room. When I woke up hours later, I expected to see Lorraine lying next to me smiling, happy as a clam at highwater. And then I remembered she'd never smile at me again, and more than anything in the world I wanted to say goodbye to her with all the people who had mattered to her. That was almost forty years ago, and I still wish I would've done that. I still regret not doing it."

"Does anybody remember our waiter's name?" Lisa interjects again. "Was it Danny? Donny?"

"Gary," Doug answers.

"Well, Gary's gonna get my heel in his ass if he doesn't bring me another Diet Coke."

Doug wonders if Lisa is addicted to Diet Coke.

"I was thinking," Michelle says, "that maybe it'd be better if I visit him later. You know, at the cemetery, after the service."

Kimmy wobbles her head as she weighs her words. "In my experience—and this is hardly scientific—I've found that being surrounded by friends and family of the departed, even if you don't know many of the people there, there's this collective energy created that helps you not have to shoulder the grief all by yourself. Because you're all there together to pay your respects, show your love, share your best memories. To heal. And as I said, it can bring closure."

"That part of my life closed when I left New York."

"Your relationship with him did, yes. But not your life with him. Your memories of Liam will stay with you for a long time. If you can reconcile his goodness with his sickness, these memories can be happy ones instead of haunting."

TWO

Michelle met Liam at the Dowhill Crest Institute, a private rehab center in Brooklyn. She was trying to kick oxy; he, alcohol. They had stepped out into the courtyard at the same time for a smoke, and he struck up a conversation with her, asking if she liked alternative music. (She was wearing an Oasis T-shirt.) She told him she was into Britpop. His preference leaned towards prog rock and (*ugh, really?*) '80s hair metal, but these differences in musical taste did nothing to dampen their instant interest—and guarded attraction—toward one another. Over the next three weeks, they sought out as many opportunities to talk (just talk) as they could find, getting to know each other in the safest space they could be.

After getting discharged from rehab, Michelle and Liam began dating in earnest, doing the things any normal couple would, but with a prickling sense that it could all crack and crumble in a moment of weakness for either one of them. They did their best not to acknowledge this, because more than anything they wanted to live normal lives. To be a normal couple.

So they went out for coffee, checked out the new movies at the multiplex, drove out to Jones Beach to walk through the sand and surf in their bare feet.

There's an unwritten rule (more of a recommendation, really) that recovering addicts should not be in romantic relationships with each other. But that seldom stopped it from happening, because fellow addicts most acutely understood each other's desires, fears, needs. They could keep each other straight.

Or they could drag each other down.

But normal couples did not worry about that. Instead, they fantasized about their future together, making six-figure salaries, riding around in nice cars, living in a beautiful house by a lake.

Their fantasy hadn't been altogether unrealistic. He had a dual degree in Mechanical Engineering/Architectural Design and was working for a top-tier commercial construction firm in Midtown Manhattan; she earned her MBA from Columbia University and landed a cushy, mid-level job with Morgan Stanley. They both had promising futures on paper. Their companies invested in them by offering generous sign-on packages and introducing them to some of the most powerful players in their industry, who invited them to some of the most exclusive parties in town. So when their substance use had gone from recreational to habitual, their respective employers protected their investments by sending them to Dowhill Crest.

There was an appreciable feeling of shame that accompanied a mandatory stint at a rehab. But there was also a bright side to be seen (if one chose to look at it in this light): they were there to get help, to get better, to *be* better. And for Liam and Michelle, there was the bonus benefit of meeting one another. From their kindred perspectives, they were destined to meet there. To be together. They would make each other stronger, happier. They would trade a harmful dependency for a healthy one—Love.

And so they did. For a while.

Shortly before moving in together, when their life was at its full-bloom rosiest, Liam took Michelle to meet his family for Christmas at their estate located a half hour outside Philadelphia. Their home—to not understate it, the place was a veritable castle—sat on a sprawling, frost-blanketed field surrounded by dense birch and pine forest.

It's like some fairytale kingdom, Michelle thought.

"Wowwww. I know you said your parents were rich," Michelle marveled as they approached the huge stone edifice in the hired town car. "But you didn't tell me they were *this* rich."

"Sure I did," Liam said.

She shook her head. "I would've remembered you saying they lived in friggin' Downton Abbey."

He chuckled. "We're not quite that loaded, but we do come from old money. Very old."

Their limo pulled around the circular driveway lined with luxury cars. It stopped beneath the covered entranceway, where they were met by a trio of valets dressed head-to-toe in black. Two of them opened the doors for Liam and Michelle while the third opened the trunk and whisked their luggage inside through a side door. Liam didn't tip them like he always did in New York.

Upon entering the manor, Liam began introducing an awe-struck Michelle to each of the three dozen nattily attired guests. First they came upon his great aunt and uncle in the foyer, who were primping themselves in a full-length oval mirror on the wall. Aunt Gerty was a grotesquely obese woman in a turquoise caftan and knitted turban. She transported herself by way of a souped-up mobility scooter embellished with cat decals. Her husband, the strikingly tall and formidably muscular Uncle Randall, sported the worst toupee Michelle had ever seen. It appeared to be made of wet straw, with green streaks—mold?—running through it.

"I hear you're working at Morgan Stanley," Randall said to Michelle, who nodded in affirmation. "I have a few senior-level associates there I can connect you to."

"Such rubbish, Randy," Gerty said. "The girl shouldn't need anybody's help to move up in the world."

"Well, a little help wouldn't be so bad," Michelle said, only half joking.

"Let me tell you something from experience, dear." Gerty regarded her with an expression that demanded she be heard and heeded. "There is a profound pride a woman derives from being self-made. Everything I've ever achieved I've earned, and not by necessity but by choice. I didn't wish to be beholden to anyone, especially to a man. Once men have a hand in your success, they think they own you or that you owe them."

"Actually, dear, one of my colleagues at Morgan Stanley *is* a woman," Randall interjected. "Vera Bel—"

"Shush, Randall. I am not addressing you." Gerty raised her index finger like an exclamation point and narrowed her eyes at Michelle. "You are the master of your destiny, dear. You work for yourself to build a future, a fortune, an empire. When your success belongs to you and you alone, nobody messes with you." She redirected her extended finger to scratch under one of her many chins. "And should you fail, it only signifies that you were undeserving, unworthy. A less desirable outcome, certainly, but at least then you know where you stand in the pecking order, and you'll be content with whatever crumbs people toss at you."

Michelle gaped at her, unsure how to respond.

"I'm sure she's up to the task, Aunt Gerty," Liam said, rescuing Michelle from her discomfort.

"The jury is still out on that," his aunt responded coolly before puttering off on her scooter, her husband following on her wheels.

"Huh," Michelle said. "I don't think your aunt likes me."

"Don't take it personally," Liam answered. "The only thing she likes is money, and anybody who makes her money. Such as Uncle Randall. Marrying a hedge fund manager has its perks."

"What does she do for a living?"

"Gerty owns—inherited—a company that manufactures all types of light military weapons. Mostly grenades. She calls them ballbusters. Named after herself, obviously."

Michelle chuckled, while her mind growled "*What a bitch.*"

As they moved into more and more lavishly adorned rooms deeper within the home, Liam continued introducing Michelle to the other attendees. Most of these amounted to the briefest of exchanges, the smallest of small talk.

An exception to this was Liam's older sister, Bethany, his only sibling. She immediately treated Michelle like they were BFFs, emitting gleeful squeals and jauntily tapping Michelle's arm as they spoke. She wore a blood-red tube dress that only served to accentuate her rawboned body. A sparkly diamond-studded band held her long Titian hair out of her face.

"Girl, you have the most stunning cheekbones!" Bethany remarked, twitching her nose. "Did you have them done in New York?"

"Pardon?" Michelle responded.

"Whoever worked on you did a stellar job."

"Uh, thanks?" Michelle said, still perplexed.

"My sister thinks you had plastic surgery," Liam explained.

"Oh, no," Michelle said to her. "I didn't have anything done. This is just me."

"*Ah bon*?" Bethany said, genuinely surprised. "Then I'm *sooo* jealous. Get her away from me, Liam. I cannot look at her!" She laughed with oddly quivering lips.

Liam's sister chatted them up for the next several minutes about all the terrific shopping in New York City. She repeatedly wiggled her nose and mouth like a hopped-up rabbit. She would have yammered on longer had Aunt Gerty not run over her foot with her scooter. Bethany scurried off to inspect the state of her recent pedicure, Gerty motoring after her, offering halfhearted apologies.

"Why does she keep doing that stuff with her face?" Michelle whispered to Liam when his sister was far enough out of earshot. "Y'know... the twitching."

"She has Tourette's."

"Really? She sounded normal. Aren't they supposed to curse or bark or something?"

Liam shook his head. "Beth doesn't have any of the vocal tics. It's all muscular."

"Poor thing. She must've gotten made fun of a lot at school."

"No one makes fun of a Fowlington," Liam replied. "Not for long."

The rest of the guests Michelle met were more distant relatives, less eccentric perhaps, but all carrying an air of unfettered wealth that made them seem almost alien to her. She wondered how Liam had turned out so normal.

The Christmas tree in the cavernous grand hall stood taller than any tree Michelle had ever seen in any home, just a few feet shy of the one erected in Rockefeller Center, she guessed. It was strung with golden, star-shaped lights and hung with hundreds of giant, gleaming ornaments. Michelle also spotted the random crude figure fashioned from twigs, hair, and what looked like strips of some kind of desiccated flesh, maybe rawhide. She asked Liam about them; he told her they were made by the children.

Michelle scanned the room for kids but didn't see any. Liam explained their Christmas dinners were an adults-only affair.

"That's kinda weird, isn't it?"

"Growing up, I saw my nannies way more than my parents," he replied, shrugging. "I'm the proud product of childrearing for the very rich."

Up until the white tuxedoed maître d' announced dinner was ready to be served, the only people Michelle had not been introduced to, or even seen yet, were Liam's parents. Everyone took their assigned seats in the dining hall at a long table covered in a red tablecloth and neatly set with shiny silverware, bone china plates, and a few communal appetizer platters featuring mousses and caviars paired with toasts and crudité. Two seats remained empty, one at each end of the table.

"My folks like to make a big entrance at these kind of things," Liam said as if reading Michelle's mind.

Michelle wondered how his parents could possibly upstage the manor's ostentatious interior.

Once the guests were settled into their chairs, the maître d' again addressed them. "Good gentlemen and fine ladies, it is my pleasure to welcome each of you to this, the 109th year of our annual Fowlington Family Christmas festivities."

Michelle stifled a shocked gasp. These days she considered herself lucky if she spent two Christmases in a row with one of her three siblings and her dad. Even then, it was always a different combination of faces—her father, this brother or that sister, sometimes one of dad's girlfriends, maybe a stray cousin she'd never met. She could scarcely imagine *all* of her family assembled together for any event in a single year, much less over the course of a century, except for, perhaps, a funeral.

"It is without further ado," the maître d' continued, "that I present your esteemed hosts, Nathaniel and Isadora Fowlington."

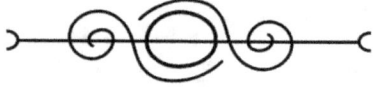

The maître d' unfurled his arm toward the broad mahogany staircase behind him. All eyes swept up to the landing where Liam's parents stood.

Nathaniel Fowlington wore a long crimson coat with glittery silver filigree and blue mink trim, a matching fur cap, and a fake blizzard-white beard. *He's dressed up like Santa Claus,* Michelle thought, *if he were attending some special royal function.* He even brandished a ruby-encrusted, carved ivory scepter. Beside him, his wife Isadora's golden robed outfit was even more dazzling, with a high-rise, ray-finned headdress and wing-like bell sleeves that she billowed with a flutter of her outstretched arms. She resembled a fair-skinned Egyptian queen.

Even without the regalia, Michelle would bet they would still exude the regal bearing of those born into wealth, power, and a centuries-spanning bloodline founded on both.

Holding one another's upraised hands, they descended the steps with deliberate grace, reveling in the reverential applause of their guests. Michelle politely joined in. Once they reached the foot of the stairs, Nathaniel escorted his wife to her chair at the farthest end of the table, kissing her middle knuckle before stationing himself at the opposite end.

"My dear family, both old and new," he said in a husky voice that boomed throughout the room. Although she wasn't family, Nathaniel's eyes rested a moment on Michelle when he said *new*; it made her scalp tingle like a schoolgirl getting her first kiss.

"We're here to observe the birth of Jesus of Nazareth, a much-vaunted man, a maverick, a martyr, and to some, a messiah. Whatever he may be, there is no doubt that he has merited his stature of distinction as one who has cultivated the indomitable faith of legions of followers across the world by launching the greatest PR campaign in the history of humankind. For that, he has earned my sincere respect. So let us raise our glasses to this simple carpenter turned self-ordained king."

Everybody did as instructed. "*Ut supra, sic infra!*" Nathaniel bellowed, then took a sip of his cabernet sauvignon. The other guests repeated the phrase—Michelle only managed to get out the "*sic infra*" part—and drank from their crystal goblets. (Liam and Michelle had been served sparkling apple cider in lieu of what was no doubt an expensive vintage wine.)

"And then," Nathaniel continued, "we have the famed figure who puts the merriment into 'Merry Christmas'—Santa Claus. For those of you here who are attending our holiday soirée for the first time…" He again looked at Michelle. "It has been a long-standing tradition for the patriarch and matriarch of the Fowlington family to don the costumes of Father Christmas and his beloved companion, Mrs. Claus. Isadora and I have built upon this tradition for nearly two decades now by dressing as different Christmas icons from around the globe. This year—"

"Happy Christmas!" a voice screeched behind Michelle.

All at once the guests turned their heads to behold a hoary old woman tottering towards them. A cream-colored nightgown draped over her, swishing on her scraggly frame like a riffled curtain. She could have been in her eighties or nineties or over a hundred, Michelle thought, being of that age where years no longer mattered because she couldn't look much worse unless she was dead. Only her emerald-green eyes hadn't succumbed to the ravages of time; they remained defiantly twinkly and vibrant.

"Mother!" Nathaniel snapped. "You shouldn't be traipsing around down here."

The old woman (Liam's grandmother, Michelle presumed) reached the dining table. "Oh, is that fig pudding?" She extended her wizened arm between Liam and Michelle, dipping her hand into the plate of goose liver pâté and scooping up a large clump.

Michelle then caught a whiff of some foul odor. Judging by all the wrinkled noses around the table, others smelled it too. A combination of rotten foods and fresh feces. A moment later, Michelle spotted the soggy streak of yellow-brown sludge on the back of the woman's nightgown, running from her butt crack to her kneepits. She almost gagged.

Liam's grandmother smushed the palmed pâte into her lips, smearing as much onto her nose and chin as she got inside her mouth.

"Please, Grammy," Liam said, unfazed by the repulsive scene. "Go back to bed. You might hurt yourself."

Liam's grandmother closed her eyes and chewed slowly, as though she were savoring what she likely still believed to be fig pudding.

"Rhian!" Nathaniel called out to a blonde servant girl who had just entered the dining hall. "Please take my mother to her room and make sure she doesn't roam off again. Give her something to drink if necessary."

"Yes, sir," Rhian dutifully responded. She gently grasped the deluded old woman by her bony shoulders. "Come, ma'am," she cooed. "You'll wear yourself out." Liam's grandmother hummed a chipper song to herself—*Mary Had a Little Lamb*, it sounded like—as the servant girl led her away from the table without a fuss.

"And clean her up!" Nathaniel barked as an afterthought. His mien betrayed a fleeting moment of irritation, then embarrassment, before returning his jovial attention to his guests.

"My apologies everyone. May I continue?"

All the guests nodded, eager to move on.

"This year I am portraying Ded Moroz, also known as Father Frost, who brings gifts to the children of Russia and Ukraine on

New Year's Eve," Nathaniel resumed, unflustered. "Like many folkloric icons, the original Mister Moroz was depicted as some malevolent being, in this case a demonic wizard who kidnapped naughty kids. But he has since become a softy in his older age, preferring benevolence over punishment. He is also customarily accompanied by his cheerful companion, the Snow Maiden, but this year our Isadora has opted instead to take on the role of the Christkind, an angelic sprite who also leaves presents for good children on Christmas Eve in Germany and Austria. Interestingly, Christkind—which translates as 'Christ Child'—is most often played by a young *female*, I'd dare say much to the delight of the menfolk at town festivities."

This comment elicited chuckles from his guests. Michelle followed suit.

"Thank you for once more indulging my penchant for long-winded oration. Now I shan't deprive your clamoring stomachs any longer!" Nathaniel lifted his goblet again in toast; everyone likewise raised theirs. "May all your coffers be ever full. May the walls around your kingdom be ever strong. And may we still be traveling in the land of the living by this time next year. *Nollaig shona dhaoibh!*"

The guests echoed the foreign—Gaelic?—phrase. (Michelle didn't even try to pronounce it this time.) Everybody then drank from their glasses, which were promptly refilled by the waitstaff.

The servers brought out the first dish of what seemed to be a neverending feast, each of its multifarious courses served to the guests from shiny silver trolleys. The holiday meal offered several foods Michelle had never tried before: French truffle consommé, foie gras croquettes, stuffed Cornish hens, champagne-poached pork jowls, lavender-infused sea urchin. Everything tasted decadent, if not always delicious. (The sea urchin was too salty and spongy to her liking.) She welcomed being able to occupy herself with eating while those sitting near her, Liam included, chatted amongst themselves about such diverse topics as corporate politics, international hotspots, and recreational hunting, none of which Michelle had much to say about.

After dinner, Liam took Michelle aside and apologized for his grandmother. Grammy's health has been declining for years, he explained, her dementia progressing more aggressively over recent months. Michelle asked if she'd be better off in assisted living. Nobody puts a Fowlington in a nursing home, Liam replied. This house is the only home she has ever known, and it's where she will spend her remaining days, his father had insisted. Grammy would die in a familiar place, around family.

Liam and Michelle mingled with the other guests, and she now found herself engaged in somewhat meatier conversations than those she had earlier, though most everyone was asking her the same questions:

"What do you do for a living?"

They acted impressed when she said she was a risk analyst with Morgan Stanley.

"How did you meet Liam?"

She narrated a sanitized version of their true story, swapping out the rehab center for a Coldplay concert.

"What do you think of this house?"

She answered variously that it was amazing, incredible, and spectacular.

Michelle also discovered she was the only newcomer at the party, which made her feel even more out of place, regardless of how warmly most everyone was treating her now.

She couldn't help sensing they were all judging her. Every word she spoke and gesture she made. Every detail of her face, hair, and clothes. And she couldn't help thinking she was coming up short in their appraisals. Aunt Gerty insinuated as much when she told Michelle she looked like "one of them New York uppies" before zooming away on her scooter. Michelle presumed she did not mean it as a compliment.

As the evening ticked down and the invitees cleared out, there remained two people who Michelle had yet to converse with at any length—Liam's parents. It was the moment she had been most anticipating, and most anxious about.

That moment arrived a few minutes before midnight. While the servants were tidying up the remnants of the party, Isadora Fowlington asked her son and Michelle to retire with her and her husband to the drawing room.

The room smelled of exotic tobacco. Flames in the small fireplace swirled and crackled. Michelle sat beside Liam on a plush leather settee. Isadora, still in costume minus the lofty headdress, was seated across from them in an oversized and overly ornate armchair, close enough to discern her expressions in the dim recessed lighting, yet far enough away to almost blend in with the décor and disappear. Having traded his Father Frost outfit for burgundy loungewear and black shearling slippers, Nathaniel perched in the furthest corner in a huge wicker chair draped with animal hides, like some imperialist king on an African throne. Both hosts nursed snifters of cognac; Liam and Michelle of course abstained, holding one another's hand instead of a drink.

They spoke for a while about nothing in particular, just idle chatter, until Isadora leaned forward to study Michelle's face.

"What is your ethnicity?" Isadora asked Michelle, as innocuously as if she were inquiring about her favorite TV show or what kind of shampoo she used.

"Uhm… white?"

Isadora snickered. "Obviously, dear. We're not blind."

Michelle blushed. Yet again she felt like she was being interrogated. Which of course she was. She was dating their only son and had to fully pass their muster, meet their undoubtedly high standards. They wouldn't want Liam wasting time on someone he did not have a future with. The Fowlingtons were affluent, influential people and nothing but the best would do for their boy who would carry on the family name. Michelle wondered if her best was good enough.

"What I meant is," Isadora said, "from what countries does your family originate?"

"Oh, from Europe mostly. Irish and German. There might be some Scandinavian blood mixed up in me, too."

"So, you're *very* white."

"Yeah… I sunburn easily."

Both Mr. and Mrs. Fowlington laughed heartily. The couple's wispy wavy hair, hawkish noses, and deep-set bright green eyes looked similar enough to make it seem like they could be related,

Michelle thought. First cousins, perhaps? She'd heard once that that sort of marriage arrangement wasn't too uncommon in old-money families like theirs.

"Sunburn! The curse of the Caucasoid," Nathaniel quipped. He rose from his chair and crossed the room to the fully stocked bar. He poured himself another cognac and leaned against the counter.

"Liam tells us your mother passed away a few years back?"

"Yes," Michelle said soberly. "She had breast cancer."

"How tragic. Very sad indeed," Nathaniel sighed. "We Fowlingtons have been blessed with many generations of cancer-free lineage, save for the isolated instance of melanoma. Does cancer run in your family?"

Michelle pondered the question a moment. "I had an uncle who got mouth cancer because he smoked too many cigars. Besides him and my mom, I think that's it."

"And how about heart disease? Or any other congenital disorder?"

She knitted her brow. "I'm not sure… I guess, maybe?"

Michelle braced herself for inquiries into her past bouts with addiction. She decided she would answer Liam's parents candidly, acknowledging that, yes, she had a problem with alcohol and drugs, assuring them she has had it under control for almost two years (as has Liam) and would continue to do so. She considered calling it a "phase," but worried that might sound glib.

Isadora tautened her lips. "My apologies, dear. We must be coming across as quite the prying parents."

"It's okay," Michelle replied. "I understand."

"Suppose it's rather hypocritical of us, as we strongly value our own privacy. We cling to it. It's not a matter of pride, mind you, but rather protection. Fortunes such as ours tend to attract the wolves and the leeches."

"Not to say that *you're* a leech, sweetheart," Nathaniel interjected.

His wife scrunched her nose abashedly. "Oh, heavens no. I didn't mean to imply that at all. We don't believe you're a... what is the term?... a gold digger."

"My mother has this charming habit of misspeaking," Liam said.

"That's alright," Michelle said. "I mean, I agree with you... I remember back when I was in elementary school, there was this girl who liked the barrettes that I wore. They were real pretty ones with all different patterns. She'd snatch them out of my hair and keep them for herself. And she was much bigger than me, a bully. She threatened to ruin my face if I ever told anyone."

"You poor girl," Isadora said. "That sounds harrowing."

"It was." Michelle knew she was nervous rambling—*why am I telling them this?*—but was now so far into her story that she just barreled on. "Anyway, I stopped wearing those fancy barrettes at school. My mom kept buying even fancier ones for me, and one day she asked me why I didn't wear them to school anymore. I told her some of the other kids were jealous of me and it made me feel bad. And she said, 'Michelle, you should never feel bad about being beautiful or being better at something than someone else. Because that's how God made you, and if people are jealous, then that's *their* problem.'"

"And you never tattled on this girl?" Nathaniel asked.

"No."

"Because you were scared of her."

"Because she was ugly and miserable. And no amount of my barrettes would ever change that."

Nathaniel and Isadora remained silent for several moments. Michelle worried that she had said something they disapproved of, that perhaps they thought her anecdote insipid or infantile. That they had decided she didn't measure up to their standards after all.

Then Isadora asked, "Do you think God exists?"

"God?"

"Yes. Do you believe in a god?"

"I do," Michelle answered, somewhat meekly.

"Do you go to church?"

She shook her head. "No. Not anymore."

"And why is that?"

"It's… uh… not my scene? Not that I'm anti-church or anything. I just pray my own way."

"Speaking for Nathaniel and myself, we believe where one worships God is not as important as how one worships Him. We are not churchgoers either, but we are observant. In our own way. It's the price we pay for the comforts we enjoy."

"Hey, it's getting kinda late," Liam chimed in, shifting in his seat as Michelle wondered what Isadora meant by "the price" they pay. "It was a long ride here from New York," he added. "Maybe we should call it a night, huh?"

Michelle wasn't tired—her nerves were still too wound—but she nonetheless welcomed wrapping up the conversation, if only to dodge the addiction questions that had not yet been raised.

"Of course. You both must be tuckered." Isadora stood, and Liam and Michelle did the same. The matriarch stepped toward Michelle and smiled at her. "I like you, Michelle. You're smart, and honest. And quite a lovely thing. I can see why our Liam is so attracted to you."

"Yes, indeed!" Nathaniel drained his cognac and approached them. "I can tell you're a keeper," he declared with a wink and a grin that reminded Michelle of a ship captain, one who had never encountered a rough sea in his life.

Over the following year, Liam and Michelle visited his parents a half dozen more times. She grew closer to them with each interaction, and they to her.

After Liam and Michelle got engaged—he'd proposed to her at his family's Summer Soirée, sliding a three carat, cushion cut diamond ring onto her finger as they sat on a stone bench in the statue garden—Liam's mother began calling Michelle "Beanie," which Michelle later learned was derived from the Gaelic word for "daughter-in-law." The Fowlingtons gave her extravagant gifts, treated her to the finest of restaurants, and regaled her with fantastic stories of their ancestors, of kings and queens, barons and bishops, warriors and even a warlock—Aldrich Bukani, a self-taught physician from Wales who had sailed across the Atlantic to introduce his unorthodox remedies to colonial America.

"Did you say he was a warlock?" Michelle asked Nathaniel while they shared a pot of tea one morning in the Fowlingtons' plant-filled, terracotta-tiled sunroom. "That's like some kind of witch, right?"

Nathaniel nodded. "That's what the authorities labeled him as," he replied. "And what they burned him for. He was a heretic, a heathen, a whoremonger, oh my!" He smirked at his own wit. "But Aldrich was in fact a spiritualist, to use the on-the-nose Victorian branding. Somebody who believed the dead not only could communicate with the living, but can have agency over them in particular circumstances."

"What kind of circumstances?"

"Well, mind you, this was the 17th century, when God and ghosts affected everything from your home to your hair. But Aldrich took his beliefs a step further, theorizing that spirits could play an active role in the lives of the living. He thought a spirit may be tethered to a person, and then help them by directing their actions. So he'd bind the soul of a deceased loved one to a relative of theirs who was suffering from health issues, mental infirmities, even financial troubles. The spirit would thus guide them onto the right path, healing them and blessing them."

Michelle sipped her tea. "You mean, it would possess them?"

Nathaniel shrugged and *hmm*'d. "You might call it that—possession. Aldrich had called it psychical aegis, which amounts to practically the same thing. At any rate, he considered it a bona fide medical treatment. And who's to say he was wrong?"

"Well, it is kinda… Hollywood horror storyish."

"You think so?"

"To be honest, I don't really believe in that stuff," Michelle admitted. "Ghosts or demons. Aliens. The Loch Ness Monster."

"When you bunch them together like that, then yes, I suppose it does sound rather absurd. Yet, I think Shakespeare expressed it best, if I may paraphrase: 'There are more things in heaven and earth, Michelle, than are dreamt of in your philosophy.' And I can attest to the truth of that."

Nathaniel nodded at her and did not elaborate.

The final time Liam and Michelle stayed together at the Fowlington estate was for Thanksgiving. It was a much smaller, more intimate gathering than their Christmas party or the Summer Soirée. Eight well-dressed individuals attended in total: Michelle, Liam, Nathaniel, Isadora, Bethany, Uncle Randy, and Aunt Gerty (with her silly cat-stickered scooter). There was also a man in an all-black suit whom Michelle had never met, introduced to her as Deacon Codswell, a longtime spiritual advisor for the family. Absent were any kitchen workers or waitstaff. Michelle wondered if they had all been given the day off.

To Michelle's surprise, Nathaniel and Isadora had prepared the holiday meal themselves, an elevated traditional carte du jour of orange-glazed roast turkey, brown butter mashed potatoes, maple-drizzled squash, and pickled brussels sprouts, capped off with a Dutch apple pie that tasted a little strange to Michelle, of some sort of spice she couldn't identify. Something bitter, almost coppery. She could only eat a few bites of it.

"Do you not like the pie, Beanie?" Isadora asked her.

"No, I do. It's good."

"Are you sure? You made a face when you—"

"Bet it's the allspice," Nathaniel cut in. "It wasn't fresh. Told you it smelled funky, Dora."

"Really, everything was delicious," Michelle said. "I'm just really full."

"Say no more, sweetheart," Nathaniel said. "Often our bellies are not big enough to accommodate our appetites. And you're such a tiny thing. Wouldn't want you to explode!"

"Especially with the staff away. Who would clean it up?" Uncle Randall joked.

"Oh, I can help clear the table," Michelle volunteered.

Isadora waved her hand dismissively. "No need, dear. Mary and Rhian are both returning at midnight. They'll take care of it."

Michelle realized she was feeling kind of buzzed, her brain a bit muzzy, her body slightly numb. Something wasn't right. She wondered if she should say something.

She speculated she might be having an allergic reaction to the gourmet food, to some uncommon ingredient she never had before. Yet this only vaguely concerned her since, truth be told, it felt really nice. She hadn't felt like this since before she quit oxycodone.

"Are you alright?" someone asked.

It took Michelle a moment to register that it was Isadora who was speaking to her.

"Y-yes. I'm fine."

"Very well then, shall we all make our way to the Thinning Room?" Nathaniel suggested with unrestrained enthusiasm.

Everyone around Michelle agreed.

"Whassa thinning room?" she whisper-slurred into Liam's ear.

"You'll see," he answered teasingly, offering her a reassuring smile. "C'mon."

They crammed into the wainscot-walled elevator—it always blew Michelle's mind that a private residence had an elevator—and rode it to the fourth floor. She didn't even know there was another floor; from outside the home, she had only ever counted three stories. There wasn't even a button for "4" on the elevator's bronze control panel. Nathaniel had pressed the first and third buttons at once, giving Michelle a smile and wink after he did it.

They disembarked from the elevator into a wide, carpeted corridor lined with flocked ivy-green wallpaper and lit with gold-leaf sconces. Nathaniel and Isadora led the procession, followed by Liam and Michelle, then the rest of the party behind them, with Deacon Codswell bringing up the rear. Michelle's light-headedness didn't much hamper her walking—it was a bit like floating in a bubble—but she still appreciated Liam wrapping his strong, supportive arm around her waist.

The corridor doglegged into another at least twice the length. Mounted on the walls between more antique sconces were framed portrait photographs of different men and women. Most of the people appeared to be over fifty or sixty years old, though a few seemed younger, with a couple probably only in their teens. The pictures looked more dated the farther they advanced along the hallway. The photos then became exquisite paintings, and then the paintings became detailed sketches on yellowed parchment, leading up to a set of raw timber doors with wrought iron handles and hinges.

―

"Are theeese… your relatives?" Michelle asked Liam as they passed the portraits.

"Yeah," he answered. "Dead ones."

Nathaniel opened the double doors and ushered everyone into a small room. As Liam led her by the hand, Michelle's eyes roved the space. Three short rows of wooden benches faced what appeared to be a low-profile stage set with a rustic wooden table and chairs, with a tall oaken cabinet placed against the rear wall. An imposing painting of a generously bearded man wearing a gray waistcoat and green cravat—the warlock Aldrich Bukani?—hung in an alcove that seemed expressly created to exhibit the artwork. The domed ceiling featured bas-reliefs depicting the phases of the moon, interspersed with abstract etchings done in a style somewhere between cave drawings and Egyptian hiero-glyphs. A bright white sphere was suspended from the vertex of the dome, serving as the room's sole source of illumination.

It's like a theater, Michelle thought. *Or a chapel.*

Liam navigated her to the stage and settled her into a chair at one side of the table, then took a seat next to her, while his family members sat down in the pews behind them. Michelle al-most giggled, wondering if they were about to put on some sort of improv show, but she could sense the solemnity in the air, a palpable sacredness charging this undeniably special room. Her skin tingled all over, something she recognized as nervousness, but with her mind cloaked in a pale fog, she found herself able to ignore it.

Codswell circled around the table and stood opposite Liam and Michelle.

"*Benenachtia*," he began. "Liam, Michelle, it is an honor to address you here today. Yes, I say 'honor,' for your union shall preserve the Fowlington family bloodline, and certainly that is something to be exalted."

Liam gently squeezed Michelle's hand and her heart danced.

"The Fowlington family is one steeped in tradition, both corporeal and spiritual," Codswell continued. "Many of the clan's venerated rituals have endured for millennia. And this chamber in which you now sit has served as the venue for many of these rituals for more than a century. In fact, some of the materials used to construct this hallowed space are considerably older than that, such materials serving to facilitate a cross-dimensional conduit, *thinning* the barrier between this world and the next."

The deacon's red-flecked blue eyes lingered on Michelle as he spoke this last sentence. She met his stare, almost spellbound by it. Codswell was a handsome man, probably in his forties, with sandy blond hair and a clean-shaven face. *Looks like a Ken doll*, Michelle concluded. She would bet he'd had some plastic surgery done.

"Aye, we fold these blessed fragments from our past into the fabric of our present to fortify it, and we sanctify our present to ensure our future is likewise blessed. Hence the reason we are here tonight, to perform the consecratory ritual of *Gálffwöting…*"

The strange word sounded to Michelle like *golf-voting*.

"This rite purifies the souls of a betrothed couple, preparing them for their spiritual synthesis, so their forthcoming nuptials and life together thereafter should be free of strife and sorrow."

Michelle tittered without knowing what amused her. Why was she feeling so loopy?

Why couldn't she always feel like this?

Deacon Codswell turned and walked toward the cabinet behind him. He opened it and collected an assortment of items from its dark shelves. He returned to the table and set the items down in front of Liam and Michelle. She tried to focus on each piece, her brain struggling to identify what they were. A purple cloth... A small, corked, black jar (or maybe its contents were black)... A silver blade with a slender hilt. A scalpel?

"Liam, Michelle, now I shall mark the flesh over your hearts, using ink anointed with both your bloods. These holy sigils will bond your spirits, each strengthening the other into mystically forged armor, so that when you venture into life as wedlocked partners, it will be infused with an indomitable energy, repelling the evils and excesses which commonly plague Man. It is written that when Aldrich Bukani received his first divine vision..."

Michelle swayed in her seat. Codswell's voice sounded farther and farther away, growing more and more distorted, as if she were underwater. Her eyes drifted to the portrait of Bukani on the wall. It rippled like hot asphalt, his stoic face stretching and swirling, mesmerizing her. Her mind hardly comprehended the pricking of her index finger, the tip being bled into the inkwell. Hands then stripped off her blouse and bra. There were other voices now, all around her. People watching her. Doing things to her.

She did not care.

She felt good.

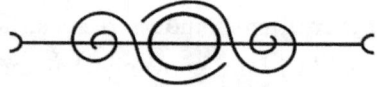

Michelle awoke with a hurricane of a headache. She was in Liam's elegantly sparse room, in the same four-poster bed he'd slept in as a teenager. Liam lay beside her, still asleep, his light snores reminding her of leaves rustling in the wind. Normally she found his snoring soothing, but not now.

Although she knew where she was, she felt disoriented, disconnected. She couldn't remember how she got back to his room. Actually, she remembered very little from the night before. It was the kind of blackout she'd experience when she got so loaded time skipped ahead.

Michelle slid out of the bed—she was only wearing her green sateen nightshirt, again with no memory of when she had changed into it—and shambled into the en-suite bathroom. After peeing, she went to the sink and washed her hands (where did that Band-Aid on her finger come from?), then studied herself in the vanity mirror. Sunken half-circles underlined her glassy eyes. Her lips were dry, leathery. She stuck out her tongue and saw it was coated in a white film. She unzipped her toiletry bag, fetching her toothbrush and toothpaste from it, and gave her mouth a full scouring. She spit the chalky foam into the basin and quickly rinsed it down the drain as if it were teeming with disease.

As Michelle fussed with her mega-mussy hair—it looked like it had lost a brawl with her pillow—her other hand scratched at an itch on her chest. She felt something there, underneath her shirt. She stretched down the collar to discover a square gauze bandage taped over her sternum. She gingerly peeled it off…

"What the hell is *this*, Liam?"

Liam jolted awake, springing upright in the bed.

"Huh? Wha? What's wrong?"

"This. This!"

He swiveled his head toward Michelle's voice, blinking the bleariness from his eyes until he could clearly see her standing in the doorway of the bathroom. She was pulling the neckline of her nightshirt down to show him her chest. There between her breasts, slathered in a clear gel, was an intense dark purple tattoo, still red and raw around its edges—a small diamond in the center of a circle that looked like it had burst apart and bent out of shape.

"H-how d-did I…" she stammered. "Where did this come from?"

"Chill out, Chelle," Liam responded to her shock with an almost patronizing nonchalance. He then took off his tie-dyed T-shirt to reveal a bandage over his breastbone. He removed it to uncover the same tattoo on his chest. "See? I got one too."

Michelle furrowed her brow. "Why?"

"It's called a bonding sigil. It's this really powerful symbol to ensure we have a successful marriage. It's like a blessing, a good luck charm that protects us from anything that could harm us. So from now on we won't have any problems with our wedding, our jobs, or anything else in our life together. Isn't that cool?"

Michelle stared blankly at him without answering.

"And you always said you wanted us to get matching tattoos, right?" Liam grinned at her, hovering his hand over the sigil. "I think these are perfect. Don't you?"

"Shit, Liam, it's *my* body," Michelle fumed. "This should've been my choice. I mean, as your future wife, I would've liked to have been at least part of the decision."

He shrugged his shoulders. "You *were*. We talked about it last night. At dinner. You were totally fine with it. Don't you remember?"

Michelle glared at him a moment longer, then shut her eyes and combed her memory. "No," she sighed. "I don't remember much of anything from last night."

"Hmm. That's weird. You know, you weren't feeling great, so maybe that has something to do with it. My dad thought there was some bad spice in the pie."

Michelle squinched her lips. "Wait… I think I… There was this room. A theater?"

Liam nodded. "The Thinning Room. That's where we did the ritual. When we got the tats."

She shook her head in frustration. "It's like there's this door in my brain that won't fully open."

"Well, maybe it'll come back to you later."

Michelle rotated her body toward the oval bureau mirror next to her. She examined her tattoo critically.

"It's kinda ugly."

"It's special, Chelle. It means you've been accepted by my family." He beams at her. "How does it feel to be the soon-to-be Mrs. Fowlington?"

"I feel like I'm gonna throw up."

Liam frowned. "Really?"

She looked at him sheepishly and forced a smile. "In a good way."

THREE

Michelle decides she's going to attend Liam's funeral that Sunday, though her heart doesn't seem in it... or rather, too much in it. To Doug, she sounds heartbroken. Maybe she is. She and Liam had a history that probably wasn't all shit and shambles. There was a time when she wanted to marry the guy. She must've really loved him once. Maybe a part of her still does—

Doug shunts aside pangs of jealousy, recognizing such a response is unhelpful, not to mention irrational. The guy's dead, after all.

"Guess I'll buy the plane ticket to Philly today," Michelle says. She and Doug sit across from one another at the IKEA dinette table in his kitchen. "Hope it's not too crazy expensive. You know, buying it almost last minute."

"I think some airlines offer discounts if you're flying to a funeral."

Michelle nods. "I'll check into that."

"Do you want me to come with you?" Doug asks somewhat reticently. It sounds terrible, going to his girlfriend's ex-fiancé's funeral, but it sounds worse having her deal with it alone.

"It's gonna cost too much, both of us going."

"We could drive there."

"Drive? How long would that take?"

Doug performs some quick mental calculations based on his memory of driving to New York City. "We could do it in one day if we wanted to. Or we could break it up into two days so we're not so beat when we get there. We can leave early tomorrow. Stop midway, probably in Ohio, and get a room for the night. Should make it to Philly the next day by late Saturday afternoon, evening-ish. We can find a motel nearby."

"Liam's parents said I could stay over at their manor house."

"Well, that would save us some money." Doug glances at his fingernails, frayed from restocking cat trees and assembling dog kennels. He puts his hands beneath the table. "Do you think his folks would mind me there?"

"I think they'll have bigger things on their mind."

Doug nods. "So then, should I pack?"

Michelle weighs the idea a moment, her tongue circling the inside of her cheek, her eyes fixed on the Petique Boutique mug she's drinking apple cider from.

"Are you sure you want to come?" she asks.

"Yeah," Doug answers, less assuredly than he intended. He rallies his voice. "Of course. I want to be there for you. If you need me."

"It might be kind of… weird."

"For you or for me?"

"Either?"

"Would you prefer I didn't go? It's okay if you do. I'd understand."

Michelle shakes her head. "I just don't want you to be uncomfortable."

"That doesn't matter." Doug leans toward her, cupping his palms on her knees under the table. "I'm not expecting it to be a barrel of laughs. But I know going will be difficult for you. I'm always here for you whenever things are difficult. And I'll be there for you too, if that's where you want me to be."

She grins at him and caresses his forearms. "You're the best, you know that?"

"So I've heard."

Michelle feigns outrage, dropping her jaw and crossing her arms. "What hussy also told you you're the best?"

"I can't help it if all the cat ladies at the mall find me irresistible."

"They better keep their paws off you," she says, cocking an eyebrow. "I've already marked you."

Doug smirks at Michelle. How much more confident she has become over these past few months. Funnier, flirtier. So much more *her*, the *her* he's fallen in love with. So different from the Michelle he first met at the mall last spring…

Doug noticed Michelle lacing and unlacing her fingers in her lap. She was nervous, he figured, though he couldn't fathom why she would be. Not for *this* job.

She looked very put together, very business-ready in her pearl white blouse and raven black blazer with a matching pencil skirt.

Gorgeous long, wheat blonde hair and a slim, slinky figure. So professional, so posh. So hot. Why did she want to work *here*?

They sat opposite one another in the food court at a black-laminate table covered with washrag streaks. Doug, the general manager of the Petique Boutique pet supply store in the Chicago Ridge Mall, wore his work uniform—khaki pants, brown shoes, and blue polo shirt embroidered with the company's bird-on-cat-on-dog logo with his plastic nametag pinned above it. He ran through the standard "tell me about a time" interview questions and Michelle provided answers convincing him that the job—a sales associate position—was well below her level of experience. Hell, she didn't appear to have any relevant experience for this job at all.

He looked at her intently when she spoke, to give her the impression that he was paying attention. And he was, but he was also admiring her drowsy green eyes, her perfect coy smile, and the smattering of faint freckles sprinkled on her cheeks.

"So why do you want to work at Petique Boutique?" Doug asked. It was the last question on his list. He wished it wasn't.

"I really love animals," she answered. "I used to have a dog. A Yorkie."

"Those are sweet dogs. I have a Jack Russell."

"Those are super hyper, right?"

"Oh yeah. I named him Rocket."

"Because he's so fast?"

"Sure is." Doug scratched his scruffy chin with the plunger of his pen. "He's so fast he can literally shoot himself into outer space."

"Wow. That's a pretty amazing trick."

"He's a great fetcher, too. I have an impressive moon rock collection."

Michelle laughed. She stopped lacing her fingers.

Doug, perusing her résumé, then asked a few impromptu questions about her interests:

What do you like to cook most? *Indian and Italian.*

What do you like to read? *Fantasy, sci-fi, autobiographies of musicians.*

What do you like to draw? *Faces, trees, city streets.*

They spent the next fifteen minutes talking about their time in New York. A couple of years before, Michelle had earned her MBA, then got hired on at Morgan Stanley. Back in his twenties, Doug had couch-surfed around SoHo as a member of an indie film collective.

They talked about what they missed about the city: the food, the culture, their friends.

They talked about why they had left. Michelle told him her father had recently undergone treatment for prostate cancer and she wanted to be closer to him, taking care of him while he recuperated. Doug said he just outgrew his dreams of becoming a filmmaker. (Which wasn't really true. When he couldn't afford to follow those dreams any longer, he moved in with an old high school buddy of his outside Chicago, then found his own place in Wicker Park.) Since then he had gone through a string of retail management jobs but was now writing an animated heist movie screenplay that he was confident would sell, or at least land him a Hollywood agent.

Michelle admitted the sales clerk position was indeed only for the short term, until she figured out what she should do next. Maybe go work as an advisor at one of the bigger financial firms downtown.

They both had grander plans for themselves.

Michelle got the job at Petique Boutique. The first few weeks of her and Doug's fledgling coworker relationship were for the most part professional. During the store's down time, they spoke at length about New York City, music (both were fans of Oasis and Radiohead), and the various pets they'd owned throughout their lives. This segued into flirty repartee and dirty innuendos. Then came the titillating brushes against one another whenever their bodies passed going in and out of the stockroom.

One night after their shifts had ended at the close of business day, Doug locked up the store and walked Michelle out of the mall to her silver Acura parked in the near-empty covered lot.

"Hey," she said. "Wanna hear this cool new band I just discovered?"

"Sure," he replied.

Michelle got into the driver's side of her car, inviting Doug to join her in the front seat. As soon as he shut his passenger door, she keyed the ignition and cued up the disc in the CD player. A song started to blast from the speakers, an upbeat synth-pop track featuring reverb-heavy guitar, electronic drums, keyboard, and maybe a theremin. The thumping bass rattled the car.

"They're called The Unravellers. What do you think?"

"I think they're a little loud!" Doug shouted over the music.

"Oh. Sorry." She turned down the volume. "I like to feel the pounding in my bones."

"Jeez. How hard do you like to be pounded?"

Michelle fixed her vampish eyes on him and said, "As hard as you can."

That did it. Acting on their pent-up desires, they kissed with instant blazing passion, their tongues taking turns doing laps in each other's mouths. He clasped her waist, she kneaded his chest. Next, their hands snaked underneath each other's clothes, exploring and exciting their more intimate parts. Their hearts began to race in sync with the music. All the car's windows fogged up.

Michelle reclined her seat and Doug wrested his body across the emergency brake, struggling to position himself on top of her, wriggling his lower torso beneath the steering wheel. They both started undoing their own pants—

Then they heard a shrill, sustained *BEEEEP*.

"Shit," Doug spat. He scrambled back into the passenger seat and the honking ceased. "Sorry. My ass hit the horn."

A pair of bright headlights illuminated Michelle's car. Doug hiked his pants back up, then wiped the condensation from his window with his sleeve. A mall security SUV making its rounds cruised by them as it swung onto the ramp to patrol the upper level of the parking structure.

Jolted out of their ecstasy, Doug and Michelle leaned back in their seats and stared at one another, hot and breathy.

The top couple of buttons on Michelle's work shirt had come unfastened and Doug was able to see the tattoo on her chest, just above the front bridge of her pink bra.

"When did you get that tat?"

Michelle reflexively placed her palm over the piece, as though she were embarrassed by it. "It was a while ago."

He angled himself closer to her. "It's interesting. Is it some sort of tribal symbol?"

She eased her hand off the tattoo to let him view it better.

"It's kinda rough looking," he continued his appraisal. "I'm guessing it was done free hand?"

"I don't know."

"Well, did he use a stencil?"

She shrugged. "I don't really remember getting it."

"Oh." Doug grinned. "You must've been drunk. Or you got it in prison and don't want to tell me. Am I right? Is that one of them jailhouse tattoos all the cool criminals are strutting around with these days?" He tapped the design with his fingertip.

"No, I've never been in jail," she said, curving her lips into a strained smile. "Sorry to disappoint you."

"I knew that already. It would've popped up in your background check." Doug brushed strands of sweat-slick hair from his brow. "So... wanna go to my place?"

Michelle regarded him a moment with half-squinted eyes, as if she were deliberating something important.

Doug wondered if she might be reconsidering taking their relationship further. They were both aware it was against company policy for coworkers to fraternize romantically, especially between a superior and subordinate. Was it worth the risk?

With their chemistry, powerful as it was, Doug thought so. He'd had his fair share of girlfriends: a children's party clown, a mortuary science student, a swimsuit/lingerie model, and a slew of others. But there was something different about Michelle. She filled the cold voids that shadowed him—boredom, loneliness, aimlessness—with something that he could only describe then as "the hots."

So hell yeah, she was worth it. He could always find another retail management job. But he couldn't speak for Michelle. She might be more strongly attracted to not getting fired.

"Tell me a secret," she said.

"A secret?" he replied, a bit taken aback.

"Yeah."

"Any secret?"

"Well, one of yours obviously. But a juicy one."

"Why?"

"So then I can tell you one of mine."

Doug mulled over her request. He didn't think he had any secrets. Nothing special anyway. In high school, he thought he got two girlfriends pregnant at the same time in his senior year, but they were both false alarms. He had done a moderate amount of recreational drugs in college, mostly weed and a tab of acid now and then. And he once set fire to a car in a grassy field—his friend Richie's '82 Toyota Corolla, a clunker whose engine had finally seized; they got arrested for torching it, charged with vandalism, and ordered to pay a $250 fine each. That was it for Doug's dirty laundry, all PG-13 rated stuff. Nothing Michelle would judge to be the kind of deep, dark secret he figured she wanted to hear.

"I'm an undercover FBI agent," he said with a straight face.

Michelle arched a dubious eyebrow. "Really?"

Doug nodded. "We're investigating if Petique Boutique is a front for the Russian mob. We suspect they're smuggling trained attack bears into the U.S. and selling them to drug lords here."

She shot him a *you're-full-of-crap* look and said "You're full of crap" in case he couldn't read her expression.

"Am I?"

Michelle narrowed her eyes and pursed her lips, grumbling "hmm." She waited for Doug to try again.

"I… uhm… okay, I also once got arrested for setting fire to my buddy's piece-of-shit car. Spent a few hours in a jail cell. Got mentioned in the crime section of the local newspaper. I was this famous outlaw in my town for like a week."

"Ooo, what a delinquent," she teased.

He nodded. "Hope you like bad boys."

Michelle's face went slack, somber. It was her turn.

"I'm an addict," she confessed.

Then she recounted the uncensored circumstances of her return to Chicago—the CliffNotes version of it, anyway—and her subsequent recovery efforts. It explained why she would choose to work at a pet store for near minimum wage. She was seeking a fresh start, taking baby steps until she could once more slip on her Versace power heels, commanding a six-figure salary and a corner office.

Michelle fished her iPhone from her pocket to show Doug the pixelated admittance photo taken of her at the most recent rehab she'd entered. Physically she looked much the same, with a single striking difference—her eyes. They were dull, lifeless. But they looked better now, Doug thought. Much better.

———

As much as he's psyched himself up for it, Doug is not ready for this. How can he be? He may as well be preparing to dive naked into an active volcano.

Michelle was right; going to Liam's funeral will be weird.

Doug tries playing out in his head all the different uncomfortable scenarios that could happen while he's there, and how he will tactfully react to each of them. Every instance he conjures ends with him uttering some platitude along the lines of "I'm sorry for your loss" or, even more cringey, "I'm sure Liam's in a better place." He hopes he'll at least get Liam's name correct and not mistakenly call him Larry or Ian to one of his family members.

Doug has only attended three funerals before. The first was for his grandmother. She adored her Douglas, always giving him gifts of candies, toy dinosaurs, and once, a Robie the Robot from RadioShack. When Doug was nine, she suffered a fatal stroke while tending her vegetable garden. He bawled all through Gramma's service at the cemetery, then would not leave his house for days, not until his mom coaxed him out to go to Abe's Arcade. When Doug was seventeen, a recent ex-girlfriend of his drowned swimming in Lansdale Lake. Viewing Rachel all gussied up in her coffin, someone he had once been intimate with, unsettled him, the images of her alive and not-alive battling for indelibility in his brain. And two years ago, his assistant store manager at Petique Boutique was killed in a car accident. Doug didn't know Josh very well, but he was somebody Doug would see several days of the week, and then one day never saw him again.

Doug figures, compared to any of those, Liam's funeral will be a breeze. He never met him, never so much as read one of his Facebook posts. He won't miss him at all.

Michelle didn't sleep over at Doug's place the night before leaving for Philly. He can understand why, though part of him feels sort of snubbed. He recognizes that's a selfish point of view to take, maybe even insensitive. But how is he supposed to feel? They say you shouldn't speak ill of the dead, but after what he put Michelle through, Liam can seriously, ceaselessly go fuck himself.

Michelle obviously doesn't share that perspective. Doug just wishes that, once the guy's buried or cremated or whatever, she will file her memories of Liam away in an unmarked container, lock it in a deep drawer, and move on.

Doug finishes packing his stuff for the trip. The funeral will last one whole day, and Michelle wants to be there for the entire shebang, which means they will be staying two nights at Liam's family home. Doug would rather be doing most *anything* else, but he'd also do most anything for Michelle. He's glad she wants him to be with her for this.

He scoots Rocket into his soft-sided pet carrier—Michelle's father kindly offered to dog-sit him while they were away—and zips it closed. After locking up his apartment, he totes the carrier and suitcase downstairs and loads up his Nissan Cube, its scarlet red paint marred with hair-thin scratches and thumbnail-sized chips, a consequence of years of parking it outside on a city street. He gets in, buckles up, and starts the engine. The digital dashboard clock reads 7:05. Good. He should be able to avoid the morning rush hour.

"Okay, Rocket," Doug sighs. "Let's get this over with."

No matter how unsurprised Michelle was about Liam's death, she is not ready for this. How can she be? They were supposed to be married, living out the rest of their lives together, keeping each other clean and sober and happy. But that's rarely how the stories of recovering addicts in love go. One will ultimately disappoint the other, and often the other starts using again too rather than leave the one they love. Michelle guesses she was lucky to be the exception. Though this kind of lucky feels like shit.

She sits on her bed in her room in her father's house, among the things that chronicle her life growing up there: photographs, awards, vacation souvenirs, stuffed animals, posters of The Stone Roses, Oasis, and Blur. Michelle stares at a photo of herself with the clarinet she had played in her junior high school band, before the partying and the booze and the drugs and the rehabs and the AA/NA meetings. Junior high seems so long ago, she muses. That forward-looking fourteen-year-old version of her doesn't exist anymore. She doesn't really think about the future now, just takes each day as it comes. And most of those days have been OK, or good, sometimes even great.

Today is not one of those days.

At least she has Doug. Michelle knows bringing him to Liam's funeral is a terrible idea for scores of reasons—poor etiquette, bad vibes, a petri dish of awkwardness. Despite putting on her best front, she wonders if Doug can sense her reservations. Yet these reservations are overshadowed by her wanting him to accompany her, support her, remind her how much better she's doing now.

She doesn't want to go there by herself and confront all those dashed hopes of her past, and the ruins of a future unfulfilled. Sure, she has conquered (no, controlled) her addiction, but when she thinks about seeing the Fowlingtons again, she doesn't feel like a survivor.

She feels like a fucking failure.

FOUR

When Liam and Michelle left the Fowlingtons' estate after their Thanksgiving stay and returned to their apartment in Brooklyn, she could sense things were different. She now felt this strange sort of energy. The air undulated around her, like waves of fresh, gentle, earthy breezes cascading over her, giving her goosebumps. This sensation intensified the nearer she was to Liam. It wasn't unpleasant. On the contrary, it comforted her, reminding her of contented times as a child visiting the lakeshore with her family during the summer.

Michelle unpacked their luggage while Liam headed out to pick up some groceries. With him gone from the apartment, she felt a palpable emptiness. She wanted to be close to him more than ever now. *Needed* him to be close to her. All the time. She tried to cast the thought aside, realizing she was being foolish. He was shopping just down the block. He'd be back any minute. And yet, Liam seemed so far away from her, for so long. It was almost unbearable.

Stop being silly, she reminded herself.

Michelle hung up Liam's clean shirts from their trip in their walk-in closet. (A servant had laundered their previously worn garments before they left.) She had never lived with a guy before, but found she enjoyed sharing a space with somebody she loved. It was like a dress rehearsal for married life, and based on how things have been going, it looked like their marriage would have a great run.

Shortly after getting engaged, Michelle and Liam had moved in together into a cute two bedroom/two bath walk-up near Park Slope. It was the practical next step in their relationship. And after the wedding, they could combine their bank accounts and she would no longer have to write him a check each month for her portion of the rent.

The wedding! Just seven short months away, and there was so much planning left to do. They'd already chosen the Fowlington estate as the venue for the ceremony—a no-brainer, it was a beautiful property—but they still had to settle on the theme, the menu, the music. Even with the high-end, and highly expensive, wedding advisor Liam's parents hired for them, it all seemed an overwhelming undertaking.

Michelle started to sort through her travel bag, putting away her clothes in the closet and drawers. As she unfolded her white pleated blouse, she noticed a faint brown stain, smaller than a dime, between the top two mother-of-pearl buttons. It looked like dried blood.

She dredged up a hazy memory of her wearing the blouse at the Fowlingtons on the night of the "ritual" (as Liam called it).

Ritual—the word had always sounded sinister to her, evoking images of cowled figures sacrificing a brainwashed virgin to some fearsome deity. Michelle hadn't been sacrificed, obviously, just marked with a Fowlington family sigil that was still tender to the touch.

As hard as she tried, Michelle still couldn't remember getting the tattoo. Neither could she visualize any details about the ritual. This bothered her at first. She had not experienced a blackout since before she quit using. But Liam was so thrilled by their new "spiritual connection"—it was all he had talked about on the ride home—that she too found herself swept up in his jubilation.

Where is he? she wondered. *He's been shopping for over an hour!*

"Jojo!" she called to her Yorkshire terrier she'd adopted five years prior. "Go fetch Liam!"

Jojo slunk from the hallway and crouched at the threshold of the bedroom, staring at her warily like she was about to commit a crime he would need to report. He'd been acting funny ever since they got back. He hadn't raced to greet her upon their return like he always did. Hadn't leapt into her lap to be petted whenever she sat down on the sofa. Jojo wouldn't even come near her or Liam now, dodging them if either came too close.

"Stop being such a pooper, Jojo. Are you mad we left you for a few days? You usually love playing with all the other dogs."

Jojo scampered away from her. No, Michelle concluded, this wasn't petulance from having been boarded for a week. Rather, it was as if Jojo did not remember or recognize them. He treated Michelle and Liam like they were virtual strangers. She worried the poor pup was becoming senile, but he was not even six years old. She resolved to take him into the vet soon, something that would certainly stress him out on top of whatever was going on with him. But what else could she do?

Michelle heard Liam's keys jiggling in the front door lock. She dashed toward it, throwing her arms around his neck as soon as he stepped into the apartment.

"I missed you!"

Gripping a brown grocery bag in each hand, Liam reciprocated by awkwardly stroking his knuckles against her hips.

"Missed you too, babe."

She held onto him as though their love depended on it.

"Hey... can I put these away? They're kinda heavy."

"Oh. Of course." She released him. "Can I help?"

"Nah. I'm good." Liam headed into the kitchen, set the bags on the countertop, and started emptying them while Michelle raptly watched him. "So I got the no-fat Greek yogurt you wanted. Some skim milk. Eggs. Wheat bread. A box of dark roast K-cups. These cheesy chips we like. And something special."

He reached into the bag and from it produced two bottles, one a margarita mix and the other a silver tequila.

Michelle's jaw dropped. "Is that actually...?"

"Yep. The good stuff. To celebrate with."

"Liam." She shook her head in disbelief. "We can't."

Since leaving rehab, they had been going to AA meetings together regularly. Maybe not as often as recommended, but enough to call themselves "recovering."

"Yes, we *can*." Liam smiled confidently. "Remember, we're protected now."

She did remember him telling her that.

"As long as we're together, our sigils guarantee we can't be hurt. I mean, it's not like we can jump in front of a speeding train and survive getting smashed. We're not immortal. But our minds

—

and spirits are much stronger now. We can enjoy ourselves and not worry about losing control."

"I… I'm not…" Michelle stammered.

"Not what?"

She could have said she wasn't ready, but that wouldn't really be true. A recovering addict was always ready for that next drink or next hit. It only took the right opportunity to present itself, the right conditions aligning to dive back into the abyss.

Michelle gazed upon the almost luminous bottle of tequila. When was the last time she had indulged in a margarita? Maybe happy hour at El Vez? Or how about any other alcoholic beverage? Ten months, almost eleven, without so much as a light beer. Day after day she grappled with each and every urge to once more stagger down that rough, rapturous road.

You'll always be a recovering addict, everyone told her. *It's a neverending battle*. She must never let her guard down, always remain vigilant in her fight against temptation.

"C'mon, babe," Liam said brightly. "It's okay."

The brittle part of her in charge of skepticism and self-preservation knew she should refuse. Resist. *Just say no, Michelle*.

"Babe?"

NO!

No.

no

"Are you sure it's safe?" The words poured from her mouth almost unconsciously.

"Yes, Michelle." Liam put on what she called his super serious face, the expression he wore when there was nothing to be afraid of (excepting, in his case, heights, spiders, and dentists). "We've been blessed by a higher power. A higher power that wants us to be happy. Trust me, we'll be fine."

She looked into Liam's eyes. She loved this man so much.

And the ritual, the tattoo… It *had* done something, hadn't it? Changed something inside of her. If she were truly immune to addiction now, shielded from its life-crippling effects of lost jobs, lost friends, and lost time, Michelle didn't really see a downside. Be it from God, magic, or some ancient science, it didn't matter. She did trust Liam. They had fought the same battles, the same demons. If he said something was keeping those demons caged, shackled, and muzzled, she believed him wholeheartedly, because her whole heart belonged to him.

He would never hurt her.

"Sooo… shall we waste away in Margaritaville?" Liam asked, cocking an eyebrow.

Michelle wanted a drink. So what? She didn't *need* it. Just wanted one.

This time would be different. She could *feel* it.

"Okay," she said, her simmering excitement now swelling, her eyes reflecting a quelled hunger rebirthed.

She pulled ice from the freezer. He plugged in the blender. They uncapped the bottles and mixed them in the pitcher. The blender's motor whirred and growled. They poured the golden slush into the largest plastic cups they had.

Then they celebrated.

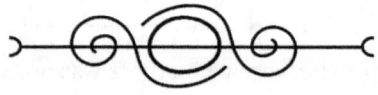

Michelle awoke the next morning feeling like hot garbage. Headache, dry mouth, nausea. Daggers of daylight streaming between the window blinds stabbed her eyes. She did not want to move, but she forced herself out of bed when she realized Liam wasn't there beside her.

Her entire body rebelled against her every action—sitting up, swinging her legs onto the floor, standing, shuffling out of the room. Everything hurt. She wanted to puke. She needed to pee.

Damn, she needed a drink.

What time was it? She squinted at the fuzzy digital clock on the stove. 12:43. After-fucking-noon. She hadn't slept that late since before she got sober.

Fortunately, she didn't have to go back to work until Monday. That gave her almost a full day to recover…

From drinking. From getting drunk.

She suddenly felt sad. And ashamed.

"Liam?" she called.

He didn't answer her.

Naked, she headed into the bathroom to relieve herself, brush her teeth, rinse her face. She studied her face in the mirror. Her eyes were grossly bloodshot, her cheeks blotchy red. Her hair sat piled on her head in a tangle like a forsaken wig.

She didn't look like herself, but rather a failed clone of herself destined to be chucked onto the trash heap of life's rejects. She worried Liam would think she was ugly now.

"Liam!" she cried out again.

Again, no reply. Maybe he wasn't home. But then where was he?

She slipped on her rose-red satin pajamas and returned to the living room. A wave of dizziness broke over her, causing her to collapse into the armchair behind her. She closed then opened her eyes, then closed and opened them again, repeating the process until the room stopped spinning, swooping, and swaying as if she were on some condemned amusement park ride.

Michelle gawked at the empty bottle of tequila Liam brought home the day before, now lying on its side on the coffee table. They had knocked back three glasses of margaritas each before taking alternating swigs straight from the bottle until draining it completely. She thought they might've had sex. Or maybe they tried and passed out.

She couldn't remember.

Where the hell is he?

Though Liam had assured her they would be protected from the alcohol's adverse effects, she sure didn't feel protected now. More like her body was mad at her. She was mad at herself. And kind of upset at Liam, but not really. He'd only wanted them to have a good time and genuinely believed they could party without consequences. Liam's family believed in a lot of strange stuff. She couldn't fault him for embracing the same beliefs instilled in him since childhood.

But she should've known better.

She did know better.

Michelle and Liam had both begun drinking and doping in college. (Hell, drinking and doping are what got them through college.) After they graduated, it continued to allow them to cope with the daily pressures of their burgeoning careers. It enabled them to function, until they couldn't function without it, until they couldn't function with it. Their work was affected, showing up late, screwing up projects, pissing off clients. Their problem became apparent to everyone in their offices. Since addiction is legally classified as a medical condition/mental disorder, their employers paid for their treatment. Next stop rehab, where Liam and Michelle met. They got clean, fell in love, and learned how to live a healthier life. A beautiful life, with a bright future.

Michelle winced when her eyes wandered to the overhead fluorescent light in the kitchen. Her headache, which had never fully receded, roared back with a one-two punch to her temples.

Fuck my life.

She averted her eyes from the blazing bulb and spotted Jojo squatting beneath the writing desk, watching her intently.

"Don't judge me, puppy," she muttered, weak and weary all over. "I'm sick."

Jojo snarled at Michelle, then bolted into the spare bedroom, hunkering under the futon like he did during thunderstorms or fireworks.

Liam arrived home carrying a box of Pinot Noir.

"You bought a case of wine?" Michelle incredulously asked him.

"Better than that," he answered, placing the box on the coffee table in front of her. He opened the flaps and extracted a variety of bottles.

"I got us some apple brandy… an Italian gin… Grey Goose vodka… coconut rum… and this awesome twelve-year-old single malt Scotch. Oh, and a nice merlot. Pick your poison!"

"I can't, Liam."

"Why not? Didn't we have fun last night?"

"I guess so… I don't really remember a lot."

"Well, I do. And I can testify that we had fun. *You* had fun."

"I feel awful now."

"That's only because your body isn't used to it. You know the best way to cure a hangover is to keep feeding the meter. Once you build up a tolerance again, everything will be right as rain."

Michelle sighed, still conflicted.

Liam regarded her empathetically. "Hey… I realize this is all pretty out there for you. I get it. I'm asking you to swallow a lot of new ideas, and it's hard to adjust your perspective. I mean, if these were normal circumstances, I'd be riding that wagon with you. But we're not normal anymore. We're *better* now."

Michelle's eyes lingered on the bottle of Scotch. "What… what if the tats… don't work?"

"But they ARE working. I KNOW they are." The force of his conviction knocked her breathless. "Don't you trust your future husband?"

Of course she trusted him. What choice did she have?

"C'mon, babe. Don't be a bummer," Liam said, his tone now assertive, almost angry.

She wanted to make him happy, to not disappoint him. She wanted to be a good wife-to-be.

She wanted another drink.

Michelle nodded.

Moments later, there was a glass of whiskey in her hand.

She drank.

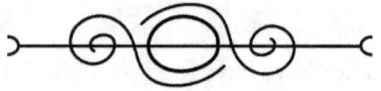

Michelle had enough presence of mind to email her boss about calling out, telling him she had contracted some nasty stomach virus over Thanksgiving vacation. Liam didn't notify his supervisor about his absence until she managed to reach him on his phone. He told her he had a sudden death in the family and he'd be back at his desk as soon as he could.

Neither of them returned to work again.

Every two or three days, Liam would venture out to procure more booze for them. At first he always selected top-shelf brands, but then stopped caring about quality altogether. Any cheap rotgut would do, the more potent the better. How the alcohol made them feel was no longer as important as how they felt without it. Their bodies and their brains demanded it, brutally punishing them if they neglected to appease them.

They didn't try to convince themselves they were in control anymore. They both knew this road, knew where it led. But they needed to keep on driving, and this was the only way they could see ahead of them, toward any destination where they could refill their tanks.

They'd keep going until they crashed.

One day, after rousing from another pickled stupor, Michelle called out for Liam. He didn't respond. She rose from the sofa and roamed the apartment in a semi-haze, making a languid effort to tidy up things, scooping throw pillows off the floor, placing dirty dishes in the sink, gathering empty bottles on the kitchen countertop. She noticed Jojo's food bowl in the corner was down to a few crumbled bits of kibble. She dragged the bag of dog chow from the kitchen cabinet and tipped it into the stoneware crock.

"Come and get it, Jojo!"

Michelle resealed the bag with its plastic clip and put it away. When she turned back around, the food remained untouched. Jojo normally came running whenever his bowl was refilled, if just to sniff it.

"Jojo! Din-din!"

Jojo didn't appear.

"Jojo?"

Michelle checked the dog's usual lounging areas—beneath the desk, under the bed, on the windowsill—without luck.

She grabbed Jojo's chain leash from the hook on the kitchen wall and jingled it, expecting him to bound out of whatever nook he was hiding in, yipping excitedly in anticipation of going to the dog park across the street.

Still no Jojo.

Michelle then heard the steeple bell ring from the Episcopal church on the corner. That *always* brought the dog racing to the front window to watch the parade of decked-out parishioners strolling to Sunday service. Once again, Jojo was a no-show.

"Where are you, buddy?"

That's when she noticed the front door, standing ajar.

Her adrenaline spiking, Michelle ran outside. She wobbled down the stoop steps, clutching the iron railing to avoid taking a tumble onto the concrete. From the sidewalk, she peered frantically up and down her block of historic brownstones and honey locust trees.

"Jojo! Jojo! Jojo!"

Sheer panic consumed her. Her breaths caught in her throat like it was a gunked-up straw. Her head reeled, blurring her vision and fouling her footing. But before she fell, two arms grabbed her.

"Michelle!"

She regained her senses, registered it was Liam holding her up.

"What's wrong?"

Her eyes widened. "Jojo's gone."

"Wha—how?"

She narrowed her eyes at him and hissed, "You left the fuckin' door open, asshole!"

Over the following days, Michelle and Liam were able to muster enough of their impaired focus to search for Jojo. They scouted their neighborhood, calling for him while shaking a packet of his favorite beef liver treats. Liam phoned the local animal shelters, many of them more than once a day, asking if Jojo were there. Michelle created a missing dog flyer featuring a photo of Jojo with his favorite toy, a plush hedgehog he'd almost chewed to tatters. They taped the flyers to trees, lampposts, and construction fences throughout a dozen-block radius of their home.

They performed all these tasks while loaded. Michelle and Liam were both so-called functioning alcoholics, having a knack for doing things even while under the influence. Looking for Jojo gave them an emotionally charged motivation, and during this time they unconsciously paced their drinking instead of binging. They told themselves all that mattered was finding Jojo, even as they were frequently diverted from this mission to get their fix.

—

After five days had passed with no luck, they began to give up hope, or rather, they drowned that hope in more booze. When leaving their apartment became too onerous, they had their liquor (and some groceries) delivered to their home. The bodega down the street eventually cut them off after an argument with their delivery guy about him taking too goddamn long and fucking up Liam's order. To hell with them; there were dozens of other stores they could order from. Liam soon depleted his bank account, then maxed out all his credit cards. Michelle let him use hers. It had an $18,000 limit. They would not go dry for a while.

Liam spent most of his time sacked out in the bed or on the sofa, sometimes the floor. He spent his few waking moments taking swigs from this bottle or another, whichever one was easiest to reach. A daily routine of chasing and embracing oblivion.

Michelle, by contrast, discovered that the alcohol was having *decreasingly* pronounced effects on her. As Liam had suggested, she seemed to be developing a tolerance for it. While she still experienced some of the typical symptoms of intoxication—slurred speech, wonky balance, erratic attention—she also felt more acutely melancholic. She was sad about losing Jojo. Sad about abandoning her job. Sad about relapsing. The booze was no longer helping her to relax, to forget, to escape. She needed something stronger.

Michelle's oxy hookup worked in the pharmacy department at a hospital in Queens. She had discarded George's contact info when she got clean, but she remembered the hospital and hoped he was still there. When she got George on the phone, he sounded only mildly surprised to hear from her after so many months. He knew what she wanted without her having to tiptoe around it. He told her his shift was ending in an hour and that she could meet him at the usual spot.

Too dizzy to drive there, Michelle caught the subway to Rego Park. She found George waiting in his matador-red Lexus in the parking lot of the Burger King. She got into the passenger's seat, immediately smelling his Drakkar Noir cologne. George was still wearing his blue scrubs and a gold crucifix pendant. He sold her twenty oxy tablets in a tightly rubberbanded sandwich baggie. (He also requested a blowjob, but she told him she didn't need the discount.)

On the subway ride home, Michelle's cell began playing its "Bitter Sweet Symphony" ringtone. Her father again. He had tried calling her at least six or seven times over the past few days. She didn't want to talk to him. He would only bum her out more. But at this point he was probably worried about her, and she did not want to upset him. She answered it.

"Hi daddy."

"Hey sweetie." He sounded relieved. "I've been trying to get in touch with you."

"I know… I'm sorry. Been really busy with work and stuff… How's Chicago?"

"Still windy, I think. Let mc ask the cow flying by."

Michelle giggled. It was an old joke of theirs, ever since they had watched the tornado movie *Twister* together.

"So," her father continued, "they moved up my surgery."

"To when?"

"Friday."

"This Friday? This week?"

"Yep."

"Why…" She choked on a lump in her throat. "Why did they change it?"

"They figure the sooner they deal with things, the better a chance I have."

"Okay." She faltered for a response that didn't give away her trepidation. "Glad they're on top of it."

"Yeah, they really are," her father concurred before changing his tone to one more humble, almost pleading. "So, I was hoping you could come here while I'm in the hospital. Maybe stay a little longer than that if you're able to. Just to help me around the house while I'm on the mend. I'll pay for your plane ticket."

"Can't Karen do it? Or Craig?"

"Your sister's been so busy lately. And Craig, he's got another thousand excuses why he can't help out his father." He sighed. "I mean, I don't want to put you out either."

"Did you try Pete?"

"Jesus, Mish. Are you serious?" Her father and oldest brother hadn't spoken to each other for years, ever since Pete joined that hippie collective—aka cult—in California. "Hey, if it's too much bother for you, I'm sure I can hire a caregiver of some sort."

That made her feel guilty, and her dad knew it. She had been raised to believe family always came first. While this lesson did not stick so well with her siblings, it resonated with Michelle. Her father needed her, and to refuse him would weigh on her like a battleship's anchor.

"Okay." The word spilled out of her mouth as inevitably as a breath. She hadn't taken any of the oxy yet, so her emotions were still running on hyperdrive. She was powerless. "I'll buy a plane ticket as soon as I get to my computer."

"I'll reimburse you."

"That's alright. You just get better."

The moment she got home, Michelle booked an early flight to Chicago leaving the next morning. She then swallowed two oxies, chasing them down with a slug of Jim Beam. It was enough to purge her anxious thoughts, right before submerging her into a dreamless unconsciousness on the sofa.

She awakened to somebody's car alarm blaring on the street outside. She groaned, spat out a garbled cuss word that sounded like "fungin." The alarm stopped after about fifteen seconds but continued to reverberate in Michelle's skull for a minute more. When the high-pitched buzz finally subsided, she glimpsed the clock on the stove and—*SHIT!*—she had less than two hours to get to the airport to make her flight.

She stomped into the bedroom and hastily packed her carry-on travel bag with five mismatched sets of clothes, her toiletries, and her iPod. Liam, conked out in their bed, didn't stir a muscle as she banged drawers shut on her bureau and squeaked hangers apart in the closet. Once she had everything, she shook Liam by the shoulders to get him up.

He gasped and gurgled and grunted before croaking, "Wha d'fuck, Chelle?"

"You need to take me to the airport."

"Wha-huh… Why?"

"Going to Chicago. My dad's having his operation early."

"Your dad?" Liam squeezed his eyes closed. "Y'gotta go now?"

"Yeah. *Right now.*"

He huffed. "Call a cab."

"You can get me there quicker at this hour."

Liam glanced toward the window, saw it was still pitch-dark out. "Christ, Chelle. What time is it?"

"Time to drive your fiancée to the airport."

Liam moaned and rolled off the bed, revealing a large sweat stain on the sheet in the shape of him. He threw on a sweatshirt, jeans, and sandals. He killed off the bottle of inky black rum they had cracked open a couple of nights before, then grabbed his keys from the bamboo bowl on the credenza. Michelle followed him out with her bag. Neither of them thought to lock up their place.

Liam rented a monthly space on the lower level of the parking garage a couple of blocks away from their apartment. He yanked the gray protective cover off his black Audi and bunched it up against the concrete wall. Michelle tossed her bag into the back seat and hopped in front. Liam puked a little on the ground beside the car, then oozed himself into the driver's side. He keyed the ignition, inputted "airport delta" into Google Maps on his GPS, and jerkily maneuvered out of the garage.

Typically, the trip to JFK Int'l Airport took forty minutes with decent traffic. But this early, almost an hour before sunrise, most of the other vehicles on the roads consisted of just taxis, delivery trucks, and police cruisers. Liam often bragged he was a "great drunk driver," like he could win an award for it. He zigged and zoomed, veered and vroomed down the pre-bustle urban streets, blowing red lights, skidding off curbs, and clipping at least one signpost—all of this miraculously unnoticed by any cops—before reaching the Delta terminal just outside of twenty minutes. Liam thought he might have set a record.

Michelle lurched out of the car, snatched her bag from the backseat, and mumbled "see ya" to Liam while charging for the automatic entrance doors. She checked in at a kiosk and printed her boarding pass, got through the security line without incident, and made her way to her flight's gate. The chaotic ride there had given her a pounding headache and a queasy stomach. In a restroom stall, she popped three more oxies, swallowing them dry. She then dropped into the just-opened bar to down a couple of double shots of whatever whiskey.

By the time she boarded the plane, she was already flying.

When Michelle landed at O'Hare, she was barely conscious and had to be taken off the plane in a wheelchair. The airline attendant, who assumed she was inebriated based on the smell of her breath, brought her to the baggage claim area where her father was waiting. He promptly drove her to the nearest hospital where they pumped her stomach. He then checked her into an addiction treatment center where she spent the next thirty days.

While her father was in the O.R. getting the cancer cut out of his butt, Michelle was detoxing at the rehab. While he was at home convalescing from his surgery, she was going to therapy sessions, sharing how she got there with a roomful of strangers who were in the same boat as she was, weathering the same storm. Every day she ate three cafeteria-quality meals, enjoyed a couple of hours of recreational time playing ping-pong or sketching in her Moleskine journal, and attended a series of group and one-on-one meetings with a counselor.

Recovery was much smoother for Michelle this time around. More like taking a refresher course than starting from scratch. She found kicking her habits to be far less grueling, less agonizing, almost as if she weren't really addicted at all. Probably because her mind dreaded re-becoming an addict. Feared it as much as drowning or choking or burning to death. Everything was easier now because she was more driven to live, committed to leading the normal life she knew she was capable of having.

And Liam being 800 miles away didn't hurt either.

Well, it *did* hurt. She missed Liam. She yearned to hear his voice, to feel his touch, to laugh at his dumb jokes. (*Why did the aluminum can crusher quit his job? Because it was soda pressing! Get it, babe? So de-pressing!*) She wanted to snuggle with him. Sleep with him. Have dinner, watch TV, go shopping with him. And marry him, like she was supposed to…

But then she reminded herself that Liam wasn't himself now. When he drank, he became lazy and moody and cold. Worst of all, Liam became toxic, reinfecting her with a disease that could have destroyed her had fate not intervened.

Upon her discharge from rehab, Michelle moved back into her father's house, at his insistence. Not that he needed to insist too adamantly; she was well aware how shitty her situation had been. Living with her dad again wasn't non-alcoholic wine and roses either, but the alternative would've been to continue that downward spiral—more like a slide—with Liam.

And still she loved him.

She avoided Liam's calls at first. Deleted his messages without reading or listening to them. Busied herself with anything that would distract her from thinking about him. This worked for a while, until her heart overwhelmed her will. She convinced herself that she only wanted to find out if he was okay. Explain to him they had to end things between them. Tell him goodbye for good but she'd always love him.

"It doesn't have to be like this, Chelle," he said to her on the phone.

"Yes, it does, Liam," she answered, lying on her bed, staring up at a small spider crawling on the ceiling. "I'm clean now."

"Then you can help *me* get clean."

"No, I can't. It's too hard… us being together. I can't do it."

"I love you so much."

"I… I love you too."

"Then come home."

"I can't, Liam."

"I miss you… and Jojo misses you too."

Michelle sighed. "Jojo's gone. He ran away. Remember?"

"Ah, shit… shit, that's right. Come back here and we'll find him."

"I gotta go. Please don't call me again."

"Chelle—"

Michelle hung up. She swore to herself that was the last time she would ever speak to him. She wouldn't accept any more of his calls. She would start a new life without him.

Except she didn't want that life. She wanted him. That's why whenever she would talk to Liam from then on, she would sneak off to places around the house that minimized the chances of her father eavesdropping on them. Liam was always drunk when they spoke, often passing out mid-conversation. Even so, just hearing his voice comforted her, an abiding if tenuous tether to the perfect life she almost had. Liam often cried, begging Michelle to come back to him. He promised he would stop being such a fuck-up. They belonged together, he insisted. They were bonded, he reminded her. They were—

"Give me the phone, Michelle."

Michelle, sitting cross-legged on a stack of slate patio tiles behind the shed, snapped her head up to see her father looming over her, his hand extended.

"No… Dad… It's not—"

"Right now." His tone was stern, undefiable. She gave him the phone.

Her father put the phone to his ear. "Liam. Listen to me carefully," he said, his voice calm and controlled. "Don't ever contact my daughter again. Not one word or selfie or emoji. If you do, I will fucking kill you."

Michelle gasped. Her father seldom swore.

"You're out of her life. You understand me?"

Michelle couldn't hear Liam but guessed he said "yessir" or some other slurred affirmative.

"Good," her dad said. "Take care of yourself, Liam." He then ended the call and passed the phone back to his daughter.

"I want you to delete his name and number from your phone. Better yet, block him."

"Okay," she answered, scarcely masking her petulance.

Her father regarded her with a combination of muted anger and sad empathy. "If you go back to him, Michelle, you'll probably wind up dead. You know that, don't you?"

"I know," she whispered.

"And if you do decide to go back, I won't help you again. I won't be here for you."

Michelle looked up at him, tears rimming her eyes. "What?"

"If you return to New York, to him, I won't speak with you again. Never. No matter how desperate you become—for money, for advice, for anything—you're on your own. I'm not bailing you out again. Not listening to your sob stories. Not doing anything more for you." He paused before quavering, "I will not be your father anymore."

"How can you say that? That's horrible."

"That's the way it has to be, Ponygirl." Michelle always softened when he called her that. Since she was a young teen, she had been a big fan of the movie *The Outsiders*. She would watch the Special Edition DVD every year with her father on her birthday, up until she left for Columbia. He thought she had a crush on C. Thomas Howell's character, Ponyboy, hence his nickname for her. What started as a tease had grown into a term of endearment. She couldn't imagine no longer being daddy's Ponygirl. That would further break her already broken heart, well beyond repair.

"I just can't do this anymore," he said.

"Okay," she muttered.

"You know I'm not bullshitting you, right?"

She nodded. She knew he wasn't.

They heard the rumble of not-so-distant thunder. The wind abruptly picked up, causing the leaves on the trees in their yard to thrash about like threatening pom-poms.

"Gonna rain soon," Dad said. "Come inside. I'm making us shepherd's pie for dinner."

They went inside and ate together in stormy silence.

Later that same week, Michelle joined the local AA group, paid for a gym membership, and applied for the sales associate job at Petique Boutique in the mall. She never spoke to Liam again.

Her brother Craig, who lived in New Jersey just across the river from Manhattan, volunteered—after a degree of prodding from their father—to collect Michelle's possessions from her and Liam's apartment, pack them up, and ship everything to Chicago.

Craig fit the classic middle child mold: overachieving, extroverted, resentful. He went from being wide receiver on his high school football team to slinging nets off fishing boats in Alaska, skipping college except for one semester at DeVry studying computer programming. He later moved to Jersey for never disclosed (to Michelle, at least) reasons, only saying it was "for work." She speculated he might be a male escort—you could accurately label him a "hunk"—and if so, she had no doubt he was the #1 hustler in Hoboken.

Michelle wouldn't have been surprised if her father did not even try asking her sister Karen to help her. As the eldest sibling, ten years older than Michelle, they had never been close. By the time Michelle had started third grade, Karen was heading off to Duke University, dual majoring in Economics and Anthropology. After their mother died, Michelle had hoped it might bring the two of them closer, but no. The sisters had seldom spoken to one another over the years, never so much as exchanged Christmas cards. So forget about her lending her time and toil to clear out Michelle's old apartment.

Michelle had FedExed her key to her brother, in case Liam didn't answer the door. He didn't, so Craig let himself in.

"Hey. Hello? Liam?" she heard him call out while he was on the phone with her. "You home?" He then whistled the Old Spice jingle.

"Jeez, Craig, he isn't a dog."

"Well, he lives like one. Looks like a dirty bomb went off in here. Smells like it too."

Michelle sighed. "He's not his best self right now."

"No kidding." Michelle heard the clinking of a gently kicked bottle. "Maybe he's at work?"

"It's possible," she answered without conviction.

Michelle guided Craig to where she kept her things, beginning with the bedroom. He pulled out her suitcase off the closet floor, set it on the bed, and loaded it with her blouses, dresses, and pants. She next had him empty her bra and panty drawer in her bureau, a task he thankfully made no qualms nor quips about doing. Last, she sent him to the bathroom to gather all her pricey makeup and perfumes. With zero room left for even one more tube of lipstick, he zipped up the suitcase.

"There's a shoebox up on the closet shelf. Can you grab that too?"

"The one with the cartoon characters all over it?"

"Yeah. It's got a lot of, uh, sentimental stuff."

"So, dildos and cock rings?"

"Ugh, god no. Gross, Craig. It's just a bunch of photos and ticket stubs and matchbooks, stuff like that."

"How dull."

"That reminds me. I need my shoes too. They're in the hall closet."

"Damn, Mrs. Marcos," her brother uttered upon beholding her stash of footwear. "I think I'm gonna need a bigger boat."

"There's a blue laundry bag in the linen cabinet in the bathroom. You can throw everything in that."

Once that was accomplished, Michelle had Craig go find a box—there were several empty wine cases scattered around the apartment—and fill it up with other sundry items she wanted: her favorite *I♥NY* mug, a framed print of Dali's "The Persistence of Memory," any mail on the writing desk addressed to her, her first copy of S.E. Hinton's novel *The Outsiders*, her teakwood bowl on the coffee table…

"Holy frijole," Craig said in a whisper. "He *is* here."

"Liam?"

"No, Justin Timberlake," he razzed while sounding justifiably creeped out. "Yes, Liam. The dude's on the floor, against the couch. Jeez, he must be out cold. He didn't wake up when I was rummaging through the place."

"Well, don't wake him. You'd probably scare the crap out of him."

"Don't worry. I have no intention of poking him or shouting in his ear," Craig said. "It's not like I'm itching to chat with him about U.S. foreign policy."

"That would only put him to sleep again." She paused as a new concern occurred to her. "He *is* breathing, isn't he?"

"Yeah, yeah. Like an obscene caller. So, am I done here?"

"I think so."

"Oh, what do you want me to do with the ring?"

Her brother was referring to her engagement ring, which she had mailed to him along with the apartment key. She told Craig to put it on the dinette table in the kitchen. She hoped Liam would not lose it, though why that would matter to her now she couldn't say.

When he was done stowing the last of his sister's belongings into his Land Rover, Craig groaned as if he had just survived a trial by fire.

"You owe me big time for this, sis."

"I know… I'll pay for the shipping."

"That's a start."

"Hey. How'd he look?" she asked before hanging up. "Liam."

"Bad," her brother answered. "Like death."

FIVE

Michelle is sitting on the front porch in a wicker loveseat when Doug pulls up to her father's house in Orland Park. She feebly waves at him, as though her hand were made of solid lead. She doesn't look like she slept well, if she had slept at all. Doug wonders if she spent the entire night on that porch staring out into space, buried in thoughts he could never truly fathom.

Doug parks at the curb in front of the mid-sized, mid-century modern home. He exits the car and fetches Rocket's carrier, with a wide-eyed Rocket inside, from the backseat. When he reaches the porch, he expects Michelle to greet him with a kiss or a hug. Instead—

"Hey," she says, rising from the loveseat. "Come inside." She ushers her boyfriend into the house with all the enthusiasm of a tour guide on the backend of a ten-hour shift.

Michelle's father, Arthur—he insists people call him Artie— owns a lucrative boat marina on Lake Michigan, and the interior décor of his home reflects his affinity for the nautical. A variety of buoys, compasses, and seashells woven into fishing nets festoon the walls. A wood ship's wheel dominates the mantelpiece above the fireplace. Through the rear bay windows overlooking the yard,

Doug can see a giant anchor, propped upright and painted white, appearing quite out of place on the manicured lawn surrounded by garden flowers.

"You kids have li'l time for breakfast before you shove off?" Artie asks, tying on a white-and-blue striped apron over his golf shirt and deck shorts.

Doug wouldn't mind a meal. They'd be on the road for hours and his body could use the fuel-up for the long ride. He waits for Michelle to weigh in, but she does not answer her father. Doug can't tell from her expression if she would rather get going or if she also wanted something to eat. She might not have heard the question at all, her mind preoccupied with other things.

"Sure, Artie," Doug finally answers for the both of them. "We have some time."

"Great," Artie says and heads for the kitchen. "Just gimme a few minutes."

While Doug and Michelle watch a cheesy crime show on TV in the adjoining living room, her father rustles them up plates of scrambled eggs, Belgian waffles, and cowboy bacon.

Artie is well-weathered for his age, tanned and toned, sporting a horseshoe mustache that's sprouting a few gray hairs. Doug has met him only once before, at a Brazilian churrascaria to celebrate Michelle's birthday. Like then, Doug finds him easygoing, easy to get along with. The polar opposite of his own father, now living in Florida with Doug's mother, which Doug guesses is just a matter of convenience for them. He's sure they have not loved one another for eons, but getting divorced would be too much of a logistical and financial hassle. (Less troubling for them was cutting their only child off when he'd decided to quit Loyola's

Poli Sci program so he could move to New York and pursue his filmmaking dreams.)

They elect to eat outside on the patio to take advantage of the unusually mild May morning. They sit at a glass top table underneath a market umbrella depicting an Old World maritime map, complete with an illustrated sea monster attacking a schooner.

"So, you two are going to Philly," Artie says, wiping a drop of maple syrup from his chin with his napkin.

"About half an hour outside it, actually," Doug answers. "A place called Burkburgh."

"Never heard of it. That's what? A day's drive?"

"It's, like, twelve hours. We're splitting it up over a couple of days."

"I was in Philly once on business, many years ago. Tried one of their cheesesteaks. It was okay. Kind of soggy. Nothing to put on a postcard."

"I hear the cheesesteak places there compete for who makes the best one."

"I bet they all claim that," Artie says.

Doug nods. "It's probably hard to prove."

"I doubt the one I had even made it to the semifinals."

Rocket, adapting quickly to his expanded (albeit temporary) territory, weaves around their chairs, pausing next to each person to beg for morsels by stroking his front paw against their leg.

"Is it okay if I give him some bacon?" Artie asks Doug.

"Sure. He likes most anything that was once breathing."

Artie offers a strip of bacon to Rocket, who greedily chomps it down. The dog then licks his chops and whines for more. Artie feeds him another piece.

———

"Hey, Karen did another of those *TED Talks* recently," Artie tells Michelle. "This one's about urban farming." He chuckles. "I never knew she was into farming, urban or otherwise. Anyway, it's pretty interesting. You can watch it on YouTube. I'll send you the link."

"Super," Michelle answers flatly. It's the first word she's said during the meal.

"Her sister is a real go-getter," Artie tells Doug. "A compulsive overachiever. She's always reinventing herself to be an expert in one thing or another, doing something with it, then moving on to the next thing. Michelle was the same way until…" He stops himself, slides a forkful of egg into his mouth. "It's just, life has been harder on her, y'know?"

Doug nods. Michelle doesn't react.

"I imagine you're eager to be done with all this," Artie says to his daughter.

"This?" Michelle asks.

"Yeah. Liam. Closing that chapter of your life."

She taps her knife against her plate, then says, "My life is not a book."

"I just mean," her father rephrases, "after the funeral, you can put all those bad memories behind you and move on."

"They weren't *all* bad."

Artie snorts. "They sure as hell weren't all good either."

Michelle clenches her jaw. "It wasn't his fault. He had a—"

"Disease? Oh, I know. It's a veritable tragedy when someone can't practice self-control, and then drags others down into the sewers with them."

"You barely even knew Liam," Michelle seethes. "You have no right to judge him."

"As a father who nearly lost his daughter because of the guy, I think I have ample reason to form an opinion about him."

"Maybe," Doug interjects, "we should talk about some—"

"You never liked him," Michelle snaps at her father.

Artie finishes taking a sip of pulpy orange juice before responding. "Matter of fact, I liked him fine, until he almost killed you."

"No, he didn't. I started using again because *I* chose to. So if you're gonna blame anyone, blame me." Michelle's eyes glisten with tears. "*I* screwed up."

"As I said, that's all in the past now," her father responds, his tone more admonishing than affirming. "Right, Ponygirl?"

Her dad calling her by her nickname does nothing to placate Michelle. Rather, it seems to antagonize her. He may as well have called her "loser" or "trash."

"Here's an idea. Maybe Karen can do a *TED Talk* about me. I can rehash my spectacular decline to her, and she can whip it up into one of her golden-tongued articles or speeches. And then she'll move on to her next personal triumph. And I'll still be your same fucked-up daughter. How's that sound?"

Her father regards her with pitying eyes. "Sounds like you're still angry at all the wrong people."

"Sure, dad," Michelle huffs. "Doug, I want to leave now." She rises from her chair.

"Uh, 'kay… I'm just gonna use the bathroo—"

"*Now,*" Michelle repeats with snarled emphasis, then storms into the house without waiting for Doug.

Doug sighs and stands. "Thanks for breakfast, and for dog-sitting Rocket, Mister Langl… Artie."

"It's my pleasure," Artie says. He gets up and shakes Doug's hand, not letting go. "Sorry the conversation went off the rails there. I was just trying to… eh, I don't know what the hell I was trying to do. The wrong thing, whatever it was."

"That's alright. Michelle's not doing so great at the moment, understandably."

The front door slams shut inside, startling Rocket while he's sniffing around the huge anchor.

"Keep an eye on her, Doug, would ya?" Artie tightens his grip on Doug's hand and leans toward him. "I'm worried about her."

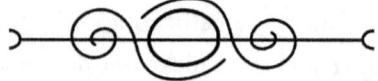

Doug worries about Michelle too. Ever since they headed out for Philly, it's as though her personality has been deactivated. For the duration of the drive to their overnight stopover in Ohio, she has not laughed or smiled, which does not surprise Doug. But she doesn't frown or cry either, scarcely shows any emotion at all. He wonders if this experience will be a trigger for her. If it will cause her to relapse.

On their first official date, a leisurely lunch at a faux-French boulangerie, Michelle told Doug—or rather forewarned him—that more than half of recovering addicts relapse. This shocked him, if only because he was dating a recovering addict and those weren't great odds. If Doug was a betting man, he would have walked away from the table.

But then, he thought, aren't all relationships a gamble?

Doug asked her what he should do if she ever relapsed.

"Just throw me back into rehab," she answered with a casual flip of her hand, as if it were no big deal.

Doug told her he'd never, to his knowledge, known anybody who had gone to rehab. This shocked her, because in her world, rehab was par for the course. (Doug was pretty sure he'd had a couple of alcoholic friends and maybe an uncle, but they never looped him in about their attempts to sober up, if they were trying at all.)

Instead of being a red flag, Doug found himself attracted to, and more than a little intrigued by, her forthrightness. Right out of the gate, Michelle told him about Liam her ex-fiancé and Jojo her ex-dog, how her substance abuse led to the ex-ing of them both. She talked about what rehab was like. She even joked about all her public displays of idiocy while under the influence, sometimes culminating with her arrest. (She said she'd once peed off a horse-drawn carriage as it trotted through Central Park, generating a variety of reactions—New York City being what it is—from shock to amusement to "Nice cooch, baby!")

But Michelle has gotten her shit together now, going to AA meetings regularly, showing up to work responsibly, waxing optimistic about her future. Doug has faith in her.

Not that he didn't ever have misgivings. Since Doug has never personally dealt with relapses and rehabs, he doesn't *really* know what to expect if it happens. This realization hit him hardest on their fourth date at the Art Institute of Chicago. In one gallery, Doug stared for a long while at Ivan Albright's "Picture of Dorian Gray," a painting created for the classic film. The titular subject, while in actuality a handsome aristocrat, was depicted in the art-work as a disgusting, decaying figure, metaphorically mirroring Gray's escalating moral corruption.

This prompted Doug to wonder if Michelle would suffer a similar regrettable—repellant—transformation should she fall off the wagon. Would he still recognize her? And did he have the fortitude to stick by her? Would he even want to?

But with this realization came a revelation: Doug has never done anything that's mattered, has never made a difference to anybody, not even himself. He's never produced his own film, never finished his college degree, never gotten married, never gave blood. He has, for the most part, only existed for the sake of existing. Work, eat, sleep, dream, breathe—the treadmill of a meaningless life. If he can be somebody who means something to Michelle, who can be there for her in health and in sickness—isn't that a measure of true love?—then it's worth it.

She's worth it.

Thus Doug dove into Michelle's recovering addict life with a blind gusto. In a gesture of solidarity, he quit drinking. He began going to Al-Anon group meetings, and sometimes accompanied Michelle to her AA meetings if she wanted him to be there. He collected a stack of informative pamphlets with sensational titles like "Alcoholism, A Merry-Go-Round Named Denial" and "So You Love an Alcoholic." When she had rough days, he rushed to be at her side. He promised he would never abandon her if she needed him, that they were in this together.

Doug isn't so certain Michelle needs him now, except maybe as a chauffeur. After driving for almost six hours, he checks them into a Motel 6 in Cleveland. He carries their bags into their ground-floor room, inspects the double bed closest to the bathroom for bedbugs (an old habit he picked up from his parents), and finds them a place nearby to have dinner.

They go to a Chinese restaurant in a shopping center across the street. Although it's crowded, they are seated in less than ten minutes. They both order iced green teas from the Asian waiter, then browse their paper menus in silence. Beneath the Chinese symbols representing the restaurant's various offerings are the English translations, or rather mistranslations. Doug reads these aloud while Michelle listlessly skims her menu.

"Old oysters ruthlessly juiced."

"Pinched duck in lustrous sauce."

"Bean curd on bed of burning flesh." Michelle smirks at this.

"Sexy chicken fried in dick fat." This last one causes Michelle to spit out the iced tea she's sipping. It also causes her to perk up, to laugh, to smile, to talk about happy things such as peacocks—there's a bunch of them all over the restaurant's wallpaper—and visiting the Rock and Roll Hall of Fame on their way home. Just enjoying herself, if only for a few fleeting minutes, without those shadows of Liam's death darkening her head and heart.

After dinner, they return to their room. Michelle hops onto the bed, propping her spine against the headboard, and idly examines the state of her fingernails. Doug finds the remote, turns on the TV, and surfs through the channels. He lands on one airing *The Outsiders*.

"Hey look. It's your favorite movie. Wanna watch?"

Michelle glances up from her curled fingers with a disinterested expression. "No."

"Okay." Doug resumes flipping stations.

"Wait! Go back!" she blurts. "That's my favorite part."

He clicks back to *The Outsiders.* On the screen, young actors C. Thomas Howell and Ralph Macchio are standing by a wire fence facing the rising sun. Ponyboy, Howell's character, quotes a poem. Michelle recites its final stanza along with him.

"*Then leaf subsides to leaf. So Eden sank to grief. So dawn goes down to day. Nothing gold can stay.*"

Still in his day clothes, Doug slides into bed beside her. They watch the rest of the movie together, then a syndicated episode of *Seinfeld* that comes on afterward, followed by a nature show about sperm whales on another channel. Michelle dozes off during the documentary with Doug's arm around her shoulders, her cheek nuzzling his chest.

By the time Doug learns that sperm whales got their name from the waxy fluid in their heads that researchers first thought was semen, he realizes he is not near tired enough to sleep. The digital clock on his nightstand reads almost midnight, though he's pretty sure it's later than that. Maybe some chips and a drink would help him unwind, he thinks. He gingerly untangles himself from Michelle, who doesn't so much as crinkle her lips as he repositions her.

Doug pockets the room's keycard and steps outside. He tries to shut the door as softly as possible, yet the click of the lock engaging sounds to him as loud as a firecracker. He flinches, hopes it hasn't wakened Michelle.

Around the corner in a grungy breezeway, a pair of vending machines—one for snacks, the other selling off-brand sodas and juices—glow like monolithic beacons in the otherwise unlit space. After spending a couple of minutes waffling about what to get, Doug uses his last few dollar bills to buy a bottle of Mr. Pibb and bags of Bar-B-Q Fritos and Famous Amos Cookies.

On his way back, he encounters a young couple sitting outside the room next to his. The guy's sporting grass-soiled jeans and a wife beater; the girl's rocking baggy gym shorts and a pink halter top. Both are barefoot and greasy haired. Doug figures they must've just come out there, dragging the chairs from their room to the concrete walkway like it was their front porch. They swap swigs from a big bottle of cheap bourbon.

Doug is perfectly fine ignoring them, preferring they do the same, but he must have a sign somewhere on him that says—

"Hey, dude. Got any weed?"

—*POTHEAD*. Since high school, lots of people have pegged Doug as a stoner. Maybe it's his frequent red-rimmed eyes caused by the rash of seasonal allergies he suffers from every spring and summer (though they haven't kicked in yet this year).

"We'll pay ya for it," the guy adds. "Whatever you want."

Evidently Doug also comes across as a drug dealer.

"Anything but money," the girl chimes in. "'Cause we ain't got none!" She chortles like a mental patient.

"Don't got *much*, she means," the guy says. "What'll, like, ten bucks get us?"

"Sorry," Doug replies. "I got nothing. Except this stuff here." He waggles his late-night haul at them.

"Aww, bummer," the guy groans. "Y'all look like you got the munchies, is all."

"Oo, they got Famous Anus cookies?" the girl says. "Fuckin' love Famous Anus."

"Want a drink?" the guy asks Doug, proffering the whiskey bottle.

"No thanks," Doug answers.

"C'mon, man," the girl implores. "We're celebrating. Party with us."

"What are you celebrating?"

"We just got hitched," the guy says proudly.

"*Married*," the girl corrects him. "I hate the word 'hitched.' I'm not a pickup truck, Austin."

"Well, I did just pick ya up and ride ya, Carla," Austin says with a smirk.

Carla playfully punches her hubby in the arm. "Shut yer asshole."

"Congratulations," Doug says.

"Thanks, bud. You sure y'all don't want a hit of this?" Austin shakes the bottle a little too vigorously, sloshing some whiskey onto his jeans.

"Nah, I'm good," Doug reiterates. "Well, I hope you two have a happy life together." He plucks the keycard from his pocket and inches toward his room.

"Oh, we're gonna be happy," the girl trumpets. "No matter what our folks think."

"They don't think we're good for each other," Austin explains. "Say we bring out the bad in each other."

"And they said there's no damn way they'll let our wedding happen," Carla adds. "But guess what, it happened 'cause nobody tells us what to do. This is *our* life."

"Dude, know what my pop said?" Austin points at the air. "He said we ain't gonna last a week. That we'll be done with each other before the ink on the marriage license dries. Which is such bull-shit."

"They don't understand how deep our love goes, man. It's like bottomless hole deep."

Austin nods. "Yeah, man. No matter what, we always gonna be together. Right, babe?"

"Always always always," Carla mutters like a mantra.

"Till death do you part," Doug recites.

"Pfft. Fuck that!" the girl barks. "Our love is forever, muther-fuckers."

"Fuck yeah."

The drunken newlyweds then kiss as though their very lives depend on mingling as much of their salivas as possible. By the time he reenters his room moments later, Doug guesses they've probably already forgotten about him.

A muffled bang jolts Doug awake.

He bolts upright in the bed and surveys the room. Dusty day-light seeps through the thin gap between the thick beige curtains drawn over the windows. He looks for anything that might have somehow toppled over, like a lamp or a chair. Sees nothing. Maybe it was the toilet seat falling closed again; he always leaves them up.

Michelle is no longer lying next to him. She had migrated to the other bed, snoozing on the right side as usual, on top of the covers, hugging her knees to her belly. She's clad in just her underwear, yesterday's outfit shed sometime during the night onto the floor between the beds.

The mysterious noise hadn't woken her. She must really need the rest, Doug reckons. He glances at the digital clock on the nightstand—8:20 AM. He decides to let her sleep a little while longer. As long as they got on the road by 10, they would be sticking to their schedule.

Still wearing the clothes he had on the day before, he leaves their room to get some fresh air, maybe hike out to the turnpike and grab a coffee somewhere. He immediately squints from the bright morning sun hitting their side of the motel. Shielding his eyes with his hand, he surveys the adjacent parking lot. Only two cars are on this side of the building: his Nissan and a rust-pocked white Dodge Caravan, which Doug guesses belongs to the white-trashy couple he'd chatted with last night. He feels kind of sorry for them—a shabby motel in Central Ohio is a pretty lousy place to honeymoon.

When he turns to head toward the main road, Doug notices a balled-up bath towel holding the door to the couple's room ajar. A sheet of Motel 6 stationary has been stuck to their door with chewed bubblegum. A message is scrawled on it in green ink:

TO WHO EVER FIND US
SORRY + THANKS

Doug leans over to peer through the window. Even with the curtains parted, it's too murky inside to make out much beyond the unmade bed and the table with the empty bottle of bourbon on it, plus two crumpled bags of Famous Amos—*Famous Anus, heh*—cookies.

Doug senses something isn't right here. He nudges the door open with his fist and steps over the towel as if it were dangerous or delicate.

"Hello?" he calls out. Nobody answers him.

The chairs that the couple had been using the night before are now pushed in under the table. A few Chinese takeout containers are neatly stacked up on the bureau, ready for easy disposal. There is a faint smell of something. Burnt matches, maybe?

Doug doesn't see any suitcases or travel bags anywhere. They could've already put them in their minivan and were having breakfast somewhere before setting off to wherever their future is taking them.

But then what's with the note on the door?

The bathroom door is open and the light is on. Doug can hear music, a twangy bluesy song, coming from it.

"Hello," he says again as he approaches. Again, no answer.

When Doug reaches the threshold to the bathroom, he identifies the source of the music, a smartphone propped on the lip of the sink. There's an empty pint bottle of dark rum lying on the tiled floor by the tub. Then he finds the newlyweds.

Oh fuck.

They're both sitting fully clothed in the dry tub, Carla in front of Austin, as if they were riding a bobsled. On her sternum rests the butt of a big silver revolver, its barrel inserted into her gaping mouth. Austin's thumb is still slotted in the trigger guard. The bullet had punched through the back of Carla's head and into Austin's left eye—*Christ, did he aim to do that?*—likely lodging in his brain since there is no blood spatter behind his head. His ruined socket appears even more ghastly beside his other eye that has frozen wide open, capturing his final instant of shock. Tears cling to Carla's cheeks, blood coats her lips and chin. There is a point on her jaw where the tears flow into the blood, a crystalline stream disappearing into a crimson lake.

Doug chokes back a sudden impulse to retch. The nausea passes as quick as it hit him.

TO WHO EVER FIND US
SORRY + THANKS

They had written the note for him, whether or not they knew it would be him.

Doug's next instinct is to turn away, but he doesn't. Looking away seems like an insult to them. Their bodies curled together in this, their last loving embrace, feels like a moment too special, too precious for him to chalk up as merely their brutal farewell to a world that would neither accept nor support their union.

Rather, it was their defiant declaration: *"Our love is forever, mutherfuckers!"*

Doug wishes this were true.

He also wishes he had never seen this messed-up scene. He knows people don't simply shake off shit like this. It sticks with you. Scars you. He knows this memory—this macabre memorial to them—will randomly pop into his mind for the rest of his life, during a dinner or a movie or a vacation…

Thinking this makes him feel like an asshole. At least he can still enjoy eating and watching movies and going on vacation.

Doug exits their room and calls 911 in the parking lot. About ten minutes later, two police cars and a red ambulance arrive. An Officer Krollins, who appears to have a glass eye, poses a series of routine questions to Doug. Doug answers most of them with "I don't know," one with "No, pretty sure neither of them was still breathing when I found them." By the time they're almost done, a midnight blue coroner's van backs into the space in front of the newlyweds' room.

After he gives the officer his contact info, Doug slips past the small crowd of gawkers and returns to his room. Michelle's up, still in her undies, peering out the window through the curtains. She grips the edges tightly against the sides of her head, as if she were bundled up against a winter wind.

"What's happening?" she asks him as soon as he enters.

"This couple died," Doug replies. "In the room next to us."

"Next to us?"

Doug nods and *hm-hmm*s.

"Oh wow. How did they die?"

"They, uh…" Doug falters telling her, worrying it might upset her more. But why would it? She didn't know them. She has never even seen them. "They committed suicide."

"Holy shit," Michelle gasps. "So why were the cops talking to you?"

"'Cause I was the one who found them." Doug then recounts the local crime blotter version of his experience.

"Holy shit," she repeats. "Are you okay?"

"Yeah, I'm fine," he answers. "How are you doing?"

"Alright, I guess." She then grimaces. "I had this weird dream last night."

"Did ya? What was it about?"

"We were on an African safari. You were riding an elephant. And I was on an ostrich."

"An ostrich?"

"Yeah. With a saddle on it."

Doug laughs through his nostrils. "That makes more sense. Where were we going?"

"We were racing each other, towards the ledge of this crazy high cliff."

"Like in *Thelma & Louise*?"

"Yeah. Kinda."

"That doesn't sound good."

She shrugs. "But we had the most amazing view."

SIX

An hour later, they have checked out of the motel wearing their funeral finery and are back on the road heading toward Philadelphia. After having breakfast at a Starbucks in a highway rest stop, Michelle once more slips into her stoicism, while Doug reverts to his role as chauffeur. For four hundred miles they travel without talking, neither knowing what the other is thinking, each lost in thoughts that smolder and sting.

Due to a monstrous traffic jam caused by a jackknifed semi-trailer on the interstate, they don't reach the Fowlingtons' hometown until after six p.m. Doug wants to grab a bite to eat someplace, but because it's so late in the day Michelle vetoes that idea. There'll be food there, she tells him. And she's not hungry anyway.

As he drives toward the estate, Doug soon realizes Burkburgh is not much of a town at all. It consists of only a tiny police station, a fieldstone firehouse, and a single gas station with a bare-bones selection minimart. No hotels, restaurants, markets, or anywhere else somebody might wish to spend some time. There's not even a town sign marking when you enter. (Doug only knows they're in Burkburgh because of the GPS.) This is a pass-through type of place. Any visitors who stay here awhile are probably invited guests of the Fowlingtons.

They cruise through the wide-open gateway fashioned from what appear to be patinated medieval spears. Doug estimates the white gravel driveway leading to the house must be more than a quarter mile in length. He also figures the Fowlingtons must've mown down vast swaths of the surrounding woodlands to free up enough space to develop their property. Michelle had told him the place was like a castle, and Doug decides that's pretty accurate, with its sun-bleached stone and iron-barred windows, though it reminds him equally of some historical prison that has received a major makeover to make it look marginally more hospitable.

Michelle directs Doug to drive up to the main entrance. He stops beneath the arched porte cochère beside a lanky, black uni-formed valet. Leaving the car's engine running, Doug gets out as the valet opens the passenger door for Michelle. Doug pops the hatchback door and starts unloading their luggage.

"Leave them," Michelle tells him. "Someone will bring them in for us."

Circling around to the driver's side, the valet nods at Doug in poker-faced affirmation. Doug puts their bags back into the car and fishes his wallet from his pants pocket.

"What are you doing?" Michelle asks him.

"Tipping the guy."

Shaking her head, she motions him over to her. "We're not at a restaurant," she chides him. "You don't tip anybody here."

"Okay." Doug sheepishly returns his wallet to his pocket. "My bad."

Doug watches the valet, now planted behind the wheel of his car, move it down a narrow alleyway adjacent to the entrance.

"Where's he going?"

"That's where the servants' door is," Michelle replies. "They'll take our bags in through there."

"Right. Servants door. Got it."

"Come on." With autopiloted purpose, Michelle leads Doug through the hammered copper entrance doors and into a foyer so grand it can rival the lobbies of those ritzy hotels he has only ever seen on TV travel shows. Its walls are lined with gigantic oil paintings of impressionistic landscapes representing autumnal roads, seaside villages, and shimmering cities. The wrought iron chandelier, swaying slightly above them, looks so old it may have been pillaged from some once powerful citadel now crumbled to dust. From its vaulted ceiling to the pearlescent floor, it's by far the largest and fanciest private residence Doug has ever visited.

In the middle of the foyer sits a farmhouse table that seems better suited to, well, a farmhouse. White paint chipping from its blocky legs, timeworn ruts gouged into its wooden top. Arranged on it is a collection of framed photographs featuring Liam from all periods of his life, from burbling infant to smiling adult.

Michelle only glances at the pictures before briskly moving on past them. Doug takes a closer gander and realizes why: set center stage on the tabletop in a burnished gold frame is a photo of Liam and Michelle embracing in front of the mansion. Her cheek nuzzles his chest. She looks happy. In love.

Doug moves on too.

He follows Michelle into the grand hall. It's nearly the size of an airplane hangar, with squeaky-clean picture windows and a dramatic mural that covers the entirety of the ceiling, depicting what appears to be a horse-mounted hunting party led by a white-bearded deity soaring above them. What they are hunting is not shown.

A somber assembly of well-dressed mourners talks amongst themselves in small, tight-knit groups. Many partake of the smorgasbord of fine foods set out on the long table in the adjoining dining hall. Right away Doug feels self-conscious; he should've worn a tie. His "nice" lime-green L.L. Bean sweater and gunmetal gray slacks from Walmart highlight him as the one obvious non-member at a posh country club gala. The parking valet is more smartly attired than he.

Doug thinks Michelle, with her elegant black dress and mid-heel pumps, fits in much better here. This bothers him, and the fact that it bothers him bothers him even more. He wonders who will be offering the other the greater degree of emotional support while they're there.

"Beanie!"

A middle-aged lady in a flowing, jet-black gown dashes toward Michelle and wraps her lace-bundled arms around her like dark tendrils. After a protracted moment, the woman breaks their embrace. Still clasping Michelle's shoulders, she appraises her with a puckered smile and rheumy eyes. "My, oh, my Beanie, you are as lovely as ever."

"Thanks…" Now Michelle's eyes well up. "I'm so sorry about Liam—"

"No need to be sorry, dear," she says. "You made my son so very happy when you were together. Liam was fortunate to have you in his life."

A tear streams down Michelle's right cheek, then another on the left. "I just wish things could have been… different for him."

"'*Accept the things to which fate binds you, and love the people with whom fate brings you together,*'" recites the lady, who Doug realizes is Liam's mother, Isadora Fowlington. "Liam loved you very much, Michelle. We cannot change what has happened, but we can cherish all the wonderful moments we've had, and those we were meant to have, with him."

Michelle nods as she wipes the tears from her cheeks with her knuckles, which only spreads the wetness around. Almost magically, Isadora produces a black handkerchief from some part of her multi-piece gown and offers it to her. Michelle accepts the cloth and blots the moistened areas of her face. She wisely hasn't worn any makeup, so she doesn't make a mess of herself other than the rosy puffiness now surrounding her eyes.

Doug clears his throat. "I'm very sorry for your loss, ma'am."

Only now does Isadora seem to notice Michelle's male companion.

"Oh, Doug…" says Michelle, as though she just remembered he's with her. "This is Liam's mother. Mrs. Fowlington, this is my friend, Doug."

Her *friend*. She said it so spontaneously Doug thinks she may have rehearsed it.

"He came to support me."

"Ah. That is very kind of you," Isadora says to Doug, giving him just enough attention to not come off as dismissive. "It's important to have friends in difficult times."

"Yeah, well," Doug replies, "what are friends for?"

"Indeed." Isadora returns her focus to Michelle. "Would you like to see him?"

"Who?"

"The guest of honor, Liam, of course."

"Oh. Yeah. Sure." Each word dribbles from Michelle's mouth as if caught on a fishing line running from her throat, attached to her reeling heart.

Isadora smiles warmly at her. "I know it can be surreal, scary even, viewing a loved one lying in repose. But I assure you, dear, Liam looks wholly untroubled. Peaceful. As if he's simply asleep."

"Okay." Isadora's words of succor do little to soothe her.

"I'll be with you every step." Isadora loops her arm around Michelle's waist. "I shan't leave your side. I promise." Almost as an afterthought, Liam's mother addresses Doug before escorting his girlfriend away. "You may join us, if you wish."

"Uh… nah. That's alright. I'll hang here. Okay, Michelle?"

Michelle nods. She already seems to be somewhere else.

"That's fine," Isadora says. "Hold on…" She scans the crowd in the expansive room until she spots someone within a cluster of people near the huge fireplace. "Bethie! Bethie hon!"

A young woman looks in their direction.

"Come here please!" Isadora calls, beckoning her with a wave of her hand.

The young woman excuses herself from the circle of men she is chatting with and sashays over to join Isadora, Michelle, and Doug.

"Bethie, you of course remember Michelle. And this is her friend Doug. Doug, this is my daughter Bethany."

Bethany bows her head once and says a cordial "hi, sweetie" to Michelle. She then proffers her hand to Doug, her genteel grin faltering whenever her lips twitch, which is often. She has a kind of Tourette's, he recalls Michelle telling him. "Pleasure to meet you, Doug."

"Likewise." He delicately shakes Bethany's wiry hand, trying not to gawk at her. Michelle had also told him Liam's sister was super skinny, but this chick is just skin and skeleton. Wearing a tight, black satin dress that emphasizes every angle of her body, her arms and legs resemble four suntanned sticks, her neck and cheeks wilted beyond gaunt, as if all the meat has been sucked or scooped out of them. Yet this is not even her most striking—or shocking—attribute. Her breasts are absurdly humongous, like two jumbo-sized balloons affixed to a flagpole. Must be a boob job, Doug decides, performed by a mad doctor who should have his license revoked.

"I'm taking Beanie to see Liam," Isadora informs her daughter. "Can you keep Doug company?"

"That's alright," Doug says. "I'll be fine here on my own."

"I can just imagine what it's like being someplace where you don't know anyone." Isadora bobbles her head a bit as she speaks, a slight edge salting her voice which Doug interprets as a *how-dare-you-challenge-my-bidding* tone. "Everybody knows each other, and you are just standing around staring at your shoes or whatnot, no one noticing you, no one caring about you. You're there but might as well not be."

"I can deal," Doug maintains. "I don't want to be a bother."

"Oh *peuh*! You're far from a bother," Bethany purrs at him. "We wouldn't want you to feel uncomfortable in our home. Nay, we *won't* allow it. So *vous* are stuck with *moi*. Would you care for something to eat or drink?"

"Sure," Doug capitulates.

"Pardon my manners, dear," Isadora says to Michelle. "Might you want something too before we head up? I know you've had a long drive."

"No, thank you," Michelle answers.

Doug can understand why Michelle is so fond of Mrs. Fowlington, more than once calling her "the sweetest thing." Toward Michelle, Isadora Fowlington is indeed amiable, unintimidating, motherly. He wonders how much she reminds Michelle of her own mom.

"I'll bring her back soon," Isadora tells Doug as she leads Michelle out of the room, the other guests parting the way for them like paparazzi at a red carpet event.

"Shall we, *mon chéri*?" Bethany cradles Doug's elbow in her palm and guides him in the opposite direction.

Michelle and Isadora take the elevator to the fourth floor.

Michelle expected to be nervous but instead finds herself... eager? That sounds weird to her, and yet that is the only way she would describe how she feels right now. Maybe her father was right. She *is* looking forward to closing this chapter of her life, and seeing Liam now—lifeless, soulless—will allow her to put that book back on the shelf. Or in a box, sealed and stored away in some hard-to-reach place.

Or maybe it's something else. She just needs to see Liam one last time, say a proper goodbye, say she's sorry. Their whacked-out shitshow ending aside, she can concede—to herself—that she misses the life they had together. It was passionate and fun and hopeful. She loved Liam. Loves him still. They understood one another better than anyone else ever could. Better than even Doug, though she loves him too, of course. And Doug's alive, so that definitely works in his favor. But a piece of her seems to have died with Liam. That's probably a normal thing, a natural thing. A good thing. Part of the healing process.

So here it is, Liam & Michelle: The Final Chapter, she thinks. Or would this be an epilogue?

Whichever, she's ready to move on.

They exit the elevator into a hallway laid with plush maroon carpeting. A succession of gold sconces fitted with amber-glowing bulbs run the length of its green walls. Michelle retains a vague memory of this passage, but try as she might, she cannot lift the veil obscuring when she has been here before.

Isadora leads her to the end of the hallway, then turns down another, longer one lined with photographic portraits. Michelle recognizes two people from the first grouping of framed photos, hanging next to each other. She stops, scrutinizes their pictures.

"I remember them… Liam's aunt and uncle, right?"

"Gerty and Randall, yes," Isadora confirmed. "They perished in a freak boating accident last summer, hit by a rogue wave. Just dreadful. I was rather fond of Randall. Though Gerty, Nathaniel's sister, she could be churlish. Her poor health—she had mobility issues you may recall—likely was what soured her disposition."

Michelle does recall Aunt Gerty, with her souped-up scooter and acid tongue, and the brawny Uncle Randall, his toupee looking much less ridiculous in the photograph than it had in person.

"That's sad," Michelle says.

"It is. But they both loved the water. I should think they are quite pleased with the manner of their passing."

Michelle nods, though she very much doubts anybody would find drowning a pleasing experience.

As they proceed to the end of the hallway, the portraits of expired Fowlington family members graduate from photographs to paintings, and from paintings to inks on parchment.

Isadora and Michelle reach a set of rustic timbered doors with tooled iron hardware. They remind Michelle of the kind of doors that grace old churches. A bouquet of small animal bones, joined with twine and resin, is nailed to the wall above them.

Michelle remembers these doors.

And the room beyond them.

Her skin tingles, her gut roils, her brain crackles. The tattoo on her chest burns hot as a stovetop. And once again she enters the Thinning Room.

Doug loads up a white bone china plate with fancy foods from the buffet table—beef wellington, lobster thermidor, squash soufflé. Most items Bethany has to identify for him. She offers him wine. Feeling so out of his element here, Doug could sure use a drink or two. Instead he opts for a glass of iced tea in case Michelle comes back before he's done with his meal.

Bethany and Doug end up in an unoccupied sitting room out-fitted with swanky sofas and fashionable armchairs, all purpose-fully mismatched. Doug guesses they were purchased for their exorbitant price tag and not for their practicality, as most of the pieces look rough in texture and/or ridiculous in design. (One severely angled chair appears to be upholstered in reptile hide.) Bethany finds them the lone comfy exception, a velvet-covered loveseat strewn with chenille throw pillows. Doug sinks into one of the cushions while she sits beside him, so close their hips almost touch.

Bethany keenly watches Doug eat. He sneaks glances at her crossed, spindly legs that remind him of a frog's limbs, all bone and tendon. He figures she must be near starving herself to keep herself looking like this, a stick-figure Barbie with titanic tits.

But hey, he thinks, *if that's what makes her feel hot, hooray for her.*

"Enjoying your meal?" she asks him.

He nods as he pops another forkful of soufflé into his mouth, which tastes like baked heaven to him. He feels somewhat guilty wolfing down the heaping plate in front of her, but he hasn't eaten since early that afternoon, and that had been only a small break-fast sandwich from Starbucks. He's famished. So she can stare at him all she wants for all he cares. Maybe it'll spur her into gorging herself on a stuffed clam or a couple of olives.

"Hey… I'm sorry about your brother," Doug says between bites.

"I love your face," Bethany says as if she hadn't heard him.

"Yeah?" Doug replies. "What about it?"

"Your brow, your jaw, the bridge of your nose. They've such well-defined lines. As though each had been sculpted separately, yet there's a harmony between them. Everything's in balance."

"Is that right?"

"Oh yes. Whoever does your work is very skilled."

Doug furrows his well-defined brow. "What work?"

"Your cosmetic surgery. If you wouldn't mind sharing your doctor's name—"

Doug chuckles and shakes his head. "No doctor did this." He circles the air around his face with his fork. "This mug is natural born me."

"*Ah bon*?" Bethany gasps. "Well, didn't you hit the genetic jackpot!"

Doug can feel himself blushing. "Guess I'm a lucky dog."

"If you're a dog, I'll be your bitch." She nibbles on her plump lower lip while also involuntarily flaring her nostrils, pretty much spoiling the intended sultry effect. "Want to bury your bone in me, Fido?"

Doug's eyebrows spring to his hairline. It's been a long time since somebody has so brazenly hit on him. Ordinarily it would excite him, top off his self-esteem tank. But nothing about any of this seems ordinary to him.

"That's really flattering, but…" he says, sipping his iced tea. "It's just, I'm with someone."

Bethany's lips spasm, warping her smirk. "Might this some-one be Michelle?"

Doug takes a moment to mull over his response. "It might be."

"So she's your girlfriend?"

"That's what *I* like to call her."

"But that's not what she is here, is she? You're her *friend*." The way Bethany says *friend* brims with mischievous teasing, border-line cruel sarcasm.

"She's just trying to make things less awkward."

"That's a tough zipper to zip," Bethany declares. "But what a big-hearted guy you are, coming to the funeral of your girlfriend's fiancé."

"Ex-fiancé. They broke up."

Bethany rolls her eyes. "Fiancé. Ex-fiancé. Boyfriend. Friend. What difference does it make?"

Doug doesn't have an answer, nor an appetite, anymore. "I think… I will have a glass of wine."

"See?" Isadora sighs. "He looks like he'll wake up any time now."

To Michelle, Liam looks neither asleep nor dead. Rather, he most resembles a mannequin, with his too perfect skin and too red lips and too groomed hair. A product of mortician chic. This is not the Liam she remembers, even on his best days. Still, she thinks she prefers this artificial-looking Liam right now. It makes everything marginally less real, less unsettling.

They've dressed him in a snazzy black wool suit and laid him out in a lidless, unembellished pinewood coffin—more of a crate, really—riddled with knotholes that Michelle imagines will allow worms and maggots easy access to him when he's in the ground. The thought makes her shudder. The casket is placed nearly up-right on a large steel easel in the center of the small raised stage.

Liam appears to be standing there, eyes closed, facing the pews like some actor or singer about to perform.

When they entered the Thinning Room, Nathaniel Fowlington, decked out in a suit matching Liam's, was dozing beside his son on a ladderback chair, gripping the neck of a half-consumed bottle of blue label Scotch. He awakens to the sound of his wife's voice. Upon seeing Michelle, he rises from the chair, spreads his arms wide, and approaches her, his mien a mixture of profound joy and sorrow.

"Michelle!" Liam's father bear-hugs her with enough force to squeeze all the air from her lungs. "Sweetheart! You came!"

"Of course…" Michelle replies once he has loosed his hold. "I'm so sorry—"

"Now now, no more of that." Nathaniel waves a repudiating hand. "That's why I left the reception. Couldn't stomach all the condolences and crying."

Michelle does not know how to respond to this, so she only nods.

None of them say anything for a while, wrapped up in their own thoughts, memories, and, in Michelle's case, guilt. Guilt for enabling Liam, for ditching him, for not helping him when she could have, when she should have.

Liam's mother fusses with her son's slim indigo tie, adjusting it so it aligns precisely along the buttons of his white shirt.

Michelle finds the gesture touching.

"He was trying to get sober for you, you know."

"W-what?" Michelle stammers in answer to Isadora's statement, uncertain if she had heard her right.

"Liam thought if he could get better, then you would take him back."

Michelle is speechless. Liam died because of her.

"Because he loved you that much," Nathaniel says.

"Oh, Jesus." Michelle feels nauseous. "I wouldn't want him to do that. I never asked him to."

"We know, sweetheart." Nathaniel's solicitous smile quickly dissolves. "But you can understand why he was thinking that way, in his condition."

"Surely Liam was not thinking clearly," Isadora adds, able to read the dismay on Michelle's face. "You have nothing to feel bad about."

Too late, Michelle thinks.

"My wife and I do have a favor to ask of you," Nathaniel says, rubbing his chin as if trying to resculpt it. "It may seem unorthodox. Outlandish, even. But please lend an ear with an open mind."

Michelle nods.

"Our family has long believed that important endeavors one could not achieve in their life should be honored after their death whenever possible. Granting a posthumous last wish, so to speak. You're well aware how much Liam cared about you. Nothing in his life was more important than you. Nothing mattered as much as spending the rest of his life with you."

Michelle is on the brink of melting to the floor in wracking sobs.

"As such, we think it fitting, if you're amenable, that you and Liam can still… consummate your plans."

"To put it plainly," a mildly impatient Isadora interjects, "we want you to still marry our son."

Michelle gapes at her, stupefied. "You... what?"

"It would be purely ceremonial, dear. Not legally binding at all, but rather a symbolic gesture of closure before we reverence the funeral rites."

"I don't know... It seems..."

"Unorthodox, as I said," Nathaniel says. "Yet, in essence, it's no different from any other tribute or memorial the living perform for their departed loved ones or respected icons. And that's all it is—a performance. One that would mean a lot to us."

"And of course, we believe Liam would approve wholeheartedly." Isadora smiles, eyes welling. "Think of it as a very special, very personal farewell for someone you once called the love of your life."

"I..." A tear runs down Michelle's cheek. Her heart punches inside her chest. Her breaths scrape her esophagus like tiny barbs. Her skin sizzles. Her body's telling her this is wrong, yet her mind reassures her because that's what minds sometimes do. No matter how fucked up one's world becomes, they convince themself that everything is fine. Otherwise they'd just break apart into so many splinters and shards that they never can be completely patched up, never be in one unblemished piece again.

Michelle has been broken before, and then reassembled into a fairly faithful likeness of herself. She doesn't want to revisit that damned, damaged version of her.

What Liam's parents are proposing need not shatter her. She only has to ignore the hammer that may be hovering over her.

There's probably no hammer at all, Michelle tells herself. *Just two grieving parents who want me to be a privileged part of their son's send-off to Heaven, Nirvana, Valhalla, whatever world they believe exists beyond this one.*

"I guess it'll be okay," she says.

Nathaniel claps his palms together. "It will be, sweetheart. It'll be splendid!"

"I'm confident you've made our son very happy, Beanie, from wherever he may be watching," Isadora says. "You will always be part of our family in spirit."

Liam's parents embrace their soon-to-be token daughter-in-law, their arms enveloping her like tree roots.

From over their shoulders, Michelle gazes upon Liam in his casket. She wonders if, wherever his spirit is now, he's amused by her discomfort. "You'll get used to us," he once cheerfully said about his family. Now, after his death, she very much doubts that will ever be true.

After her visit to the Thinning Room, Michelle rejoins Doug in the grand hall and grabs something to eat from the buffet table. She is still not very hungry but manages a few bites of a buttered dinner roll and a ramekin of fruit salad. A valet then escorts them to their assigned room, where their bags are already waiting for them on the ottoman at the foot of the bed.

Michelle is extraordinarily grateful she and Doug were not given the same room her and Liam had shared whenever they'd stayed there. Their accommodations are in another wing on the opposite side of the manor house. It features less frilly bed linens, blander wallpaper, and no fireplace. Instead of a view of the pool and gardens, their window looks out onto the groundskeeper's shed. It's still quite lovely and cozy, but Michelle cannot help but think she has been downgraded. She's fine with that.

Michelle takes a quick shower, brushes her teeth, and slips on her pajamas. She is still thinking about Nathaniel and Isadora's bizarre request, trying to come to terms with it. But she realizes there's no way she can make herself comfortable with the idea. It's like getting an OB/GYN exam… or going to the funeral of someone close to you.

She considers the situation from another angle: what harm would it do? Michelle can't see any, and by putting the focus on Liam's family and not on herself, honoring their request seems less of a discomfort, more of a good deed.

Michelle sits down at the foot of the bed and tells Doug what happened with Liam's parents.

"Wait…" Doug, hunched forward in a heather gray damask armchair, looks up from the word game he's been playing on his phone. "What do they want you to do?"

"They want to hold a mock wedding for me and Liam."

"Are you kidding? That's fucked up."

"No it's not. Not really. It's just… unorthodox."

"Whatever," Doug huffs. "You told them no, right?"

Michelle shrugs. "I said I'd do it."

"What the hell, Michelle. Are you nuts?… I know *they* are." Doug's expression lands somewhere between disbelief and disgust. "Why would you agree to that?"

"It's only symbolic. For closure."

"Closure for who?"

"Liam."

"He's dead. That's as closed as you can get." Doug rises from the chair—the room spins a second, likely from the glass of port he had with Liam's sister—and begins pacing the floor. "Having this bullshit wedding means nothing to him."

"It'll mean something to his family."

"So? You don't owe them anything."

"Yes, I do."

"And what's that?"

Michelle thinks about what Liam had gone through for her, at the end. "I just do."

Doug throws up his hands. "I can't believe you're seriously entertaining this."

"It's just pretend, Doug. Like when we play Father Dick and Sister Suckgood."

"That is *not* the same thing. At all."

"My point is, the wedding isn't real. It's like a play. I'm just *acting* like a bride for a day. It's kinda sweet."

"It's kinda sick," Doug says. "I mean, are you gonna have to kiss him?"

"Him?"

"Liam. Your groom. The *corpse.*"

Michelle's lips mouth words which have not yet formed in her brain. "I, uhm, don't know," she finally stammers. "I didn't ask… Probably not."

"Even if you don't have to give the guy a peck, it's still messed up." Doug walks over to the bed and looms over her, his hands on his hips. "Tell them you're not doing it."

"I already said I would."

"Then tell them you changed your mind."

"But, I haven't."

"This is insane, Mish. You know it is."

"Doug," Michelle says, exasperated. "I really need your support."

"I can't support *this*. I don't understand it, and I don't understand how you can go along with it after everything that guy put you through."

"It wasn't all Liam's fault."

"Fine. But you and him, that's in the past now. That goes for his weirdo family, too. They can't expect you to do something that is obviously gonna make you uncomfortable. And possibly give you nightmares for the rest of your life."

"I *want* to do this, Doug." Michelle looks at him beseechingly. "Please, can't you try to understand?"

Doug shakes his head. "No. I can't. This is not what we came here for."

"Not you. But it may be why I came here. What I need to do."

"Jesus Christ," he snaps. "I gotta get out of here."

Michelle frowns, lips quivering. "You're leaving?"

"I'm just going for a walk… I need to think about…"

Doug doesn't finish the sentence. He storms for the door and out of their room. He doesn't see Michelle start to cry.

Doug spends a few minutes wandering the dimmed hallways and common rooms of the huge home. With all the guests and help turned in for the night, the place is eerily empty and quiet. The faint footsteps of Doug's black oxfords echo around him, giving him the sense that someone is following right on his heels. He knows it's just his imagination, but still finds it unsettling.

He takes the elevator down to the ground floor, locates a door leading to the yard, and heads outside.

What the fuck is wrong with her?, he asks himself. Michelle probably thinks he is being close-minded and bullheaded, but c'mon, she's intending to marry her dead ex. Even if it is fake—*symbolic*—the whole idea is crazy. And creepy as fuck.

But what can he do? He can't forbid her, won't walk out on her. Maybe if he explains to her in a levelheaded tone how much it upsets him and why… but why does it upset him so much? Why should he be jealous of a guy who's being prepped for the grave? It's not like Michelle can run off with him, go on a honeymoon, buy their dream house, have his kids, and live happily ever after.

Still, he's beyond bothered by it.

It disturbs him.

And it disturbs him even more that Michelle doesn't seem disturbed by it.

Doug strolls through the still lit-up flagstone patio, weaving around the funky modern furniture and skirting alongside the glimmering mosaic-tiled pool. For some reason, maybe because of the late hour, he feels like he's trespassing here. Moving past the terrace, he stumbles upon a statue garden situated behind a line of immaculately manicured hedgerows. It's darker here, the tall hedges blocking most of the exterior houselights. He passes several life-sized stone figures portraying what he presumes to be renowned adventurers and exalted warriors, maybe a robber baron or two.

One sculpture in particular catches his attention. Double the height of the other figures, it appears to be made of polished white marble instead of porous stone. The lushly bearded, skyward-gazing male figure, garbed in some type of toga or cloak, looms over Doug like some noble colossus musing on other worlds beyond this one. On the cubic plinth beneath it is engraved the word *BUKANI*. Doug wonders if this is a god the Fowlingtons worship, or at least revere enough to erect a ten-foot-tall statue of it.

Even in the wan moonlight, Doug can discern the meticulous level of detail that went into sculpting the piece, from the folds of its cloak to the whiskers of its beard. Except for the monocolor of the marble, Bukani almost looks alive.

Like a curious child, Doug wants to touch it, feel how smooth it is. He reaches out his hand, strokes the toes of Bukani's booted foot—

"*Sir!*" a lordly voice thunders above him.

Doug's head snaps up to see the statue's scowling face looking down at him.

"*Kindly keep your hands off the art!*"

Gasping, Doug recoils several steps before fleeing from the figure. He blindly runs through the labyrinth of hedges like a coked-up Jack Torrance, taking random rights and lefts that he hopes will lead him back to the house. In his frantic state, he takes a wrong turn that instead leads him into a brick wall. He pauses. He thinks he can hear Bukani, or whosever voice it is, laughing in the not-distant-enough distance.

The laughter soon trails off into an oppressive silence. Doug collects himself as best he can, then backtracks through the darkness, navigating the towering shrubbery with his outstretched hands, praying he doesn't again encounter that admonishing, animatronic statue.

For that's what it *must* be, Doug reasons. He triggered some mechanism designed to stop people like him from leaving their greasy fingerprints all over the sculpture.

Even so, that shit was freaky.

Doug spots one of the manor's exterior lights. He threads his way toward it.

When he turns a corner around a hedgerow, he almost steps on a body. He halts with a jolt, letting out a short, unmanly shriek. The near full moon casts enough illumination for him to make out the form lying on a striped blanket spread out on a patch of grass.

It's Liam's sister, and she's nude.

"Oh, shit!" Doug blurts and jerks his foot back.

Bethany yelps in surprise.

"Sorry!" He whirls away from her, all set to bolt in embarrassment.

"Wait! Doug!"

He freezes.

"It's okay. You just startled me," she says consolingly. "Come hang out with me awhile."

"Are you still…" Doug faces her again. Bethany is now sitting up, reclining on her hands which are splayed on the blanket. She smiles at him, making no effort to cover herself. The glow of the moon highlights her white-as-milk teeth and creamy skin. Her stomach concaves like a soup bowl underneath her starkly outlined ribs. The cool air has hardened her nipples to lethal-looking scarlet points.

"Yeah, you're still… there," he answers himself.

"What are you staring at?"

"Sorry." Doug averts his eyes again. "I wasn't—"

"I'm kidding, sillysaurus. You can look at me all you want." Bethany shimmies her shoulders, jiggling her enormous breasts. Doug imagines them sloshing. "It's nice to have someone appreciate my tits." She tilts her head coquettishly. "Do you like them?"

"They're, uh… impressive."

"They better be, for what they cost. But it's worth it. I like to grab people's attention."

"Yeah… they stand out."

"Why, thank you, Doug." She flashes him another Tourette's-twitchy grin, her nostrils dilating at the same time.

Doug skews his lips in a semblance of a smile.

"I was just catching some beams," Bethany says, gazing into the sky. "They open up the pores."

Doug also seizes the opportunity to peer up at the moon, big and bright in an otherwise inky void. "Oh yeah? I didn't know that."

"*Bien sûr*. The moon is very powerful. It regulates the tides and our sleep. Inspires artists and lovers. Sometimes even drives men mad."

Doug continues to scrutinize it, a celestial object he has seen a thousand times before, one that now, as hard as he resists the thought, reminds him of a boob. Bethany's boob, to be precise.

"Something wrong, Dougie? You seem kind of… off?"

"Well, it's probably because you're, uhm, completely naked."

"I can't believe you're that much of a prude," Bethany scoffs. "No, something has upset you."

Doug shakes his head. "I'm fine." Looking again at her, he finds himself less taken aback by her casual nudity.

"So, why are you prowling around our gardens this late?"

"Just getting some fresh air. Shaking off the day."

She squints at him. "Did you get into a fight with Michelle?"

"No," Doug replies more defensively than he intended. "Why would I?"

"Maybe because she's your girlfriend and she's marrying my dead brother."

Doug glares at her. "So you know about that?"

"I'm to be her maiden of honor, so to speak."

"Great," Doug says, smoldering. "Sounds like a big fucking country bear jamboree."

"Hm-hm. You're jealous," Bethany diagnoses him.

"Why the hell would I be jealous? As you said, your brother's gonna be the next Happy Meal at McMaggot's."

Bethany arches an eyebrow at him.

"Sorry," he sighs. "That was an assholey thing to say."

Bethany flicks a dangling lock of her hair from her brow. "That didn't bother me. My family doesn't bury our deceased, so maggots will have to go dine elsewhere. But I think you proved my theory—you're possessed by the green-eyed monster." She growls the words *green-eyed monster*.

Doug grits his teeth. "Okay. Maybe a little."

"Poor guy. This must all stick in your craw."

"My craw's been better."

She regards him for a moment, much like a snake sizing up her prey. "What if you did something to even it out? Level the ball field."

"You mean playing field."

"Even better."

"Such as what?"

Bethany fans her legs apart, presenting herself to him. With her pubes shaved, even in the wan light, Doug can pick out almost every detail of her cosmetically perfect pussy.

"You can fuck *moi*," she says.

"No," Doug responds emphatically. "I can't."

"Why not? Because of Michelle?"

"Yeah. I would never do that to her."

"But she's hurting you, *non*? Don't you want to balance things out?"

"Cheating on her isn't balancing anything. I would just feel like shit about it."

Bethany frowns. "Well, that stings."

"It's nothing against you. I just respect the relationship I have with Michelle too much."

"And do you think she respects it as much as you?"

Doug doesn't have an answer to this. Of course he hopes that Michelle feels the way he does, but in this circumstance it's difficult for him to gauge her feelings. Or perhaps he shouldn't be gauging them at all. This isn't about Michelle respecting him. It's about her paying her respects to someone she once cared about a lot. Doug realizes judging her on how she should best do this makes him come across pretty shitty.

Bethany rises sinuously onto her feet and slinks toward him, stopping close enough so he can feel her steamy breath on his face. "Then how about a blow job? That's not actually cheating."

Doug gawks at her. "Yes, it is."

"Okay, but it's not *major* cheating. It's a minor dalliance. And I'm *amazing* at it."

"Nah. Not interested."

"Aww," she pouts. "You're rejecting me?"

"No offense. I just can't."

"You mean you *won't*."

"Same difference."

"Such a good boy, Dougie, yes you are. You deserve a treat."

Bethany takes another step toward him. He takes an equivalent step away from her.

"Hey, I'm gonna go back to my room now."

"At least test-touch my new tits," she says while she twiddles her nipples. "Tell me, from a guy's perspective, if they pass rigid inspection."

"I'm sure they're fantastic."

"Go ahead… I want you to play with them."

"I can't—"

"Please, Dougie." She tugs at her nipples harder, moaning insistently. "Suck on themmm… pleeeasssse…"

"Uh, holy crap." Doug clenches his jaw in revulsion. "I think you're… bleeding."

Bethany stops tweaking her nipples and examines herself. A pulsing trickle of sangria-red blood leaks from one of them, streaming over her fingers and dripping off her knuckles. The purse-string sutures at the top of her left saucer-sized areola have torn, allowing it to flap over itself like a folded slice of salami.

"Oh, *merde!*" she blurts. "I wasn't supposed to… you know… they're still healing from the surgery." She sounds mortified.

Though Doug nods sympathetically, his continued appalled expression betrays him. Bethany reads his face and grimaces. She snatches her sheer pink robe hanging from some branches on a hedge, throws it over her shoulders and flounces away, muttering something Doug just catches before she disappears from sight: "I bet you have a tiny pecker anyway."

When Doug returns to their room, he finds Michelle sitting up in the kingly bed, a thick hardcover book open in her lap. He spies a full-color illustration of beetles on its yellowed pages. She must have gotten it from the bookcase, he figures, which he had also perused earlier to find mostly editions of early science and philosophy treatises, along with a handful of classic literature, plus a folio of sheet music for a piano concerto Doug has never heard of (not that he's heard of many).

"What are you reading?" he asks.

Michelle flips back to the title page. "It's called *Fabre's Book of Insects.*"

"So you're reading about bugs?"

"It has nice pictures. And it is pretty interesting. Like…" She riffles through the pages back to the one she was on, holding it up for Doug to see. "These dung beetles roll balls of shit around."

"Don't we all?" Doug quips.

Michelle snorts in amusement.

Doug wonders if he should again broach the subject of their disagreement—it wasn't quite a fight—or if he should just let it go and act like nothing happened. Recognizing that wouldn't resolve anything, he decides to take the most peaceable path, the one that would make Michelle happiest, relatively speaking.

"I've been thinking, Mish… and I think I'm being selfish," he says. "You're right. As insane as I think it is, I guess there's no harm in you doing that thing tomorrow, if that's what you really want to do. And it will help you… deal with it, I guess. So I won't object. But, if you don't mind, I'm gonna sit out the ceremony. Maybe stay here and read about those shit beetles."

Michelle closes the book and contemplates her boyfriend as he slouches at the foot of the bed. "No, you're not the one being selfish. I totally should have considered your feelings before I agreed to this… *thing*." She sighs. "I'll just tell the Fowlingtons that I changed my mind and I'm not doing it."

"That'll bum them out big time."

She nods glumly. "I know. But you're here because of me. *For* me. And you matter a hell of a lot more to me than putting on a make-believe wedding just to make Liam's parents happy."

"You sure?"

"Yeah. I am." She says this like she's ready to draw up a contract and sign it.

Doug grins at her. "For the record, you mean a hell of a lot to me, too."

"I'll jot that down in my files."

"Be sure to include that I'm the best boyfriend ever."

Michelle chuckles. "Wanna come to bed, #1?"

Doug nods. He's suddenly very tired. And very relieved.

As Michelle sets the book on her nightstand and switches off her lamp, Doug strips to his T-shirt and underwear and slips into his checkered pajama pants. He slides under the covers beside Michelle and kisses her goodnight.

The snow-white sheets feel soft and silky against his skin. The patchwork quilt blanket drapes over him snugly. The spring mattress supports him as if he's floating on placid water, the goose down pillows cradling his head like a cloud. Doug shuts his eyes.

It would be the least comfortable sleep he's ever had.

SEVEN

Michelle and Doug rise at a quarter to seven the next morning to get ready for breakfast at eight. Doug grumbled to himself upon finding the calligraphic "Itinerary of Funereal Proceedings" card that had been slipped under their bedroom door. He didn't realize Liam's bon voyage bash would be an *all-day* affair: Full English Breakfast, Chorale Lunch, Memorial Impartings, Dinner, Cortège, Final Rites, Reception. At least there appears to be a three-hour intermission after breakfast; he can go back to their room then and catch a nap.

While Doug watches Chris Farley *SNL* skits on his phone—to his irritation, there is no TV in their room—Michelle takes a shower. The walls of the stall—to her disappointment, there is no tub in their room—feature a tacky, tiled mosaic of nude water nymphs lazing on oversized lily pads.

At least the tilework serves as distracting eye-candy while she bathes. Normally she enjoys the hot water spattering against her skin, but today it feels like a barrage of pins pricking her. She stays in just long enough to sluice her body and soak her hair. By the time she turns off the faucet and steps out, the air in the room is still dry and cool. The mirrors haven't even steamed up.

"Shower's free!" Michelle shouts to Doug as she pats herself with a large Turkish bath towel, then wraps herself in it.

"OK," he answers over Chris Farley's voice shouting, "I live in a van down by the river!"

Standing before the beveled vanity mirror, Michelle chooses to braid her hair in a Dutch fishtail, a style Liam had especially liked on her. She knows how she wears her hair today does not really matter, but it feels right, a small tribute to someone she once dreamt of spending her life with.

As she crisscrosses the three strands of hair starting at the crown of her head, she studies herself in the mirror, focusing her eyes on their counterparts staring back at her. *Is something wrong with them?*, she muses. She leans in closer to her reflection. *Yes, there is something wrong.* Her eyes are lightless, lifeless. And then she recognizes them—it's the very same stare captured in her last rehab admittance photo. The same day she left Liam.

A chill fans out from deep within her, making her shiver.

Her joints lock. Her muscles freeze.

She cannot move.

Fog crests around the edges of the mirror, creeping further toward the center, like some fast-moving fungus, until Michelle's reflection entirely clouds over. Within the blurred background behind her, she discerns a dark shape approaching her.

Her heart races as the human form draws nearer. Her mind yells at her to turn around and flee, but her body remains rigid. She wants to scream, but her mouth holds fast, her lips cemented shut. All she can do is watch while the slender figure grows closer with each gliding step.

It reaches a hazy hand toward her.

———

Then she smells it—the acrid tang of acetone, like nail polish remover. The way Liam stank before she left him, when he was so pickled in booze it poured from his pores.

"*Liam?*" her brain asks without being able to speak it.

The figure touches her bare shoulder, and with that touch she knows for sure.

"*Michelle,*" Liam says.

Raw terror seizes her. A gasp erupts from her mouth and her muscles instantly defrost.

She whirls around, wholly expecting against all logic to behold the man whom she's there to mourn to be standing right in front of her, his face mere inches from hers...

Instead she sees Doug, naked and wet, wiping himself down with a towel.

"This house has fantastic water pressure," he says, impressed. "That shower really loosened up my muscles. It was like a Shiatsu massage."

Michelle stares at him, still speechless.

"What?" he asks. "Can't I enjoy a shower here?"

She nods stiffly, affecting an encouraging smile, then ducks out of the bathroom.

"I'll be ready in a minute," Doug calls out behind her as he squeegees the condensation from the mirror with the heel of his hand.

By the time they come downstairs, Michelle has brushed off her hallucination (*not* apparition) as just her mind screwing with her. Her nerves, her guilt, her grief commingling into a treacly stew, it's no wonder she's rattled enough to imagine things.

To imagine Liam.

His smell.

His touch.

So fucking eerie, she thinks.

Yet she also ponders what she would have said to him if he were actually there. *Goodbye? I'm sorry? I'll always love you?* Was there anything left to say?

Michelle and Doug arrive at the patio for the scheduled alfresco Full English Breakfast. Seated at the dozen tables are fewer than half the mourners who were in attendance the night before. Michelle assumes those still here are the closer family members (she recognizes some of the faces from other functions) and perhaps some longtime friends of the Fowlingtons. Anybody who is important enough to merit the privilege of being present at Liam's funeral, and presumably his wedding.

Michelle dreads the uncomfortable conversation to come. She'd almost rather be back in the bathroom, hallucinating playing tag with Liam.

They spot the conservatively dressed Nathaniel and Isadora sitting at one of the round pedestal tables in the very middle of the terrace. Both Fowlingtons wave them over with overdelighted smiles, as if Michelle and Doug were the eagerly awaited guests of honor.

Doug strokes Michelle's arm and tilts his head toward their hosts, encouraging her to lead the way.

They each take a seat in one of the two available ironwork chairs. The couples exchange pleasantries, talking about how well they slept, how beautiful this house is, how lovely the weather is forecast to be. ("An auspicious omen," Nathaniel remarks.)

A weedy-looking waiter comes to ask them if they have any special meal requests or dietary restrictions. All respond that they are fine with the menu as is, though Michelle sees Doug looking confused by the more exotic offerings. He leans into her ear and asks in a whisper, "What's black pudding?"

Before Michelle can answer him, Isadora segues into the subject of wedding preparations, telling Michelle that after breakfast they would fit her for her bridal gown, of the very same design worn by Fowlington brides for generations.

"It's such a, uh, honor, it really is… truly," Michelle fumbles through her mentally practiced speech, "but I can't, uh, y'know… accept it."

The Fowlingtons stare at her mutely.

Michelle explains herself as best she can. Her voice is halting and breathy, yet she powers through, wrapping up with "I'm just not comfortable doing it… so… I hope you understand."

Nathaniel inhales sharply through his nose, exhales through his gritted teeth. Isadora glowers at Michelle with seething intensity, as if trying to telepathically drill into her mind to take control of it and retract her reneging. Michelle looks away from them, her eyes settling on a curled birch leaf on the ground.

"That's disappointing to hear," Nathaniel says, the words rife with venom.

"Disappointing," Isadora parrots him in a husky monotone, followed by several more seconds of lingering silence.

"I mean, I can say something at the service," Michelle adds. "Like, a eulogy or whatever." She glances at Doug and squeezes his knee. He auto-nods in a feeble show of support.

"I'm laying my only son to rest," Isadora continues, "and you are *uncomfortable*."

Michelle's cheeks flush. "I'm sorry—"

"I don't need your apologies," Isadora snaps. "I need you to display some basic human decency."

"Dora—" Nathaniel interjects.

Isadora barrels on. "You were his betrothed. You loved him, yes?… And then you left him… *C'est la vie*, I suppose. But now you're unwilling to carry out a simple act to honor the life you once had together, the devotion you once felt for one another. I los—" She chokes on the word. "I lost my child, the fruit of my womb, the torchbearer of our family name, the shining light of my world. But *your* discomfort… that must be so overwhelming."

Michelle doesn't know how to reply to this. She flutters her jaw in the hope the right response will come to her. It doesn't.

Isadora purses her lips as though holding herself back from continuing her harangue. Her hand makes a trembly fist on the table. A tear streams down her cheek. "Excuse me," she rasps as she rises from her chair, then beelines toward the house.

Michelle watches Isadora until she disappears beyond the propped-open French doors. Doug keeps his eyes lowered, his fingertip tracing the floral patterns on the tabletop. Nathaniel remains behind with them, his expression unreadable.

"Should I go talk to her?" Michelle asks no one in particular.

"Do you have anything else to say?" Nathaniel answers.

Michelle doesn't know what to say, but she knows she needs to say *something*. As trite as it may sound, Mrs. Fowlington has truly been like a mother to her, treating her as if she were already part of their family. And Michelle knows with all her heart that she will miss Isadora, not only for her boundless kindness and generosity, but also for her unfailing faith in Michelle, believing she was best suited to become her son's legal, loving partner.

It's been a long time since anyone believed she could be the best at anything.

Michelle follows Isadora into the house. She does not want this day, probably their final one together, to be marred by hurt and bitter feelings toward her—caused by her—on top of all the other horribleness the poor lady must be going through. Michelle vows she will remedy this situation, somehow. She doesn't think she could live with herself if she cannot.

Michelle asks one of the help, a gnomish woman in a plain black frock, if she knows where Mrs. Fowlington is. The servant, kneeling on the floor scrubbing a red stain from the carpet, points her in the direction of the drawing room.

Michelle finds Isadora sprawled on the dark leather settee, facing the fireplace.

"Mrs. Fowlington," she says as she approaches her.

Isadora, gaze fixed on the glowing hearth, doesn't respond.

"I'm sorry. I didn't mean to upset you." Michelle stops next to the fireplace and studies her. The firelight flails in Isadora's eyes and makes the wet streaks on her cheeks seem like veins of gold. Michelle thinks she looks so beautiful, and so sad, which makes her feel even worse.

"I'm just trying to do what feels right," she continues. "And I... I don't want you to think I'm a bad person."

Isadora sits up and swivels her body toward Michelle. "Oh no, Beanie," she says, shaking her head with conviction. "I could *never* think you a bad person."

Isadora glimpses her maudlin reflection in the framed lithograph of a beehive hanging on the wall across the room. She wipes her face with her fingertips, smearing around her tears into still-glistening smudges.

"Dear, I'm a mess," she moans. "Please forgive me for my... outburst."

"You're fine. It's okay."

"You're like a daughter to me," Isadora continues. "There are times, frankly, that I've been more fond of you than of Bethany. She can be a handful. Nathaniel and I spoiled her as a child and, well, we have our regrets." She sighs. "Liam was different. Oh, we doted on him too, gave him everything he could ever want. But he seldom asked for anything. Never demanded anything. Not even when he needed help. We'd have to literally drag him to, you know, those places—substance rehabilitation clinics. Liam would get better for a while. Then inevitably the cycle repeated. But he never once asked us for help. I don't think he thought he really had a problem. That, I suppose, *was* the problem. How does the maxim go? The first step to recovery is realizing you have a problem."

"*Admitting* you have a problem."

Isadora shrugs. "Amounts to much the same thing."

Michelle knows it doesn't but does not correct her.

"My greatest worry is that Liam will be so very lonely without you."

Michelle squinches her face. "I don't think he's lonely now. I mean, when you're gone… you don't feel those kind of feelings anymore, right?"

"You don't understand." Isadora sits up straighter, laces her hands in her lap. "Do you believe there is life hereafter?"

"Like a heaven?" Michelle answers.

Isadora nods.

"I think so."

"The life hereafter is one of our family's most steadfastly held beliefs. As such, we practice many customs in this life to pay reverence to, and prepare for, the next one. Liam is at this moment in a state of transference, transitioning from the corporeal to the spiritual. This is a crucial period for him, one of great and terrible consequences if we do not provide him with certain earthly favors, however symbolic, so that he may exist in bliss beyond this world. That's why it is so important you carry out the ceremony. If you do not wed him, he will go into the afterworld eternally forlorn, a soul divided from his mate."

Michelle exhales. "That's a lot to take in."

"It seems a lot to take *on*, yes. But before you know it, it'll be over and you will be on your way back to Chicago. Back to your normal life. *Ce n'est pas la mer à boire.*"

Michelle grinds her teeth, mulling this over. "I don't mean to sound rude, but if this is just a symbolic thing, can't somebody else fill in for me?"

Isadora leans toward her, a grave expression contorting her face. "No, dear. It *must* be you. You and Liam have been marked for one another, same as Nathaniel and I had been marked."

Isadora pulls the collar of her cashmere blouse down to expose a tattoo on her chest, identical to the one Michelle and Liam shared. The bonding sigil.

"Just because Liam is no longer with us doesn't mean your connection to him is severed. Like the ink that graces your flesh, you and he are still tethered by the indelible memories you have of your time together. At least do this for him, out of respect for his memory. You owe him this final kindness."

Owe him this final kindness—the words twist in Michelle's already knotted gut. Perhaps it is her debt to Liam, one that she can pay in full today. More than that, though, it would be both a commemoration of her love and a plea for his forgiveness. She doesn't expect he will answer her, but she wants to believe, as the Fowlingtons do, that he can still hear her, wherever he may be. That by itself seals her decision.

Michelle nods. "Okay. I can talk to Doug again. I'm sure he'll understand."

"And if he does not?"

Michelle swallows, realizing she may have let slip that Doug was more than a friend to her, that she had lied about him. She calculates some avenue of damage control that would satisfy Mrs. Fowlington but not trivialize her boyfriend.

"I just want to do the right thing," she says, dodging Isadora's question.

A moment passes when Isadora does not react at all. Then a beaming smile stretches across her face. "Of course you do, dear."

She presses a small silver button attached to the apron of the cherrywood end table beside her. "Now let's have some tea!"

Isadora's instant switch from despondent to delighted jars Michelle. "Uhm… alright."

The same servant Michelle came across cleaning the carpet enters the drawing room. "Yes, ma'am?" she says.

"Two cups of the Sarnathian tea, Agnes," Isadora tells her. "Mild, please."

Agnes nods and withdraws from the room.

"We have the finest herbal blend you'll ever drink," Isadora says with a twinkle in her eye.

Michelle recalls how the Fowlingtons always boast they have the finest of everything, from food and furniture to clothes and cars. The benefits of being filthy rich, she supposes. If you got it, flaunt it.

But why then, Michelle wonders, are they burying Liam in a cheap-ass wooden box?

Doug has never felt more awkward in his life than he does at this moment.

Right after Michelle follows Mrs. Fowlington into the house, their breakfasts arrive at their table. Doug asks Mr. Fowlington if they should wait for the ladies to return before they start eating. Nathaniel shakes his head and gestures for Doug to go ahead.

The older man stares unblinking at Doug while he eats, much as one might watch a fly crawling up their arm before swatting it. Doug makes a valiant effort to ignore him—he is very hungry after all—but manages to finish only half his plate while Fowlington leaves his own untouched.

"Do you not care for the food?" Nathaniel asks dourly.

"No. I mean, yes… it's really good," Doug babbles. "It's just, y'know, filling. All the meat and beans. And whatever this is." It looks to him like a hockey puck. "It's delicious. Is this the black pudding?"

"It is. It's also called blood pudding."

"Oh really… blood pudding…" Doug gulps. "First time I've ever had it. So, made from blood, I guess?"

"Yes. Our recipe uses Iberian pig's blood."

"Wow," Doug says, feigning being impressed. "Iberian, huh? That's like, uhm, the good stuff… Aren't you going to have any of yours?"

"I'm afraid I've lost my appetite."

"I'm…" Doug clears his throat, stalling for something to say and how to say it. "I'm sorry your wife took what Michelle said so hard."

"It's not her fault," Nathaniel replies thoughtfully. "I suppose it's difficult for young people in this skeptical age to understand, much less embrace, certain mystical traditions, even those that have survived for millennia. Ours is a very traditional family. For generations, our traditions have served as the foundation—the stone and mortar—of our clan. As such, you could say we're both emotionally and spiritually invested in its preservation. So you can see how Michelle's refusal to take part is… hurtful."

"I'm sure she didn't mean to offend you."

"Of course not. And yet, that is the heart of the matter."

"Well, I… uhm…" Doug puffs out his cheeks and lets the air escape his mouth.

"Doug," Nathaniel continues, raising up and twirling his index finger. "You seem to have some influence over Michelle, do you not?"

"What do you mean?"

"I noticed she repeatedly glanced your way when she was rescinding her participation. Seeking your solidarity, I presume."

"I guess she values my opinion. We're pretty close."

"Then might you sway her to perform the ceremony today?"

"I don't think I should do that," Doug replies. "It's her decision, not mine."

"Yes, indubitably," Nathaniel counters. "But perhaps you can discreetly make her more amenable to our objective."

"I don't think that'd be—"

"I'll compensate you," Nathaniel cuts him off.

"You'll what?"

"Would ten thousand dollars suffice? As a gratuity for your lobbying for us."

Doug doesn't mask the astonishment on his face. "Are you serious?"

Nathaniel smirks. "I never jest about money, my boy."

It's enough money for Doug to pay off his credit cards, buy a new computer, and finally replace the brake pads on his car that have been making this grinding metal noise for months whenever it rains. There might even be a little left over for him to take Michelle on a fun vacation to Orlando or Niagara Falls.

Ten thousand bucks is enough for him to accept that his girlfriend mock-marrying a dead guy might not be such a big deal.

But then, some sixish sense nags at him, warning him it is not worth it at any price.

Still, *ten thousand dollars*…

"I'll talk to her," Doug says. "But I can't promise anything."

"Of course. There are few guarantees in life. But you *will* try?"

"Yeah, sure," Doug squeaks. "I'll do my best."

Nathaniel's steely eyes bore into him so intensely Doug wants to look away but dares not. He bets the old dude can smell a bead of bullshit in a rose garden.

"That is all I can ask," Nathaniel says, clasping his palms together.

Their waiter stops by their table to check on them. "May I bring you anything else, sirs?" Doug is thankful for the interruption.

"You can clear our plates," Nathaniel answers.

"Yes, sir."

"And do fetch us both a cup of coffee. The Sarnathian roast. Strong."

"Very well, sir." The waiter nods, collects their dishes into an uneven stack, and takes them inside.

"We stock the finest java beans in the world," Nathaniel tells Doug haughtily. "Yields a much more sublime beverage than that mass-produced dreck peddled on every street corner across the country. You are in for a treat, young man."

Doug flashes Mr. Fowlington a polite grin. How he wishes he were drinking a cup of that burnt-tasting joe in Chicago right now. How he wishes he were back in his room upstairs. How he wishes he had never come here at all.

"So, how long have you and Doug been together?"

While Michelle hasn't outright told Mrs. Fowlington that she and Doug are dating, she supposes it must be obvious.

"Almost a year," Michelle admits, her voice tinged with guilt. She now sits on the drawing room settee beside Isadora, who is much less distraught now, more inquisitive. To Michelle, it feels a bit like she is sharing a therapy couch with the woman, being psychoanalyzed by her. *Maybe she's trying to figure out if I might still bail on the wedding.*

Michelle isn't so certain herself.

"He's quite different from Liam, isn't he?" Isadora remarks.

"Yeah, he is. Doug's... very down to earth. A realist, I guess." Michelle strokes the rim of the porcelain teacup she's holding with the pad of her thumb. "Liam was a dreamer. Always saw the bright side of everything, and convinced others to see it too. At least, he convinced me... for a while."

On the verge of choking up, Michelle takes another sip of her tea. Isadora was right, it is pretty yummy. It has a fragrant floral aroma, with a touch of citrus, and tastes sweet and a little smoky. There's a hint of a metallic flavor—saffron?—that Michelle finds unusual but not off-putting.

"Seems like you still care for my son," Isadora says.

Michelle nods. "That's why I came."

"And to say goodbye to him."

Michelle nods again. She senses Isadora is assessing her responses, studying her, empathizing with her. All Michelle aches to do is say only those things that will assuage the sorrow the dear woman must be bearing.

Isadora smiles. "Mmm. Knowing it is just goodbye for now does bring some degree of comfort. We are all on the same path, going in the same direction, toward the same destination where all our ancestors and the loved ones in our lives converge. Liam believed that, and I hope you do too."

"It sounds nice." Michelle wishes she could take back this response, thinking it came off lame, or worse, patronizing.

"Did Liam ever tell you about the first time he died?"

Along with the hisses and crackles of the fireplace, Michelle notices another ambient sound, a dull buzzing, persistent but not unpleasant. It's a sound she has experienced before when a primo high kicks in, growing louder as it disperses throughout her body, until she feels swaddled in a protective bubble, floating above herself.

Michelle lazily shakes her head. "The first time…?"

"He was six, playing on the terrace," Isadora continues. "His toy—an aeroplane of some sort, I believe—wound up in the pool. Liam went to retrieve it on his own, only to somehow fall into the water. He'd not yet learnt to swim, and he drowned. Thankfully, Nathaniel found him, fished him out, and resuscitated him. Our little boy had been gone for maybe three minutes."

Isadora's voice breaks as she utters this last sentence. She sips her tea to moisten her throat before she resumes.

"When Liam was lucid once more, I asked him what he had seen when he had crossed over, what he'd observed of the world beyond this one. And he said he did not see anything. Just black. Dark. There was nothing there, he swore to me. Nothing at all."

The buzzing in Michelle's head intensifies.

"Well, that would not stand with us. A week later, we locked Liam in a small room with nary a window or lamp. No light at all. He was immersed in total darkness. Then we instructed him to explore the space and identify ten items solely by touch. At first, he begged and cried and screamed for us to let him out. We told him we would not until he had completed the assigned task. He then made several wild guesses, naming commonplace things like a book, a chair, a shoe. But we had arranged the room to only contain unique pieces—a stuffed fox, an antique globe, a ripe pineapple, and such. Liam needed to find the items to ascertain what they were, all without the aid of sight. It was challenging for him, but within five hours he had succeeded. We released him and instilled this lesson: just because one cannot see anything does not mean nothing is there."

"Sounds kinda…" Michelle gropes for the term. "Traumatic."

"Perhaps it was," Isadora replies. "But trauma does tend to be a most persuasive teacher."

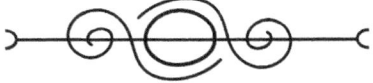

Doug has difficulty keeping his head up and his eyes open. All his muscles have gone soft as overcooked spaghetti. His brain seems submerged in a sludge that his thoughts can hardly wade through. His body demands hibernation-level sleep.

"Are you alright, young man?" he hears Mr. Fowlington ask, sounding like he could be a mile away, not sitting five feet across from him.

"I think I… need… t'lie down," Doug responds and sluggishly tries to rise from his chair. He teeters forward, bumping his belly against the table and capsizing his half-drunk cup of coffee.

"Sssorrr," he slurs as he plops back down into his seat.

"Oh my," Nathaniel says. "Bethany!"

On cue, his daughter materializes beside Doug and places a gentle hand on his shoulder.

"Dougie, what's wrong?"

"It seems Mr. Cunningham is feeling unwell," her father says. "Can you help me take him to his room so he may rest?"

"Of course."

Nathaniel and Bethany each grasp one of Doug's shaky arms and hoist him to his feet. They guide him inside the house and into the elevator, ride it up to the third floor, then steer him toward his accommodations.

Doug has never felt so sapped of energy. There was that time he went under anesthesia for the extraction of his wisdom teeth, but that was a quick lights-out. This is different. Though his body cries for sleep, his mind remains semi-clear, aware he's being led to his room by Liam's father and sister. His instincts tell him he should fight unconsciousness—that something is *wrong*—yet he somehow knows it would be a losing battle. He wonders if this is what it's like before slipping into a coma. Then a moment later, he realizes he doesn't care. He just needs to fucking crash.

Nathaniel and Bethany unclasp Doug's arms and let him flop onto the bed in his room. Nathaniel lifts his legs by the ankles and swings them over, laying his heels on the walnut footboard.

The old man pulls off Doug's cheap oxfords and clucks in disgust. "The boy didn't even think the occasion important enough to polish these. Look at this—scuffs, water marks. The laces are even frayed." He drops the shoes to the floor like they were repugnant articles of trash, rubs his fingertips together as if there were some greasy residue left on them.

"Should we undress him?" Bethany asks.

"Do as you wish, sweetheart," Nathaniel says as he heads for the door. "Just don't dawdle here too long. It's nearly time."

"Yes, Father."

Nathaniel pauses at the doorway. "And check in on Grammy before you head down. Rhian told me she didn't touch much of her breakfast. She might be hungry by now."

"I will, Father."

Doug hears Nathaniel's hollow footsteps exit the room and tail off down the hall.

Bethany sits down on the bed beside Doug, her weight barely making a dimple in the mattress. She places her palm flat on his chest, as if to measure his heart rate. She then unbuttons his shirt and draws her icy-smooth fingernails down his sternum.

She grinds the tip of her index finger into his right nipple. "Can you feel that?" she breathily asks him. "Does that feel good? I want to make you feel good."

Doug does not feel much of anything. With what dwindling strength he has left, he can only part his eyelids a mere sliver, just wide enough to see the nebulous shape of Bethany as she presses her lips against his.

"I'll come back later, my li'l *bonbon*…" she says after her unrequited kiss. She then licks his cheek like an overexcited dog, accompanied by the minutest sensation of her squeezing his crotch. "When you are more… responsive."

Bethany rises from the bed and pirouettes toward the open door. In his peripheral vision, as she walks out of the room, Doug watches her shake her bony ass at him, ostensibly for his pleasure. But he wouldn't give a shit right now even if she were shooting Chinese fireworks from it.

Before he shuts his eyes again and allows oblivion to overtake him, Doug perceives dozens of indistinct, but indisputably human, shapes crowding around the bed. Their faces are so dark and blurry they seem malformed, monstrous. Some appear to be wearing peculiar clothes—costumes?—dresses and hats and robes that Doug thinks may originate from other historical eras, though damned if he could name which ones.

"*Who are you?*" he wants to ask them—he's far too stupefied to be afraid—but he hasn't the power to move his mouth. Not that it matters. His mind at this moment probably would not register their answers anyway.

A moment later, nothing matters to him at all.

Michelle remembers this feeling. As if all the molecules that make her up were flitting out into the farthest reaches of the universe, then returning to wash over her in warm waves of pure pleasure. Sensuous clouds caress her naked flesh. Tranquilizing scents of lemon and lavender waft over her.

The three angels—whom Michelle arbitrarily calls Ecstasy, Exhilaration, and Euphoria—swim around her in a rhythmic, rhapsodic dance that makes her smile all over. Like nothing bad will ever happen to her again.

In a word: Heaven.

When Michelle was sufficiently drugged from the tea, three servant women, all clad in white, sari-like wraps, had entered the drawing room and escorted her to a lavishly appointed washroom suite with a large obsidian bathtub as its centerpiece, a heated slate floor (*so divine!*), and brass lamps like the ones Michelle has seen in movies set on old sailing ships. As she took in these sumptuous surroundings, the women completely undressed her. They then ushered her toward the tub, encouraging her to step down into it and immerse herself up to her neck in the milky water. Michelle found it unpleasantly hot at first, but soon adjusted to the temperature. Each of the women grabbed a sponge, dipped it into the water, and mopped every curve and cleft of Michelle's body. One scrubbed between her legs so tenderly she almost climaxed.

And we'll all float on okay, she dreamily sings to herself. *And we'll all float on alright.*

The women assist Michelle out of the tub, pat her dry with soft towels, and anoint her with fragrant oils. They trim her nails, tweeze her brows, and balm her lips. They style her hair into a lofty bouffant, weaving in green ivy and jasmine flowers. Lastly, they dress her in a simple yet elegant sage-green linen gown with a ruffled hem, knotted shoulder straps, and a plunging neckline that prominently displays the "good luck" tattoo in the valley between her breasts.

The women parade her before a full-length mirror. "There, Miss Langley," says the one who Michelle has christened Ecstasy. "See how beautiful you are?"

Michelle does see. She doesn't recognize this person at all.

"Blessed me, look how stunning you are!"

Mrs. Fowlington stands at the threshold of the washroom, appraising Michelle as though she were a masterful work of art. The servants spin her around to face the matriarch.

"Yes, you are a supreme vision, Beanie." Isadora approaches Michelle and tweaks a sprig of ivy in her hair. "You may well be channeling the image of the Divine Empress herself. Liam will be quite pleased."

But… Liam is… dead…

Isn't he?

Michelle isn't sure if she said these thoughts aloud, but if she did, Mrs. Fowlington has chosen not to respond.

"Which footwear would you prefer for her, ma'am?" asks one of the servants.

Isadora considers the question for a moment, then shakes her head. "No shoes. She has such handsome feet, don't you think?"

The servant women agree.

A slightly stooped, middle-aged man attired in an all-black suit enters the chamber. A red velvet patch covers his left eye; he averts his good eye toward the floor, away from Michelle. She vaguely recalls him… a priest, or something like that?

"The venue is ready, Mrs. Fowlington," the man announces.

"Thank you, Deacon," Isadora says. "Michelle, you may remember Deacon Codswell. He conducted the Gálffwöting ritual for you and Liam."

Michelle shivers at this, more out of reflex than recognition.

"Alas, his skills proved subpar." Michelle catches Codswell wince. "Since then he's brushed up on his sacramental praxis. We expect today's proceedings will be far more competent, yes?"

"They will, ma'am," Codswell assures both Mrs. Fowlington and Michelle.

Isadora nods with satisfaction. "I shall let Nathaniel know the ceremony will be starting soon. Be sure to sufficiently salve her chest." This order is given to the servant Michelle calls Euphoria. "We will suffer no errors this time."

Though the instruction was not directed at him, the deacon cows a bit more.

Isadora leaves the washroom, and the women sit Michelle on a wishbone chair. Euphoria then slathers a white cream on and around the tattoo. It makes Michelle's skin tingle.

She is mildly startled when Deacon Codswell kneels beside her, his face a canvas of shame and regret.

"Miss Langley," he croaks. "I've wanted to apologize to you personally. You cannot imagine the anguish I have endured since I learned of my failing. The ritual was meant to ensure that... you and Liam were supposed to have been shielded from any consequences stemming from your... vices." Codswell shakes his head. "I do not know what had happened. But I accept blame for this aberration, this tragedy. And I shall make amends for it today, I swear to you. I have already paid my penance."

He flips up his eyepatch to reveal the sunken socket beneath, sewn shut, the lid branded with a small squiggly symbol.

Codswell rises to his feet. "I will not fail you again, milady. Either of you." He bows his head at Michelle, turns around, and exits the suite.

All Michelle can do is giggle.

Michelle is shepherded to the Thinning Room by a couple of male attendants who look enough alike to be twins, both pasty-faced and slick-haired and decked out in dark, broad-collared cloaks. They remind Michelle of malnourished Draculas. This thought amuses her.

Her brain still ebbs and flows, races and slows, shrinks and billows in wondrous symmetry. Every step she takes electrifies her with anticipation; her 16th birthday, church confirmation, and college graduation all rolled into one. She thinks everything is just as it should be.

It's my wedding day!

But a distant voice in her mind reminds her that it's not. Not really.

As soon as Michelle enters the sacred space, all eyes fall upon her. Seated on the wooden pews are the dozen or so members of Liam's extended family. On the small stage stand Liam's mother and father on one side, Liam's sister and Deacon Codswell on the other. Between them, still propped upright in his casket, is Liam.

The attendants, gripping her by the arms, lead Michelle up the short set of stairs onto the stage, lifting her so she doesn't trip over herself. They bring her to a halt about three feet in front of the casket while continuing to hold her erect. She strains to keep her head raised, her eyes open.

There's a silk pillow behind Liam's head. His eyes are closed, as if he's sleeping.

But he's not sleeping. He's dead.

She can hardly hear that part of herself.

Deacon Codswell begins to speak. His oration sounds mostly garbled, almost gibberish to Michelle. She catches the odd word here and there—*matrimony, sanctify, eternal*—but primarily it's a string of discordant rumblings, like an out-of-tune talk radio station reverberating in her mind.

An attendant spritzes something onto her chest from a green glass spray bottle, instantly chilling the flesh. He then jabs the area around the tattoo a few times with what appears to be a sewing pin. Michelle hardly notices, the pinpricks feeling to her like a Q-tip dabbing her skin. The attendant nods at Codswell.

The deacon produces a rolled-up segment of black oilcloth. He opens it to reveal a shiny silver knife with a long, slender blade and an ivory handle. It reminds Michelle of the knife her dad had used when he took her fishing.

Codswell starts to cut around her tattoo. Michelle again feels nothing more than the slightest pressure. As blood trickles down her cleavage, her mind drifts to…

Her father driving them to the lake where he moors his cabin cruiser at the marina he owns. They motor out to somewhere in the middle of the water to reel in bass, trout, and perch.

With a surgeon's precision, Codswell slices underneath the tattoo, peeling the skin back as he goes.

Her father filleting their catch right there on the boat, expertly separating the meat from the bones. She relishes the times watching him be the perfect dad… the times before her mother got sick… before all the hospitals and doctors and chemo… before the rot overwhelmed Mom's body… before she said her last 'I love you' before she couldn't say anything anymore before she was gone forever—

Michelle lets this melancholic memory recede as she dazedly watches Deacon Codswell place her carved-off tattoo into a gray ceramic bowl that Bethany cups in her palms. He next removes Liam's matching sigil in a similar manner—his wound does not bleed at all—and adds it to the bowl with Michelle's. It reminds her of wet Play-Doh.

Nathaniel, bearing a tall-necked crystal decanter, moves beside Bethany and pours a partially congealed green liquid into the mortar. He then uses a gold pestle to mash and mix the contents. Once he is done, Isadora steps forward and dips her thumb into the grisly paste. With her coated fingertip she first applies a brown oval in the middle of Michelle's forehead, then spreads the goop onto her slack lips. Isadora does the same to her son.

Liam's family falls back to allow the attendants to bring Michelle closer to Liam, supporting her body mere inches away from his waxen face.

Isadora's voice echoes distantly in her mind: "…*he'll wake up any time now…*"

The deacon says something she cannot understand, possibly in a foreign language.

The attendants tilt Michelle's head forward till her lips touch Liam's in a semblance of a kiss. She feels not a scintilla of emotion during this, not horror nor distress nor disgust, even when Liam's mouth expels a whoosh of frosty air into hers.

The attendants then ease Michelle away from him. Her lips trail thin webs as they part from his, then break off and dissolve into nothing. They position her beside Liam's casket and turn her around toward the audience. Everyone is standing now.

"Dear brethren," Deacon Codswell says, his words far more intelligible to her now. "It is my privilege to present to you, hereby bound and blessed in thine eyes and those of the Divine Ones, Liam and Michelle Fowlington. May their eternal spirits be evermore woven together."

The spectators applaud.

Through her still bleary vision, Michelle scrutinizes them. There are many more people here now than there were when she arrived. And some of them are wearing the strangest outfits. Old-fashioned, ancient. She wonders who they are, then guesses they all must be Liam's family. Now her family too.

She smiles.

Michelle ambles along near the head of the procession with Liam's immediate family and Deacon Codswell, who has donned a black robe that makes him look like a sorcerer from some fantasy movie. Following them are more than a dozen—*dozens?*—of other family members come to pay their last respects. Ahead of everyone lies Liam in his closed coffin, transported on a two-wheeled cart pulled by a chestnut-colored Clydesdale horse.

What huge hooves, Michelle thinks. *And the feathery white fur on its lower legs looks like it's wearing fluffy boots.*

She is still dressed in her wedding garb, still barefoot. While she steps on jagged pebbles and pine needles, they don't hurt her. She knows it's chilly—there is a garden of goosebumps budding all along her arms—but this does not bother her either. And she knows her chest is bleeding, staining the collar of her gown a dark crimson, yet this concerns her no more than if it were just a minor sunburn.

As dusk settles in, they follow the orange-dappled dirt road leading them deeper into the forest of towering evergreens. Michelle never knew how far the Fowlingtons' property extended into the surrounding woodland. They must've been walking for an hour—maybe? Right now time seems irregular, unreliable.

When she peers up at the dense canopy overhead, she doesn't see any birds flying around or perched on the branches. In fact, she doesn't spy any wildlife at all. No deer, squirrels, snakes. She senses something is wrong here.

Or something is wrong with her.

There is nothing to worry about, Michelle tells herself. *I'm among family, and they will always help me, love me, protect me. They promised!*

They finally reach a wide circular glade with verdant, well-tended grass. In the center of this space is a rectangular, waist-high platform built from chiseled blocks of gleaming white marble. Wooly green moss blankets its base like a Christmas tree skirt. It gives the illusion the structure sprung from the earth.

The horse-drawn cart stops beside the platform. A quartet of attendants divide themselves up on each side of the casket and lift it using a pair of long planks laid underneath. They carry the wooden box to the platform and set it on top, leaving the timber planks in place as they move away.

Deacon Codswell steps in front of the bier and addresses the congregation of mourners.

"Welcome, brethren, to this serene and sacred space, where we will consecrate the passing of a beloved member's body unto spirit. We call to our ancestors, whose feet have walked and whose hands have worked this very earth, whose enduring breath we now breathe here as one, whose wisdom resounds still in our hearts and minds. We honor you and ask you to accept Liam Tyrus Fowlington so he may abide among you in everlasting peace and love. So shall it be."

Tyrus. Michelle doesn't think she ever knew Liam's middle name.

"And we call on the gods and goddesses of the Otherworld," Codswell continues, "all powerful and knowing, whose blessings have generously filled our coffers and cupboards. We revere you and ask you to protect our Liam, to nourish and nurture him, so he may dwell eternally in bountiful health and happiness beyond this plane. So shall it be."

The zealously delivered homily evokes memories in Michelle of her mother's funeral. There had been so many beautiful bouquets and wreaths all around her that they almost obscured her casket, as if in vain effort to prevent anyone from being reminded that a once living and loving person—*Mom*—would do neither again. Michelle had found it more sad than soothing.

Here, though, Liam is surrounded by trees, which Michelle judges more fitting than fresh cut flowers piled high, destined to be discarded later. The tall trunks of the pines reach toward the darkening heavens, their roots anchoring them to the hallowed earth, their branches rustling in the breeze like the whisperings of angels.

Codswell spreads his arms in supplication. Michelle thinks the drooping sleeves of his robe resemble crow's wings.

"Let us praise our ancestors and gods in hymn!" he bellows.

The deacon begins to chant in a throaty yet lilting language Michelle does not recognize. The congregation joins him on the second verse. Their chorus of voices swell and swoop in the air around Michelle, enveloping her, enrapturing her.

At the end of the hymn, Codswell pauses dramatically, then repeats three disyllabic words in the same foreign tongue he had been singing: "*Vima, Lavra, Nuto.*" After the third recitation of this phrase, great tentacles of yellow flame roar up from beneath the stone platform, quickly engulfing Liam's casket.

The fire reduces the coffin to cinders in less than a minute, revealing the human form it contained, now completely ablaze.

Liam transformed by fire. Cleansing him. Curing him.

"Beautiful," Michelle says aloud.

A gust of wind blows across the pyre, sending glowing embers of Liam—*My husband!*, she reminds herself—into the air. The embers waft over the congregants, flitting about them like fireflies on a warm summer evening.

"Beautiful," Michelle says again as a flake of ash muddies the single tear that flows down her cheek.

EIGHT

As Doug groggily awakens, he turns his head and peers out the window next to the bed. At first he believes the darkness outside to be caused by his impaired vision, induced by a bitch of a headache. Once his migraine wanes and his eyesight clears, though, he realizes night has indeed fallen.

What the... it was just morning... wasn't it?

He also realizes he's back in his guest suite at the Fowlingtons. He has zero recollection of how he got here from the patio, the last place he remembers being. It's as if a big chunk of time has been chopped out of his day—with a blunt hatchet.

What. The. Fuck.

Doug struggles to sit upright and pivots his body until his legs dangle off the mattress. He cracks the joints in his neck and surveys the room. He wonders where Michelle is.

"Mish?" he calls out. She doesn't answer.

Doug retraces his steps—or rather her steps—trying to recall what she was doing with him before he blacked out. Yeah, that's right... she went inside after upsetting Mrs. Fowlington, leaving him with Mr. Fowlington, who'd offered him ten thousand bucks to persuade Michelle to tie the pseudo-knot with his dead son.

Doug is fairly sure he agreed to do it, or agreed to try. He bets he could have haggled up the price, ten G's being chump change to a guy like Fowlington. Then again, for all Doug knows, that deal could be null and void by now. What time *is* it?

He hears the faint thrum of stringed instruments emanating from somewhere inside the mansion. These are soon joined by a piano, and maybe a flute. The Fowlingtons must be holding some sort of chamber recital, Doug figures, which seems a weird thing to do at a funeral, but then that seems pretty on-brand for them. Who knows what eccentric shit they've planned to memorialize their son's death? Doug doesn't want to know. He does not even care about the money anymore. He just wants to get Michelle and get the hell out of this madhouse.

Doug shambles into the bathroom, stoops over the sink, and splashes cold water onto his face. As he dully looks at himself in the mirror, he recognizes how much he feels, as Bethany had put it, *off*. Like he had spent hours in the sweltering sun, then took a deep, dreamless nap, waking up shaky and scattered.

What the hell happened to me?

It occurs to him he may have been drugged. That kind of shit happens all the time in movies and TV shows. In real life, too, so he's heard—the CIA spiking drinks with LSD, chicks roofied in bars, dudes in hotel rooms waking up in a bathtub full of ice and missing a kidney. Doug checks himself. Nope, no fresh surgical wounds anywhere on his torso. He's only a little relieved by this.

He knows *something* happened to him.

Where is Michelle? Doug wonders again. His worry for her growing, he reaches into his pants pocket for his cellphone. Not there.

Doug exits the bathroom. He finds his phone on top of the still-made bed. As he is about to call Michelle, he glimpses, lying on the leather-top writing desk across from the bed, a beige envelope. He's certain it wasn't there when they arrived.

As he steps closer, he can see his full name—*Mr. Douglas Roy Cunningham*—penned on the front in neat script. He picks up the envelope, opens it, and fishes out a cheque from Nathaniel H.W. Fowlington written to him for $10,000. On the memo line is jotted "In Appreciation."

In appreciation of what? Doug never talked to Michelle. Or did he?... No, he's almost positive he hadn't. So then why would Fowlington pay him? Unless maybe he's buying him off. Buying his acquiescence. His silence. His stay-out-of-our-way-if-you-know-what's-good-for-you.

Doug questions, as he tucks the check into his pocket, if it's enough to quiet the guilt already picking at his conscience.

Doug tries calling Michelle, but it goes straight to her voicemail. He doesn't leave a message, instead texting her: "Where r u?" No response.

He slips on his shoes and skulks out of the room into the hallway. Even with all the electric candle sconces, the passage remains murky, as if the merlot color of the walls and ceiling were sopping up most of the light.

The instruments are a bit louder and clearer out here. (Yeah, there is definitely a flute.) Doug imagines the music is covering up the sound of his footsteps on the hardwood floor. His instinct tells him this is a good thing, though he's not exactly sure what he is afraid of. Just that he should be.

Hoping to find Michelle, Doug follows the music. He figures it's coming from downstairs, probably the grand hall. He vacillates between taking the stairs or the elevator down, then decides the elevator might be less conspicuous.

He makes it midway down the hallway when he senses something—the feeling that someone's watching him.

"What are you doing up?" asks a crackly voice.

Startled, Doug whips his head to the right to behold, slouched in a doorway, an old lady. Bordering on ancient, really, her face being a topographic map of wrinkles and veins. Her wispy white hair looks like tufts of cotton have been glued willy-nilly onto her scalp. Impossibly, she's even thinner than Liam's sister. All papery skin and withering bones, almost transparent. Doug is surprised she can still stand there on her own without crumbling under the sheer weight of gravity.

"Um, sorry… what?" he says. The woman wears a sleeveless, pastel blue nightgown blotted with a miscellany of stains. Doug convinces himself it's just food—ketchup, mustard, chocolate.

"Don't give me any smart talk," she growls. "You go on back to bed now, Liam. Choppity chop!" She makes a quivery dicing motion with her hand.

"Oh, uh… I'm not Liam," Doug replies.

She sneers at him with her plum-purple lips. "It's too late to be playing games. If you cannot sleep, why not try counting all the stars on your ceiling?"

Lady must be senile. "Sorry, ma'am. I think you got me mistaken for somebody else."

The crone squints at Doug and slowly nods. "Ahh, I bet you were aiming to sneak a bite of Bundt cake, hmm? Go on then." She shoos him away while seeming to have some kind of hand seizure at the same time. "I won't tell your mother. It will be one of our little secrets."

She smiles a smile that would give a dentist nightmares.

"Ohh-kay," Doug says, welcoming the out. "Goodnight." He carries on toward the elevator.

"Doesn't Grammy get a nighty-night kiss?"

Doug halts, steels himself with a deep breath.

"No," he says without turning around and continues walking.

Doug takes the elevator down and heads into the grand hall. An elegantly-dressed quintet of musicians—violinist, cellist, flutist, clarinetist, and pianist—are playing some jazzy number in an airy corner of the immense space. They sound really good, Doug thinks, all bouncy and bubbly like a New Year's setlist. Then he remembers this is supposed to be a funeral. Seems the Fowlingtons are sending their son off cocktail party style.

More than a dozen guests—*mourners*—hang around the hall, talking and laughing amongst themselves. Everyone holds a glass of wine or a mixed drink. From their slack expressions and ungainly movements, Doug guesses it is not the first round for any of them.

A small group disperses in front of him, revealing Michelle lounging on a camelback chaise sofa. She is wearing her cotton candy pink cardigan sweater, sunflower yellow accordion skirt, and chunky heel sandals. It looks like she wound up her hair into some sort of tall bun; a few strands have come loose from it and hang haphazardly over her forehead. Doug also sees she clutches a highball glass in her hand, half filled with some honey-yellow liquid and ice cubes. He hopes it's just iced tea, but judging by her droopy eyelids and slumped posture, it is more likely some type of whiskey or brandy. And he suspects it's not her first one of the evening either.

"What the hell are you doing, Mish?"

"Heyyy, Doug," she replies, canting her head so she can fix her reddened eyes on him. "Where you've been?"

"Upstairs, in our room. I, uh—" Doug gropes for a plausible answer. "I wasn't feeling well."

"Oh, poor baby," she coos. "Feeling better now?"

"Yeah, but that's not important. You're drinking."

"Very observant, sir." She swirls the ice cubes in the liquor. "I am indeed."

Doug regards her incredulously. "But… you know you can't do that."

She puts on a shocked face. "Whyyy not? I'm a grown ass… piece of ass!" She titters at herself.

Is she playing dumb?, he wonders. *Or is she too drunk to appreciate the seriousness of this?* "Your sobriety," he says.

Michelle huffs. "It's just one drink."

"Bullshit. You're plastered."

"I'm grieving, asshole!" she barks at him. "This"—she raises her glass—"is one of those get-free-outta-jail cards."

"No, it isn't, Michelle. It's relapsing."

"It's none of your business."

Fed up, he snatches the glass from her hand.

"Jesus Christ, Doug! You're overreacting." She sits up, spine straight, chin upraised, in a parody of someone who is under the influence of nothing but themself. "I'm fine."

"This… none of this… is *fine*." Doug sweeps his arm around the room, until it collides with Nathaniel Fowlington's shoulder.

"Is something wrong, Mr. Cunningham?" the patriarch asks.

Doug experiences a flash of fear at the man's sudden presence, but this is swiftly overridden by his uncontainable outrage.

"Yeah, there's something wrong." Doug gestures toward Michelle's glass as if it were a case-breaking clue. "Michelle's been drinking."

"So she has. And?"

"Annnd… she shouldn't be."

Nathaniel nods, unflustered. "I believe the occasion calls for some imbibing. I'm sure you can understand."

"No. I don't understand."

"I suppose you wouldn't. Simply put, as an honored guest in our home, we consent to Michelle enjoying any comforts we can provide. Libations included."

Doug gawks at him, dumbfounded. "But, you *know*, right? You gotta know… What she and Liam went through. Why they broke up. How your son died."

An equally insouciant Isadora appears beside her husband. Michelle melts back down into the sofa.

"Michelle has been in recovery for months," Doug continues exasperatedly, this time directing his words toward Mrs. Fowlington. "And she was doing great. Now *this*. You letting her drink. It's like you're restarting her addiction. Enabling it."

"I think you're being a wee melodramatic," Isadora says with infuriating nonchalance.

"You gotta be kidding me, lady." Doug shakes his head at her. "Michelle could have just as easily died there in New York too. Would you have wanted that?"

"They would have been together, then," Isadora answers. "My son would not have passed on alone."

"*Seriously?*"

"Things would've been less complicated as well," Nathaniel adds. His wife nods.

"Holy shit," Doug says. "You people are pathological."

Nathaniel partially curls up his lips in what Doug can only describe as a smirk. "We are merely of a different stripe, my boy. You have your way of viewing the world, and we have ours. You see Michelle as a fragile thing, always teetering on the edge of that dark pit she's fought so exhaustingly to claw out of time and time again. We, however, see her presented with an opportunity to attain perpetual happiness, to be filled with a glorious light that allows her to exult in a perfect existence free of misery and burden. Isn't that what you want for her, Mr. Cunningham?"

"I just want her to be healthy," Doug replies.

"Surely you're aware there is no cure for addiction," Isadora replies matter-of-factly. "Sooner or later drugs or alcohol will be her undoing. Her fate is already written… at least on this earthly plane."

"Fuck the both of you!" Doug spits, his eyes darting between them.

Neither Fowlington reacts to his outburst. Doug registers that the recital music has stopped and his is the lone resounding voice in the hall.

He turns around and grabs Michelle by her wrist. "Come on, Mish. We're leaving."

"I don't wanna go," she squawks, feebly resisting him as he hoists her from the sofa.

"We *need* to go. Now."

"Nooo," she whines, but has scarcely any fight in her to fend him off.

"Should she not decide for herself when to leave?" Nathaniel says.

Doug stares the shorter man down. "I think you should mind your own damn business."

"Perhaps it is you who should mind yours," Nathaniel retorts, meeting Doug's buzzsaw gaze with his razor glare. "Seeing as you are the only one here who is *not* family."

Adrenaline pumping, Doug tugs the tottering Michelle along behind him past the Fowlingtons and across the room toward the elevator. He balls his free hand into a tight fist, expecting some asshole to block his path. But the other guests merely watch them for a moment before resuming their conversations, nobody taking any action to stop them, as if no one really cares they're going.

As if it doesn't matter at all.

Doug's apprehension escalates with every step he takes on their way back to their suite.

The last twenty-four hours have been a pageantry of red flags which he had chalked up to filthy rich folk weirdness. Yet now he senses something more serious—more sinister—is afoot here, though he can't articulate what that could be. What began as a tingling at the base of his skull has turned into the full-throttled revving of all his muscles while his mind goes on high alert for anything that might thwart his singular goal.

"We're just getting our stuff and blowing this joint," he tells Michelle as he continues to tow her alongside him.

"We should stayyy," she mumbles in response. "These people are sooo nice to me."

"Yeah," Doug says. "They're the bee's knees."

"Riiiight? C'mon, let's just stay 'nother hour or two."

"No, Mish. It's rude to overstay our welcome." Doug hopes this trumped-up excuse will satisfy her.

"Is it?" she replies with a bemused expression. "Well, we have to least say goodbye. It'd be rude not to."

"We'll send them a thank you card."

Approaching their room, they encounter the manor's black-suited, poker-faced parking valet waiting for them by their door, his arms linked behind his back. Doug sizes him up. He's skinny as asparagus, with gaunt cheeks, a pigeon chest, and wearing what appears to be an orthopedic left shoe with a three-inch sole. Doug is pretty sure he can take him.

"Sir. Madam," the valet addresses them. "I understand you are planning to depart."

Here it comes, Doug thinks and constricts his fist as solid as a cannonball. He does some quick combat math. *I'll punch him in the jaw, then sweep out his legs, then kick him in the gut, or maybe the groin—*

"We have packed your belongings and stowed them in your vehicle," the valet continues. "It is parked out front for you, fully fueled, with the keys in the ignition. You should be all set to go. Unless you wish to double-check your room, in case we missed any items?"

"N-nah. That's okay," Doug splutters, unclenching his hands and feeling a bit foolish. He has no idea how they'd managed to clear out their room so quick, but he isn't about to hang around jabbering about it. "I'm sure everything's good. Thanks."

The valet nods and offers to escort them out.

Less than five minutes later, Doug and Michelle are back in his Nissan Cube, cruising down the Fowlingtons' long driveway at a speed faster than prudent, the gravel crunching beneath the tires like a hard rain. Michelle is already dozing off beside him. Doug had to help her into the car, burping in his ear as he strapped on her seatbelt. He hopes she'll sleep off the alcohol and wake up normal, able to put all this behind her.

Doug glances in the rearview mirror. The mansion has more than two dozen Palladian windows spread across its façade, and he can swear there's someone peering out every one of them, observing their flight. He wants to flip them off but thinks better of it. After all, he is leaving unscathed, with a full tank of gas, and a cheque for ten thousand dollars in his pocket. He's actually come out ahead. It's like winning a jackpot at a shitty casino you never wanted to go to.

Doug has driven an hour and a half on the I-76 before his tightly wound nerves finally unravel into some semblance of calm. Those crackpots are now far enough behind them that he can treat the experience as one of those gripping stories you share with friends around a firepit. *Escape from the Fowlingtons!* Though it wasn't so much an escape as it was a dramatic departure. Still, with a little embellishment, it might make for a good script.

When a big rig thunders by them in the right lane, Michelle stirs. She gazes out her window at the passing highway.

"Where are we?" she asks.

Doug is glad she sounds like her sober, if sleepy, self again. "Still in Pennsylvania. We just passed Harrisburg."

"Ugh," she snorts. "I hate Harrisburg."

"You do? Why?"

"'Cause it's boring as hell. City's all blowhard politicians and ultra-Christians and cow lovers. Hardly a shot glass worth of personality between them."

"Really?" he replies with a chuckle. "You seem to know a lot about Harrisburg. When were you there?"

She scrunches her brow. "I… I wasn't… Must've read about it somewhere."

Maybe she isn't quite herself after all.

"Hey, I'm starving," Doug announces. He hasn't eaten since breakfast at the Fowlingtons. Blood pudding, he recalls before shunting aside the distasteful (but actually quite tasty) memory. "How 'bout we grab a bite somewhere?"

"Sure," she answers as listlessly as humanly possible.

Doug exits the highway onto a service road flanked by brightly lit gas stations, dimly lit bars, and closed fast food joints. He's fortunate enough to find a Denny's open at this hour. He parks in its almost deserted lot.

He unbuckles his seatbelt and opens his door. Michelle stays in her seat, staring straight ahead of her like a movie is about to start.

"Coming?" Doug asks.

"I'm not hungry," she answers.

"You were, like, ten minutes ago."

"I changed my mind. And my stomach."

He looks at her appraisingly. "That's okay. Come in and keep me company."

"I'm tired," she sighs. "I'll wait here in the car."

"I don't think that's such a good idea."

"Why not?"

"I… I just think you shouldn't be alone."

"Why not?" she asks again, then leers at him. "Don't you trust me?"

Maybe not, he thinks. *Not right now.*

"Why would you say… no, it's not that. I just don't want to eat alone."

"It's not a big deal, Doug."

"Please, Mish… What happened today…" His mouth takes on semi-exaggerated shapes as he tries to articulate what he wants to say. "It was kind of, y'know, messed up. You know that, right? So can't we just, like, chill out together like normal couples do? So things can feel normal again."

"Jesus, Doug," Michelle groans. "You are so fucking needy."

This pisses him off. He wants to yell at her, call her inconsiderate and ungrateful and worse. Then he reminds himself that she isn't herself at the moment, that she has been through a lot this weekend. "Fine. We'll go to a drive-thru somewhere—"

"I'm kidding, butthead!" she blurts and rolls her eyes. "Let's get you your Grand Slam breakfast before your tongue fumbles any more."

Doug smiles at her. She might've mixed up her sports terms, but at least she's being agreeable.

The petite hostess leads them to a large booth in the rear of the restaurant. Michelle plops down into the vinyl seat first, with Doug sliding in next to her. The only other patrons in the place are a bushy-bearded old man drinking a cup of coffee and a young couple with a rambunctious toddler in a Frankenstein's Monster mask (even though it's months away from Halloween). The kid is dancing to "Girls Just Want to Have Fun" playing on the overhead speakers.

A frizzy-haired waitress reeking of cigarettes takes Doug and Michelle's order. Doug gets his Grand Slam breakfast and a Coke. Michelle says she doesn't want anything. He orders her a vanilla milkshake and a plate of French fries, both favorite late-night treats of hers and, he hopes, good for diluting the effects of any alcohol left in her system.

"You need to have something," Doug stresses to her after the waitress walks off. "You're gonna feel like crud later if you don't."

"I'm. Not. Hungry."

"Well, maybe you will be when the food is in front of you."

Michelle dumps several jelly cups from the metal caddy onto the table and methodically stacks them into a pyramid.

"Whatcha doing? Making a mini replica of King Tut's tomb?"

She shrugs, then knocks over the pyramid with a flick of her finger. She reminds Doug of a petulant six-year-old.

"Are you mad at me?" he asks her.

Michelle glares at him. "No, Doug. I'm much happier being here in this Denny's than in some beautiful house with a comfy bed, delicious food, and people who care about me."

"So mad it is," he says wryly. "Y'know, I dragged you out of there because *I* care about you. Those people are a bad influence."

"They're family."

"No, they're not, Mish. They're not even your friends. They just needed you to star in their freaky show."

"Fuck you."

"Fine. Be angry. But I don't regret *helping* the girl I love." He almost said *saving*.

Their waitress returns with their food. The cook has made the components of Doug's meal—pancakes, eggs, and bacon—into a smiley face. He picks up his fork and dives in. Michelle doesn't touch her fries or shake; doesn't even glance at them.

"C'mon, babe," Doug says after swallowing his first mouthful. "Eat something."

She narrows her eyes at him and starts chewing on her fingernails.

"Cute."

She pauses, says "yummy," and continues gnawing.

"Listen, I'm sorry, OK?" Doug capitulates. "I honestly thought I was doing the right thing. I was worried about you and, uh... and that's it. So can we just go home, kick back, watch *Law & Order* together? Maybe we can bake a cake. Plant a tree. Overthrow the government. Form a whole new government promoting a cake and tree-based economy."

Michelle snickers at this.

"Hooray. I still amuse you. Points for me."

She holds up two fingers on her right hand.

"Two points?" he asks.

She nods.

"What do I get for wrongheadedly looking out for you?"

She purses her lips as she mulls it over. She then raises three fingers.

"Three points. That's five in total… How about for me doing all the driving?"

One finger goes up.

"And I also apologized for my wrongheadedness."

Two more fingers.

"That's what? Eight points now? OK, going for the win here. When we get home, I am going to give you the most spectacular orgasm you've ever had."

Michelle cocks an eyebrow as she ponders this, then unfurls her index and middle fingers.

Doug beams. "Fuck yeah! Perfect ten… But it's just two for the orgasm?"

With her eyes fixed seductively on him, Michelle takes her extended fingers, lowers them beneath the table and slips them up her skirt, high up between her thighs.

Doug's smile falters. His eyes widen.

She once more presents him with her fingers, their tips now glistening, and places them against his lips. He accepts her two digits into his mouth and sucks on them for a fleeting moment until she extracts them.

"Go on and eat," Michelle says as she inserts the straw of her milkshake between her lips. "Before it gets cold."

Less than half an hour later, they're back on the road. Doug restarts his GPS destination for home, though he doesn't really need it. Once they're on the I-76 again, he won't be changing highways for another three hundred miles. He decides he's going to do the trip in one shot, without stopping anywhere for the night. He just wants to get home.

Google Maps points him in the opposite direction from how he had gotten to Denny's. Maybe it's to circumvent an accident or road work on the highway, he speculates. Doug drives along the service road for ten minutes before the GPS steers him onto a more rural, remote street named Log Hatch Pike. The lighting here is sparser, with just a single lamppost every quarter mile or so, then none at all. There's also much less traffic; they pass only one oncoming car—an old, red Ford pickup—then see no other vehicle lights in front of or behind them for miles.

"Seems like Lady GoGo"—that's what Doug and Michelle call the British-accented Google Maps voice—"wants us to do some late-night sightseeing in the boonies. Oh look babe, there's a tree. And another one! And another! Hey, that looks like Spruce Willis.

I loved him in *Die Hardwood*!"

Michelle doesn't even crack a strained smirk. Usually she's at least mildly amused by Doug's goofy shticks, worthy of an eyeroll from her at minimum. Right now, though, she does not react at all, vacantly looking out the windshield at what empty road she can see ahead of them in the car's high beams. It's what her father, a U.S. Navy veteran, calls the bulkhead stare, a classic symptom of battle fatigue. Doug doesn't think Michelle is suffering from a bona fide form of shell shock, but he's still concerned about her.

"You okay, Mish?"

"Yes," she answers curtly, coolly.

Doug waits a couple of minutes before speaking again. She obviously doesn't want to engage in conversation, but he loathes the silence between them now.

"Mind if I put the radio on?" he asks her.

"Fine," she says.

Doug pushes the power button on the stereo and rotates the tuning knob, finding nothing except static, one country music station, and some evangelical preacher haranguing his listeners about the "Satan-suckling media." Doug switches the radio off and wishes his CD player still worked. He settles for the drone of the car engine and the whir of the spinning tires as the soundtrack for this trip. Michelle remains in her zone; that is, zoned out.

Fine fine, Doug inwardly chants to himself. *Everything's fine. Fine as wine.*

He can't believe she was drinking tonight. Can't believe those Fowlington fuckers let her, encouraged her even. Can't believe it doesn't seem to bother her, after how committed to staying sober she has been these past few months.

No. Everything is not *fine.*

A frigid draft bristles the hairs on the nape of Doug's neck. He rubs the affected area to warm it, then fiddles with the electric window controls, suspecting one of the rear ones is ajar. But no, they're shut tight.

A minute later, the draft comes again, raising goosebumps on his neck.

What the hell? Doug theorizes the air blowing from the vents must be circulating through the car and hitting him from behind. The A/C, however, is set at its lowest setting, to keep his windows from fogging up. It's not possible the flow could be strong enough to loop around and reach him.

A few seconds later, it happens again. It feels like somebody is breathing heavily on his skin.

The thought creeps him out.

"Hey Mish," Doug says, trying to distract himself. "Want to play twenty questions?"

Michelle doesn't respond.

"C'mon, babe… Okay, I'm thinking of a place. What's your first question?"

She says nothing.

"Is it in this country, Doug?" he asks himself, welcoming the sound of his own voice. He then answers himself with a jaunty "No, Michelle, it's not."

He glances at her. She remains silent, still.

"Is it on Earth?" he resumes the game with himself. "Yes, it is… Is it in Europe?… Yes indee—"

Another puff of arctic air—another breath—strikes him from the backseat.

Doug continues trying to rationalize it: a hole somewhere in his car; some kind of rare weather phenomena that occurs within confined spaces; his imagination.

He ultimately chooses to attribute it to the latter because it's the simplest, soundest reason. And because the idea that somebody might be sitting right behind him scares the shit out of him. But really, how could someone be hanging out back there without him noticing until now? Not possible. So he pays it no further mind.

Until it happens again. And again.

He thinks he can hear it now. Rough, raspy.

Just look back there, dumbass, a part of his brain chides him.

No fucking way, another part of his brain replies.

What if it's some maniac getting ready to plunge a knife into you?

That would really suck for me.

You need to defend yourself. And Michelle.

Doug considers pulling over to the shoulder of the road, then promptly reconsiders it. They are in a pitch-black portion of the middle of nowhere; stopping here is all the levels of *HELL, NO!* And who says the dude isn't waiting for him to do exactly that, to prevent Doug from crashing his car as he's being stabbed to death and consequently killing them all. Even the most bloodthirsty of maniacs must possess a sense of self-preservation.

The icy breaths quicken, as if the breather is becoming more excited, more thirsty.

Doug thinks about commenting on how chilly it is inside the car, as a sort of implicit warning meant for Michelle, but worries this could also alert any insane stowaway that he's on to them.

Doug doubts Michelle would acknowledge anything he says to her right now anyway.

He formulates a plan. He'll keep driving until he runs across any open business, like a gas station or convenience store. Then he and Michelle, acting as easygoing as possible, will get out of the car and go into the place under the pretense of using the restroom or to buy snacks. As soon as they are safe inside, Doug will call the police. Maybe he'll also tell the clerk about his suspicions and have them lock the front door of the store.

He only has to go another 2.7 miles until he turns left on what appears on the GPS to be the main thoroughfare through whatever town they're in.

Just another few minutes on this fathomlessly dark road.

The guy in the back seems to have scootched toward Doug. The breaths feel closer now, more insistent. They're bone dry and deathly cold. So cold that Doug thinks he sees, in his peripheral vision, exhaled clouds dissipating next to his cheek.

Doug desperately needs to see who is behind him. Needs to size up the threat mere inches away from him. Needs to know if he should act *now*, not wait 2.3 miles.

As casual as possible, he moves to adjust the rearview mirror so he may get a glimpse of the unwelcome passenger in the weak light of his phone's GPS screen. Doug grasps the mirror's frame and wriggles it—it makes a squeaky noise he's never noticed before—directing it toward the back until he sees...

Nothing. Nobody. Just an empty seat.

Just my goddamn imagination.

"You can't have her," Michelle growls.

Doug turns his head toward her. "What did you say, Mish?"

"She's mine," she replies without looking at him, tendrils of wintry vapor spilling from her mouth.

What the hell's wrong with her?, Doug thinks as he returns his narrowed eyes to the road.

Eyes that then widen in terror.

Clustered together on the road ahead are more than a dozen ghostly figures lit up yellowly in the Nissan's high beams. Men and women in sundry styles of clothing standing there, watching with their coal-black eyes as Doug zooms toward them at 40mph, unconcerned they are about to be mowed down.

The instant he identifies what he's seeing, Doug reflexively cranks the steering wheel to the right, swerving around the creepy crowd and hurtling the car along the grassy shoulder of the road. It sideswipes a line of tall trees before he slams on the brakes and brings them to a juddering halt.

Doug loosens his terror-grip on the steering wheel, stammer-sighing "holy shit" as he lets his heart rate slow to a more sedate Mach 1.

He hears Michelle crying beside him.

"Oh god, Mish," he says, alarmed. He pivots toward her. She's hunched forward in her seat in a fetal position, her spine heaving in sync with her breaths.

"Are you okay?" he asks her. "Are you hurt?"

She shakes her head. "They won't let me go," she snuffles.

"Who won't?"

She doesn't answer him.

Doug yearns to hug her, tell her everything's going to be okay. Instead, he peers into his rearview mirror to inspect the road behind them. Seeing only unyielding darkness, he reaches over into the popped-open glove compartment and grabs his emergency flashlight from it.

He rolls down his window and shines it down the road.

All he can see now, stretching across the cracked pavement, are the slender shadows created by the car's rear fender, twigs and pebbles, and a dead opossum. The people have scattered. He pans the light into the adjacent forest. No trace of them there either. He shuts off the flashlight and rolls up his window, verifies the doors are locked.

Doug eases the car back onto the road and promptly accelerates to just above the speed limit. He glances over at Michelle, still curled up into a protective ball. Only now she's staring at him, her cheek resting on her knee, wearing a thin smile.

"You alright, Mish?"

"That was fun," she answers then looks away from him, the smile remaining on her face.

Too tense to drive, Doug stops at the first motel he comes across, the sketchy-looking Easy Come Easy Go Motor Lodge, located off the town's main drag next to a gun & tackle store. While Michelle waits out in the car, Doug enters the motel's small, spartan front office and checks them in for the night. The heavily tattooed desk clerk—his bald head is entirely inked with skulls, flames, and an evil Gumby—gives him a white plastic keycard for a ground-floor room.

"It's right near the vendin' machines," the clerk tells him as if it's a selling point for the place.

"Thanks," Doug says.

"Where y'all headed?"

"Home," Doug replies. "Chicago."

"Groovy. I've had their pizza."

Doug nods, slips the keycard into his shirt pocket. "Thanks again—"

"So where y'all comin' from?" The guy must be bored, Doug guesses.

"A funeral," Doug answers, hoping it will cut short the clerk's chattiness.

"Damn," the clerk says. "Was it anybody special?"

What a fucked-up question, Doug thinks, but then the guy's got a demonic Gumby tattoo on his scalp. For a dude like this, there are no fucked-up questions.

"Hey, I should go take my girlfriend to our room. She's not feeling well."

"Oh, yeah. Sure sure. Sorry to hold ya up, bud." To his credit, he sounds genuinely apologetic. "Been a slow night, y'know?"

"Gotcha. Thanks again."

"Have a goodnight. Hope your old lady feels better."

"Me too," Doug says, adding before leaving the office, "And no, it was nobody special."

The clerk grins doltishly, wishes him goodnight again.

Doug cannot get a handle on how Michelle is doing. Over the last three hours, her mood, when she's exhibiting one, has swung from amused to melancholic to mean. She's definitely... *off*. (He can hear Bethany's voice in his head saying the word with him.)

He hopes a good night's rest will restore her to her normal self. If not, it's going to be a long ride home.

Doug drives his car around the building and parks outside their room. Upon entering, he wrinkles his nose from the pungent odor of lemon furniture polish over—but not overpowering—the stubborn traces of mildew and cigarettes.

Michelle immediately lies face down on the queen-sized bed, on top of the leaf-patterned covers, and shuts her eyes. She does not shed an article of clothing, not even removing her shoes. Her suede purse, still slung on her shoulder, dangles over the side of the bed.

Watching her relax takes some of the edge off Doug's edginess, enough where he feels like he can get some rest himself. He kicks off his sweaty oxfords and shucks off the scratchy Walmart slacks he has been wearing the last couple of days. He considers taking off Michelle's dress sandals, but not wanting to disturb her, decides against it.

He goes into the bathroom to pee and rinse the bilious taste from his mouth. Returning to the bed, he gingerly lowers himself onto it, switches off the rust-pocked lamp on his nightstand. He looks over at Michelle, now fast asleep, snoring softly. Soon he too dozes off to the white noise of passing traffic outside.

The dusty digital clock on the nightstand reads 12:47 AM.

Doug has slept less than two hours. He's still dog-tired, but his intuition woke him up, prodding him that something is up.

Something's wrong.

He sits up in the bed, rubs the film from his eyes, and turns on the lamp.

Michelle is no longer lying next to him.

"Michelle?" he calls out.

She doesn't answer. The top of the blanket on her side of the bed is still slightly warm to the touch.

Doug sees the bathroom door is wide open and the light's off. He checks it anyway. Upon switching on the light, he imagines the redneck newlyweds lying dead and bloody in the tub. (A crummy thing for his imagination to be doing to him right now.) A blink later, they're gone. Michelle's not in there either.

Doug exits the bathroom and parts the tatty curtains over the room's large front window. In the poorly lit parking lot, he can see his Nissan Cube—he winces at the sight of the tree-inflicted gouges along the passenger-side doors—as well as a blue Harley-Davidson motorcycle and an exterminator's van with a big model rat on its roof. Two vending machines hug the kitty-corner wall a few feet away.

But no Michelle.

Doug throws on his pants and shoes and exits the room on a mission to find her. He stands outside their door, looking all around, trying to determine in which direction she might have headed. Several moths flit around the recessed bulb above him. A plump, gray one lands on his cheek. He snatches it in his fist.

"Michelle!" he calls into the night.

The night doesn't answer him.

The insect still trapped in his hand, Doug almost crushes it but opens his fist before he does. It flies away, low to the ground in an aimless zigzag. Doug guesses he wounded its wing. Seconds later, however, it's fluttering about like normal, as if it just needed to shake off a cramp. It flies skyward, toward a flickering street-lamp visible over the motel's roof. A moment later, a small dark shape—a bat, probably—swoops down and devours the moth.

Can't escape fate, boy, he recalls his father saying every time Doug fucked up.

But he's not going to fuck *this* up. He'll get Michelle home safe.

Doug tries reaching her on his cell. An automated message informs him her voicemail is full.

He drops in the front office, asks the tattooed clerk if he has seen a skinny girl with long blonde hair.

"Nope. You're the last person I've seen tonight."

Fuck. "What's around here, that's open now?"

"Just the gas station on Whitechapel. And Vital Signs."

"Vital Signs?"

"It's a bar across the street."

Shit.

Doug darts out of the office and, jogging at a brisk pace, he makes it to Whitechapel Avenue within a couple of minutes. The street is lightly traveled and brightly lit, dominated by a series of strip malls composed of closed hair salons, takeout restaurants, mobile phone dealers, and other cookie-cutter brick and mortar stores.

And the bar.

Contrary to its name, Vital Signs Cocktail Lounge shows no indications of life. Sandwiched between a pizza parlor and a print shop, its solid steel entrance door looks like one found in a prison or psych ward. A neon Budweiser sign in the front window pulses erratically in its death throes. Only the cracked plastic "*OPEN*" placard propped on the sill informs customers that they are indeed open for something akin to business.

The interior is dim and dingy and dismal, pretty much what Doug would expect from a small-town dive bar. The TV on the wall broadcasts a billiards competition, perhaps compensating for the lack of a pool table in the place. An old jukebox sits beneath a grimy fan. No song plays on the machine. It looks more suited to a museum.

Just two people are in here, neither of whom looks like they would appreciate music or pool at the moment anyway. A single bartender with a scraggly white goatee and a wrinkly plaid shirt leans behind the counter with his arms crossed, lost in thought. Seated on a padded stool at the far end of the counter is Michelle. In front of her sits a fluted shot glass, empty. She stares down at it, into the syrupy dregs of whiskey clinging to the sides, possibly wishing for it to refill through sheer mental will. When that fails, she raises her index finger to get the bartender's attention, then points at her glass.

"Last call," the bartender tells her as he snatches a well-loved bottle of Jack Daniel's from a shelf behind him.

Before the bartender can pour, Doug cups his palm over her glass. "She's cut off," he says.

"You know her?" the bartender asks.

"She's my girlfriend."

Michelle dips a hand into her purse and fishes out a twenty-dollar bill. She slaps it onto the counter. "One more," she insists.

"No," Doug emphatically says to her. "You're done."

She shakes her head and blows a spittly raspberry at him, an action which causes her stool to wobble. Before she keels over, Doug grips her upper arm and steadies her.

"Stop it, Mish! We're going."

"Shouldn't she be the one to decide that?" the bartender asks. It's less of a question, more of a challenge.

Doug remembers how Nathaniel Fowlington said something similar to him before they left his estate. He remembers how angry it made him.

"She's an alcoholic," Doug says. It's less of a declaration, more of an appeal to the man's sense of decency.

The bartender shrugs. "Most of my best customers are."

Doug badly wants to punch the bartender in his stupid, soulless face. Instead he digs into his pants pocket and pulls out his wallet. He plucks a twenty-dollar bill from it and lays it on top of Michelle's money.

"She's done here," he tells the bartender with finality. "You can lock up this shithole now."

Doug shepherds an uncoordinated Michelle back to their motel room, his arm girding her waist so she does not trip over something or herself. She's too tanked to protest the forced march much beyond her slurring an occasional swear word, which he presumes to be directed at him. Once inside their room, he guides her to the bed. She topples onto it and conks out in seconds.

Doug first puts her purse on her nightstand but changes his mind, instead stowing it in the bottom drawer of the credenza. He takes off her shoes this time, setting them on the floor beneath the flimsy luggage rack. Her pink cardigan sweater has bunched up around her torso and stretched across her chest, straining its enamel buttons to the brink of popping off. Doug delicately undoes them starting at the collar. He unfastens the second button, exposing a patch of white. After the third one, a blotch of reddish brown appears. He finishes unbuttoning the sweater and parts it. Right above the center bridge of her baby blue bra is taped a square gauze bandage, stained with blood.

"Jesus," Doug mutters. "What the hell did they do to you?"

He supposes she could have injured herself by scratching or slashing her chest on God-knows-what, but his gut's telling him this wasn't her doing. The Fowlingtons hurt her. Why, he doesn't know. But he does know intuitively and indubitably that those mutherfuckers did it.

Doug feels a compulsion to peel the bandage off and inspect the wound, but elects to leave it alone, fearing he would tear away the fresh scabbing and wake her up. He folds over the top blanket from his side of the bed to cover her, then switches off his lamp.

Shit shit shit. Doug isn't sure what to do. Michelle once told him that if she ever relapsed, he should just "throw" her in rehab. It seemed a simple enough plan when she was doing fine. Now, though, he wonders if it might be overkill. He has no idea what rehab costs, what's required to check in, if he would be obligated to take care of anything he's not prepared for.

He needs an expert second opinion.

Doug slides his cell phone out of his pants pocket and steps outside, quietly shutting the door behind him. He strides a few feet into the parking lot, near enough to keep watch on their room but far enough for Michelle not to hear him. He scrolls through his phone's saved contacts and dials a number.

Kimmy, Michelle's AA sponsor, picks up on the third ring.

"Hey, Kimmy? This is Doug… Michelle's boyfriend…"

"Oh, hi Doug…" Her tone alternates from confused—Doug has never called her before—to concerned. "…Is everything alright?"

"Uhh, shit, sorry for calling you so late."

"No problem, hon. I was up reading. What's going on?"

Doug tells Kimmy that on their way home from the funeral, Michelle relapsed, but she's safe and sleeping right now. "What should I do?"

"You get her butt to a meeting ASAP," she replies as naturally as if he had asked her what her favorite movie or color is.

"*Kimmy!*" her girlfriend Lisa hollers in the background. "*Have you seen my Liz Clairborne's?*"

"They're probably in the hall closet where they always are," Kimmy answers her.

"*That's where I'm look—Oh, here they—Fuck me! The cat shit in my shoes!*"

"Seems Zsa Zsa pooped in Lisa's pumps," Kimmy tells Doug.

"We're kinda in the middle of nowhere here," Doug tells her.

"Shouldn't matter," Kimmy says. "There're addicts in Everytown, Nowheresville. And where there are addicts, there are AA meetings. Unless you're in the desert?"

"No. We're in Central Pennsylvania."

"Almost as desolate," she jokes. "But you can bet your bippy there'll be a meeting not too far from you. Hold on, I'll send you something."

Kimmy texts him the link to an AA group locator.

"Thanks, Kimmy," Doug says.

"Thank you, Doug, for taking care of her. She's lucky to have you in her life."

After he hangs up with Kimmy, Doug visits the website she forwarded him on his phone. He locates a 9 a.m. meeting the next day at a community center less than ten miles away. He figures he should keep a close eye on Michelle overnight as she sleeps off the booze, making sure she doesn't wander off again or puke all over herself. In the morning they can pick up breakfast somewhere, then swing by the meeting. After that they'll get back on the road home. They might even reach Chicago by nightfall if they don't stop too often. Maybe Michelle will be able to drive awhile so he can catch up on some z's.

Doug buys himself a Coke from the vending machine to help him stay awake through the night. He unscrews the cap off the soda, releasing the loud *WHOOSH* of carbonation. This reminds him of the cold breaths behind his seat in the car, which in turn reminds him of those spooky peeps standing in the middle of the road. The memory makes him shudder, and he quickens his steps toward the refuge of his room.

As he unlocks the door with his keycard, Doug hears the purr of a vehicle's engine as it pulls into the lot. He glances toward it and squints, its bright, blue-tinged headlights blinding him.

He ducks into the room and shuts the door louder than he intended to—*Shit*, he mouths to himself—but it doesn't matter.

Through his speckled vision he sees Michelle's bedside lamp is on and tipped against the wall. The tilted shade trains the lamp's harsh light across the bed.

Michelle sits bolt upright and motionless, mannequin-like, on the far edge of the mattress, with her back to Doug. The blood-stained bandage from her chest now lies partially crumpled on her pillow, like a grisly piece of abstract origami.

"Mish?" he says. "You okay?"

"She belongs to me, Doug," Michelle answers. But it isn't her voice. It sounds deep and hoarse, like a man's.

"What?"

Michelle rises and rotates mechanically toward Doug until he beholds a startling, surreal vision between the drawn curtains of her sweater. From the raw, yawning wound in her chest protrudes part of a face—Liam's face. Only his mouth, nose, and one eye are visible, grotesquely framed within the split and stretched flesh above her bra. His salmon pink lips are semi-flaccid, semi-snarled, like those of an aggrieved dental patient who's been injected with too much Novocain. Liam's milky iris is replicated in Michelle's own eyes. Dead eyes staring at Doug.

"What the fuck?" Doug mutters.

"Michelle is mine!" Liam's face shrieks. "Mine forever!"

Doug questions his sight and his sanity. This must be a hallucination, he presumes, maybe a residual effect of whatever drug Nathaniel Fowlington might've slipped him in his food or drink.

Illusion or not, it demands a response.

"The hell she is," he growls at Liam.

"It's too late, Doug." Liam's mouth drools something red and gloppy. "Let her go… and move on."

"No, no, no," Doug repeats, shaking his head. "This can't be real."

"Of course it's not." Liam grins and gurgles. "How could it be?"

A car horn beeps twice outside.

"Our ride's here," Liam says. "Don't follow us. You're in no condition to drive."

Doug thinks the bastard's mocking him.

Michelle heads for the door, her movements stiff and jerky.

Ignoring his common sense to keep his distance (or his disbelief), Doug advances toward Michelle in an attempt to defend her, protect her, help her somehow, someway. In the split second before he reaches her, he must choose between clamping onto her shoulders and holding her in place—while staying out of biting range of Liam—or punching Liam in the nose, which might also hurt Michelle.

Liam/Michelle makes the choice for him. With the back of her hand, she slugs Doug in the jaw, much harder than he'd think her capable of, rattling his teeth and shooting convulsive ripples down his body. His knees wobble, then buckle. He staggers sideways, his body slamming into the nook between the wall and TV console. Dazed from the blow, he barely discerns the blurry form of Michelle opening the door to outside.

"Stop!" he blurts.

She doesn't stop.

Doug scrunches and unscrunches his face as the ringing in his head abates. Bracing his hands on the TV console, he heaves himself to his feet and scrabbles for the doorway.

He sees Michelle climbing into a silver convertible.

"Michelle!" Doug yells.

As he primes himself to lunge toward the car, another figure blocks his path. Someone super slim, wearing what might be a white tennis outfit—a short pleated skirt and a tight tank top that hardly contains a pair of the most ridiculously large boobs he has ever seen.

He knows these boobs.

The instant Doug recognizes her, she spritzes him in the face with a small spray bottle of something that smells like a heady perfume of exotic spices and vinegar. It burns his eyes. He feels dizzy again. His muscles seize and he collapses backwards onto the floor. His larynx clenches up, hence he can neither speak nor scream. Panicked, he concentrates on breathing evenly through his nostrils, fighting to not pass out.

"Sorry, *mon chéri*," Bethany Fowlington coos at him, "but family always comes first."

The motel room's door shuts with him still inside. Moments later, he hears the muffled revving of an engine, then the sound of tires squealing on gritty asphalt.

Doug can only lie there, immobilized, listening to Bethany's car speeding away from the scene, followed by the surf-like hum of his blood coursing through his brain.

NINE

Over the next two plus hours, Doug summons all his willpower to regain control of his body while impotently staring up at the motel room's popcorn ceiling. He is first able to wiggle the index and middle fingers of his right hand, tapping them on the cool coarse carpet underneath him. He thinks he can move his big toes too, but it's hard to tell for sure while wearing shoes.

Soon he can flop his limbs—looking like a huge fish plunked on a pier, he imagines. Minutes later, he can sit up and oscillate his head, painfully cracking the vertebrae along his neck.

Doug spots Michelle's sandals beneath the luggage rack. He figures she must have gone out barefoot. He worries she did not button up her sweater and that she's riding shotgun in Bethany's top-down convertible with her bosom on bold display in her semi see-through bra.

That and her ex-fiancé's face jutting from her chest.

But that must have been a hallucination, right? The Fowlingtons could have somehow doped him again before they left the estate with some delayed-release, LSD-like drug so he'd be easier to deal with later when he started tripping. And they probably dosed Michelle with something, too. Why else would she leave willingly with Bethany like that? This is the only explanation that makes sense to him.

Goddammit, none of this makes any sense!

He guesses they must be on their way back to the Fowlington estate. He hasn't the slightest idea why they would be taking Michelle back there, but he knows it's not to roast marshmallows and sing kumbaya.

Doug commences the strenuous process of getting up on his feet. He flips onto his hands and knees, crawls over to the bed, and presses his cheek against the side of it. He then hooks his chin on the edge of the mattress and swings his arms on top of it. He squirms his upper torso onto the bed, rolls onto his side, and uses his hands to jack himself upright. All of this takes him nearly thirty minutes.

He digs a semi-gnarled hand into his pants pocket and scoops out his cell phone. Pressing the screen with the middle knuckle of his other hand, he calls 911 and in a gaspy, gravelly voice reports Michelle's kidnapping.

While waiting for the police to arrive, Doug stretches his legs, flexing the muscles and bending his knees until he feels they can support his weight again. The cops show up maybe ten minutes after he hung up with them.

There's a commanding rap at the door. Doug rises from the bed like a zombie clambering out of a grave and, taking measured, mindful steps—"One sec! I'm coming!"—answers it.

Two uniformed police officers stand side by side in the same straight-spined stance, both wearing steel-gray shirts and navy-blue pants which fit them so crisply they could've been sculpted onto their bodies out of clay. They are the same height, the same weight, likely the same age. One has olive skin and sports a mustache that resembles a well-used Brillo pad; the other is the polar opposite, blond, fair skinned, and clean shaven. Doug reads the shield-shaped patch on the mustached one's shoulder: OXBORO TOWNSHIP POLICE. Doug does not know where Oxboro is, other than it must be in Pennsylvania. He experiences a twinge of foreboding that he may never leave this damned state.

"Mr. Cunningham?" the mustached cop says.

Doug nods and invites them in.

The officers enter the room and size him up. Their postures remain rigid, ready.

Doug presents a rundown of the series of events—omitting a few details so he doesn't come off as cuckoo for Cocoa Puffs—which led to him calling them. Holding a pen as if it were a whisk, the pale cop jots select info on a mini spiral pad.

"Do you know who she left with?" the mustached cop asks. Doug notices he didn't repeat the term he had used: *kidnapped*.

"Yeah." Doug nods. "The family of her dead ex-fiancé."

"And why would she do that? Go with them?"

"I'm not… uh…" Doug flounders for a response. "It's hard to explain."

"Please try. The more information we have, the better we can assist you."

Doug opts to come across clueless instead of crazy. "For some kind of ritual, I think? Maybe. I'm really not sure. You'll have to ask them."

"Was your girlfriend removed from the room by force?"

"Kinda. Pretty much, yeah."

"Did they have weapons?"

"No, no weapons."

"So then, did they drag her out, tie her up, gag her? Anything like that?"

"No." Doug senses he is losing their attention, that they are about to dismiss his concerns as ungrounded and frivolous. He rallies a tone of distress. "But she wasn't in her right mind. She was, like, brainwashed, y'know? And Bethany knocked me out with some sort of knock-out spray."

"Who's Bethany?"

"The sister."

"Of your girlfriend's deceased fiancé?"

"Yeah. Ex-fiancé."

"How many alleged abductors were there?" *Alleged.* There's that equivocality again.

"Just her, I think."

"Any idea where Bethany brought her?"

"Probably back to their estate."

"Whose estate is this?"

"The Fowlingtons."

The officer with the notepad stops scribbling and speaks for the first time: "Nathaniel and Isadora Fowlington?"

Shit. These cops know who they are. Doug wonders if all the police in the region have been paid off to cover up the Fowlingtons' crimes, or to at least not investigate any wrongdoings reportedly perpetrated by them. Such as a kidnapping.

"Have you consumed any alcohol tonight?" the pale cop asks Doug.

"No. I haven't."

"You smell a little boozy, sir."

"Like I told you," Doug replies defensively, "I was at the bar across the street before, so maybe something got on me. But I wasn't drinking. I was there for five minutes, tops."

"To get your girlfriend."

"Yeah."

"Who went there by herself."

Doug can imagine what the cops are conjecturing. He sighs and nods.

"Did you take any sort of controlled substance or other medication tonight?"

Bastards are flipping all of this around on me, Doug realizes. And he never even mentioned the part about Liam's face in Michelle's chest.

"No," Doug answers. "Nothing."

"Okay, I think we have enough to go on, Mr. Cunningham," the mustached cop declares.

The other takes down Doug's phone number and address.

"We'll look into your girlfriend's whereabouts and get back to you when we can clear things up."

"What should I be doing in the meantime?" Doug asks.

"Go home and wait for us to contact you. These things usually turn out to be some kind of misunderstanding. I'm sure your girlfriend had her reasons to leave with Ms. Fowlington, and she just didn't want to upset you or hurt you."

"Or maybe she was afraid of you," the pale cop adds.

"No way," Doug insists. "I swear it wasn't anything like that."

"As we said, we will look into it and notify you as soon as we find out anything."

The officers leave the motel room, leaving Doug frustrated and angry. Even if the police aren't in the Fowlingtons' pockets, Doug doubts they believed much of what he had told them. (A reaction the Fowlingtons no doubt would be counting on.) It'd been a waste of time, and he has no time to waste.

Doug considers calling Kimmy again, or Michelle's dad, but what would it accomplish? They're both hundreds of miles away. There's nobody else close by he can contact for help, nothing else he can do except go after Michelle himself and figure it out when he gets there.

Which he knows is not a great plan. It's impulsive and reckless and just plain stupid.

But he has done some impulsive, reckless, stupid stuff in the past and things had worked out fine.

Here's hoping.

Doug lurches out of the motel room into the parking lot. He glimpses the taillights of the black-and-white squad car pulling out onto the street. They cruise away at a leisurely speed.

Doug heads to his car, opens the door, and folds himself into the driver's seat. He keys the ignition, half expecting it to not start, or to blow up like in a mafia movie. Neither happens. The engine sputters to life like normal.

Clutching the steering wheel as if it was the edge of a cliff, he coasts to the road and turns in the opposite direction the cops had gone, toward the last place he wants to go.

But go there he must.

Because if he doesn't, Doug fears he may never see Michelle again.

For the duration of the one-hour-and-forty-minute drive back to the Fowlingtons—in between stressing about what the hell he's doing—Doug thinks of Michelle, reminiscing about their last ten months together: their first date at a Japanese hibachi restaurant when she laughed so hard she spat sake all over the chef's grill; collecting enough sea glass at Montrose Beach to fill a mason jar that sits on their kitchen window sill; going to the Lincoln Park Zoo where they imitated all the animals (her impressions of the meerkats and penguins were especially spot on); the weekend of his 30th birthday when they'd binge-watched all the *Lord of the Rings* movies including the animated one from the 1970s; having sex in the backseat of his car under Fourth of July fireworks at the Navy Pier.

Doug also envisions their future together: he will propose to her on the boardwalk by the lake, surprising her with the ring in an ice cream sundae or possibly via trained seagull; she'll say yes with the most joyful tears filling her eyes that will royally mess up her mascara but she won't care; they'll have an inexpensive yet awesome wedding in her father's yard with a pit BBQ reception and live Celtic music; maybe they'll raise a couple of amazing, not-fucked-up-at-all kids; and they'll grow old happily together in a beautiful home with the perfect view of the sunset from their deck.

Then Doug wonders if it's too late for any of that now, if he's too late to save Mich—

No!, he snaps at himself. He can't start thinking like that. He dispels the doom and gloom from his mind, replacing it with one of single-minded purpose: to locate and liberate Michelle.

Doug reaches the entrance to the Fowlington estate and finds its tall, imposing gates closed. The brick walls that surround the expansive property must be at least eight feet high and capped with iron spikes, making it virtually unscalable. He also notices glints of yellow light bouncing off the lenses of four security cameras installed in cubbyholes carved into the masonry columns on each side of the gate.

He isn't getting in this way.

Doug drives on past the entrance, hoping he was not detected by any guards or whoever's inside watching the security monitors. The wall parallel to the road ends about three quarters of a mile down, cutting sharply to the right at a 90° angle. Branching off the paved road is a barely discernible dirt one running alongside the perpendicular wall; it's sheer luck that Doug spots it in the periphery of his headlights. Speculating it might be a service road used for deliveries or utility visits to the home, he turns onto it.

He negotiates the bumpy road, seeking another point of entry into the estate that he hopes will be less scrutinized and provide him an opportunity to slip through either in his car or, if necessary, on foot. He goes maybe half a mile to encounter more uninterrupted solid wall, the iron spikes replaced by concertina wire.

Shit. He deliberates going back, plowing his car through the front gate, and praying such a brash, desperate tactic somehow works in his, and Michelle's, favor.

In his rearview mirror, Doug sees the twin white gleams of headlights some distance behind him. He doubts it would be a delivery van or utility truck arriving there at this hour. Probably a security vehicle responding to him trespassing. With impenetrable wall on his right and night-shrouded trees to his left, there is nowhere for him to turn around, so he continues to drive slowly onward, the road growing darker and the woods getting denser before him.

Don't lose your shit now. Doug ill-conceives a half-assed plan. When the guard pulls him over, he can pretend he's lost, ask for directions to the highway, then figure out another way onto the grounds that might not entail him going full *Dukes of Hazzard* through the entry gate.

He expects its emergency lights to start flashing any moment. The vehicle accelerates, gaining on him fast. Rather than swirling orbs set ablaze on its roof, Doug observes its two headlights merge into one. Must be some optical illusion, he thinks. A trick of the mirror or something.

The vehicle—a motorcycle, maybe?—speeds up even more, getting close enough to kiss his bumper. Doug thinks it's going to ram into him. Instead, it careens sideways and rockets forward until it is keeping pace right next to the driver's side of Doug's car. He glances out his window to see who's crazy enough to ride so near him you could trap a starved sparrow between them.

It's not a *who*. It's a *what in hell?*

Two people on a mobility scooter glower at him. The driver is a corpulent—bloated, to be more accurate—woman in a one-piece swimsuit, her rat's-nest hair matted down to her head, the flesh on her arms and face sagging like gross globs of melting wax. Seated behind her with his hands clasping her shoulders is a brawny, bald man in swim trunks. Doug realizes the guy doesn't fit on the seat with the enormous woman; he's literally sitting on air. Even more unsettling is that these people, and their scooter, appear ripply and washy, almost transparent, like a film projected on fog. But it isn't foggy out, and this is no movie. It's something otherworldly. Something terrifying.

The scooter suddenly veers left a few feet, then jerks hard to the right, seemingly intent on slamming into the car. Bracing for the impact, Doug tightens his grip on the steering wheel. Rather than smashing his door, however, the man, woman, and scooter pass *through* it, then *through* Doug, then putter beside him on the passenger side, still inside the car.

"You can't knock him off the road, Gerty!" the man shouts. "We're intangible!"

"I know that, you moron!" the woman barks back. "Just want to scare the shit out of him!" She then swivels her swollen head toward Doug and opens her mouth unnaturally, almost comically wide, revealing a knotted mass of shimmery black eels. They untangle themselves, slither down her chin and across her cheeks. An extra-large, slimy-looking one stretches horizontally outward from her maw. It strikes at Doug with serrated teeth.

Doug yelps in horror and recoils from the serpentine creature. He cuts the steering wheel left, barreling the car into the forest. His right tires hit the sloping foot of a triangular boulder, upending the boxy vehicle onto its left wheels for a couple of seconds before tipping onto its side. The car skids along the ground like a runaway train until jamming between a pair of close-growing fir trees. The collision shatters the windshield and caves in half of the roof. Pine needles rain on Doug through the breach, causing him to flinch and snort.

Once the prickly shower ceases, he reopens his eyes and reorients himself. His body is twisted into a corkscrew, his scapula uncomfortably butting against the driver's door, one knee mashed against the center console, the other lodged beneath the dashboard. The car's engine has stalled, the headlights killed. He can hear liquid dripping, see steam spewing from the hood.

The phantom scooter freaks are gone.

Doug tests each of his limbs. Thankfully, nothing hurts, nothing's stuck. He brushes the pine needles and glass bits from his face and hair, unbuckles his seatbelt, and crawls out the busted windshield. He discovers his right ribs are tender and sore, but not bad enough to be broken.

He scans the inky woodland all around him. His eyes haven't yet adjusted to the darkness; the luminosity of the full moon penetrates the canopy just enough for him to perceive the different degrees of black. Then he makes out a faint greenish-yellow glow through the trees. That must be from the Fowlington estate, Doug figures. He heads toward it while trying to keep his spine straight to avoid aggravating his bruised ribs.

As he draws closer, the glow becomes brighter and greener. Doug begins to wonder if it's not originating from the mansion, but rather some nearby factory or an outdoor sports arena. (Not that the Fowlingtons would live anywhere near places like those.)

He hikes almost five minutes before he reaches a clearing in the forest and, within it, the source of the light. It's not Fowlingtons' home or a chemical plant or a Minor League baseball field.

It's a ship.

An old ship—the type that pirates or explorers voyaged on, Doug imagines—stands in the middle of the woods, no signs of traversable water anywhere. It must be as long as three city buses. Two masts, their sails furled, tower from the vessel, both taller than the surrounding trees. A bowsprit protrudes from its prow like a gigantic unicorn's horn. A thick dark stripe running along its side is painted with images of the moon's phases, interspersed with arcane symbols Doug doesn't recognize. The whole thing emits a chartreuse green light that reminds him of how radioactive waste is depicted in movies.

His first instinct is to run like hell, because he wouldn't be at all astonished to learn that is where it came from. Then he hears somebody call out to him in a booming brogue:

"Ahoy, Mr. Cunningham! Please join me, won't you?"

On the ship's deck, at the top of a raw timber gangplank that extends out to the forest floor, stands a spindly old man with long white hair and a long white beard, looking like Santa Claus after a crash diet. His complexion is even whiter than his hair, except for the web of capillaries creeping from the bridge of his nose and across his cadaverous cheeks. He wears a burgundy smoking jacket, beige cargo shorts, and a butt ugly pair of cherry red Crocs.

Every molecule in Doug's body screams for him to flee this vision—it surely cannot be real, but why take the chance?—until the old man speaks again.

"Come now. We can discuss the matter of Michelle."

"W-what about her?" Doug asks.

"Whatever it is you want to know, Mr. Cunningham."

Doug hesitates to respond or react.

"Please don't be leery of me," the old man says. "You are my guest, and I have no intention of being an inhospitable host."

Doug is inclined to believe him, if only because he sees no other viable option that might help him help Michelle.

He ascends the gangplank. The wood flares a brighter green under the weight of his footsteps. If the ship is radioactive, he muses, he's definitely contracted cancer of everything.

The old man greets him at the summit with an affable smile. "Welcome aboard *The Night Queen*, Doug!"

"How do you know me?"

The old man chuckles. "I don't *know* you. But I am well aware of who you are."

"And you knew I was coming here?"

"I can't say you were expected. But I am not surprised to see you."

"And who are you?"

"Pardon my manners," the old man answers. "I am Aldrich Bukani." He says his name like it has import.

Doug stares at him blankly.

"You could say I am the forefather of my family's beliefs."

"Wait…" Doug replies, pointing at him. "Bukani? There's a statue of you in the garden, right?" He gestures his thumb in the direction he reckons the gardens are.

"Aye, I am he," Aldrich answers like some smug Civil War-era orator.

"Ah, okay. I thought that was supposed to be some god."

223

"I suppose, in a way, I am a god to them. Over the centuries they have added their own frills and flourishes to my research. Transformed it into a veritable religion. At the risk of sounding blusterous, I find it quite flattering."

"Over *centuries*? So you're telling me you're what? A ghost?"

"I prefer the nomenclature 'spirit,' but for your purposes I think either is acceptable."

"Uhh hmm" is Doug's response to this affirmation. He still knows he should make a break for it, or at least freak out like most people would in this situation. But at this point, after all the *Beetlejuice*-ish things he has encountered within the past twenty-four hours, he's beyond those sorts of reactions.

"Where's Michelle?" he asks.

"How about we take this conversation below?" Aldrich suggests. "Where it's homier."

"I'm fine talking here."

"Don't be mulish," the old man scoffs as he moves toward an oblong doorway that Doug presumes is for accessing the bowels of the ship. "I promise I shan't tear your soul apart or anything ghastly like that." He takes a step over the threshold leading down into the hold and pauses. "Come now," he says amiably, beckoning him with a twirl of his hand.

Doug takes a fortifying breath and follows Aldrich, ducking through the squat entryway and descending a narrow set of rickety stairs. While the nuke-green phosphorescence lessens the further they proceed, the reek of bilgewater and burnt wood intensifies.

Despite Bukani's reassurances, Doug does indeed fear for his soul—and everything else of his—as he presses on deeper toward whatever awaits him.

If he had to take his wildest guess what the hold of an old ghost ship would contain, Doug still would've been far off. Strings of red Chinese paper lanterns and tropical tiki lights festoon the rafters. In the middle of the space is a purple-felt pool table with ball-and-claw legs, and against both walls stand a variety of classic arcade game machines: *Pac Man, Donkey Kong, Frogger, Joust,* and a KISS pinball machine. At the stern end, a leather club chair sits in front of a mint-condition 1970s TV cabinet console with built-in radio and record player. Currently showing on the 20" screen in vivid color is *Point Break*, its audio blasting astoundingly clear from the twin speaker panels.

It's Aldrich Bukani's man cave.

Even dead, the dude's living it up.

"Fancy a game of snooker?" Aldrich asks Doug as he lowers the TV's volume using a brick-sized remote. "Or we can team up for a tourney of *Joust*. I've never played it with two players."

"Where's Michelle?" Doug asks again.

Aldrich sighs with disappointment. "She's at the estate. But I imagine you knew that already."

"What are they doing with her?"

"It is mostly done," Aldrich answers. "There's just one step remaining in the ritual, then Liam and Michelle's spirits shall be tethered together on this earthly plane for eternity, however long that lasts. 'Eternity' is such a nebulous term. Speculative, even. Still, it's rather romantic, is it not?"

"I need to see her," Doug demands.

"Why?"

"I need to help her."

"She doesn't need your help anymore, Doug."

"That's not true!" Doug blurts, shaking his head. "She needs me now more than ever."

Aldrich crinkles his brow. "For what?"

"To stop whatever's happening to her."

"And what do you think is happening to her?"

"I think… I *know* she's in danger."

"Michelle is fulfilling her destiny. And if you truly care for her, then you will let her achieve immortality with her true love. Liam."

"She doesn't love him," Doug asserts. "Maybe she did once, but not anymore."

"That is of no consequence," Bukani counters. "Michelle was pledged to him. Marked as his. And now she's consecrating their union as intended."

"Liam almost killed her!"

"They shared a weakness of the flesh. That will no longer be of consequence, either."

"Oh god." A realization so obvious and heinous slams Doug in the gut. "They're going to kill her, aren't they?"

"They are freeing her, Mr. Cunningham. Certainly you understand now that physical death is not an end, but a transfiguration. I'm quite content with mine. Everything's upgradeable!"

"But Michelle didn't choose this!"

"She didn't? Did she not accept Liam's proposal to marry? Did she not promise herself to him? She is simply carrying out her obligation."

"That's bullshit," Doug growls. "It's not fair."

"I shan't recite that tired trope," Aldrich grumbles. "My research in metaphysical healing was revolutionary. It would have benefitted all of mankind, all over this world. In no manner had I blasphemed God. In truth, I was doing His work. And yet I was burned to death for it by priggish, puritanical minds in this very vessel... Was that fair?"

"Maybe it wasn't. But your actions, your research, they *were* your choice, right up till you got whacked. If Michelle is killed—murdered—by your people while she is under their influence, that's not her choice. Your people are plotting her death, totally ignoring how she feels about things now."

"And how do you know that to be the case?"

"How do you know it's not?"

"They have a pact," Bukani reiterates. "Pardon my callousness, but it's her fault if she did not read the proverbial fine print."

"Did they even give her anything to read? Or did they just give her enough drugs so she didn't know what the fuck was going on? 'Cause that's what you did, didn't you?"

"*I* did not give her anything."

"Well, your family sure as hell didn't give her a chance to decide for herself what she wants. But everyone else gets what they want, don't they? Even Liam, and he's dead."

"*Chance*," Aldrich says ruminatively, stroking his luxuriant beard. He walks over to the leather armchair and eases himself into it. "That word calls to mind my journey to the New World, a journey undertaken on this very ship, on a mission to share my knowledge with those who had settled this land. Halfway across the Atlantic Sea, we were struck by a merciless storm. Terrible, towering waves thrashed our hull, ferocious winds tore our sails. Many of my crew were swept from the deck whilst trying to fasten down the rigging. We were helpless against Mother Nature at her most furious. I had resigned myself to my fate, to be cast into the depths and devoured by fish and fowl.

"And then I prayed for God to preserve me, to provide me another chance to carry out my noble work. Does that surprise you? Yes, I am a man of science, of intellect, but I am also a man of unwavering faith. And the Lord rewarded my faith in Him by quelling the storm and sparing my life. He gave me that chance I prayed for. I presume, Doug, that you have a comparable faith in Michelle, staunchly believing she loves you so much that she would renounce the covenant drawn between her and Liam?"

"Yeah," Doug replies confidently. "I do."

"Very well then. While life may not be fair—ha! I said it after all—I do consider myself a fair man. If you truly believe there is a chance you may divert Michelle from her destiny, then I shall presumptuously play the role of God and bestow upon you the chance you wish for. That is, to save her. Correct?"

Doug nods. "Yeah. Sounds good. How's that gonna work?"

"That is for you to suss out. I shall furnish the opportunity; you shall formulate a strategy. But…" A scrimshaw pipe appears in Bukani's hand; he sticks it in the corner of his mouth. "I shan't let you go in blindly. I think the maxim '*Before you judge a man, walk a mile in his shoes*' would be apropos in this circumstance."

"What do you mean?"

"Not everyone has gotten what they've wanted, Mr. Cunningham," Aldrich answers cryptically. "Understand that and you may understand why you cannot save everybody."

TEN

Doug has no clue what the hell is going on now. One moment he's on a colonial-era sailing ship in the woods talking with its spectral captain in a pimped-out cargo hold, the next he's seeing a life flash before his eyes—but not *his* life. From his own POV, he witnesses a stream of somebody else's memories in quick succession: a child's arms flailing in a swimming pool; a gang of prep school brats gleefully stomping him with their cleats; chugging a bottle of rum while a bunch of frat guys cheer him on; being extracted from a wrecked Porsche Spyder; lying in a hospital room bed (more than once); getting locked up in a jail cell (more than once as well); puking on a girl's back while he's screwing her from behind (also vomiting on a city sidewalk, into a dirty public toilet, in the rear row of a college lecture hall).

Intercut with this harrowing montage are snippets of bizarre ritualistic activities featuring knives and fire, runes and masks, blood and booze. It's all like some frenetic art film.

Then Doug finds himself splayed out on a spongy sea-green couch in some strange home. His head is spinning so viciously he has a tough time focusing on anything around him. It seems to be a small place—an apartment, maybe a condo. Although all the window blinds are shut, he can tell it's daytime from the slivers of sunlight seeping between the slats. He's surrounded by mostly empty bottles of liquor. Whiskeys and vodkas and gins and rums and tequilas litter the tabletops, countertops, and floors, looking like the aftermath of some riotous party that he has no memory of attending.

Doug starts to sweat and shiver at the same time. His palms feel clammy and swollen, his mouth as dry as dust. He suffers an urgent thirst beyond any he has ever experienced before.

He frantically gropes through the debris nearest him until he latches onto a half-full pint of Jack Daniels. He unscrews its cap and guzzles it, making sure every last drop dribbles down his gullet.

The relief is immediate and almost indescribable. A combination of tranquility and torpor overcomes him, conquers him. He surrenders to it willingly, welcomingly.

He feels calmer, in control again.

Yeahhh… that's better… okay…

Now he needs to figure out what's happened to him. Needs to find out where he is and how he got here. He needs to… needs to… needs…

I need another fucking drink.

Doug scans the area around him with radar-like precision. He homes in on a *3 Rings Wine & Spirits* bag set on the kitchen counter, packed so full its thin white plastic has stretched close to bursting, making its Ringmaster logo appear deformed, diabolical. Doug lunges for it as a hungry—thirsty—animal would. He peels the bag off its contents: large bottles of dark rum, vanilla vodka, and peppermint schnapps, each equally tempting.

Doug's hand selects the schnapps, it being the tallest bottle, and he opens it with all-consuming zeal. He swigs a third of the sickly-sweet syrup, paying his stinging esophagus no mind in favor of satisfying his bestial cravings.

He hunches over the counter and, still clutching the neck of the bottle like a pacifier, he idly gawks at the big black refrigerator across from him. He spots an unfamiliar photo affixed to the door by a banana-shaped magnet.

Doug totters toward the fridge, gripping its handle to steady himself while he examines the image: a smiling Michelle stands in front of a stone fountain with another guy—Liam. Doug's eyes roam to another picture stuck to the fridge below it: Michelle and Liam posing cheek to cheek in the soft light of a votive candle at a linen-covered table in some ritzy restaurant. And another: a strip of snapshots of them together in a photo booth, making silly faces at each other.

Where the fuck am I? Doug thinks as he once again surveys the place.

He glimpses his reflection in a full-length mirror mounted on the closet door across the apartment. Only it doesn't look like him. Puzzled, he lurches toward the mirror, his fuzzy vision becoming clearer as he gets nearer to it.

No. Fucking. Way. He rakes his trembly fingertips down his nose, mouth, and chin, feeling the pressure of his touch on a face that is definitely not his own.

It's Liam's.

Doug figures he *must* be hallucinating this time. Maybe Al Bukani hypnotized him and is performing some Jedi-level mind-fuckery on him.

A distant part of Doug's brain implores him to quit drinking as he again raises the bottle of schnapps to his lips.

Yeah. Just a hallucination. Gotta be.

Doug staggers over to a cozy-looking armchair and plops into it, relishing the sensation of his body—Liam's body—sinking into its plush cushions. He shuts his eyes, obliterating the world around him that is plainly not real, not his.

Gotta be. Gotta be. Gotta be, he repeats to himself over and over, until passing out.

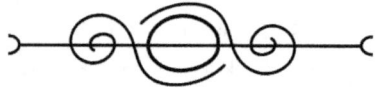

When Doug comes to, the first thing he makes out through his crusty squinty eyes is Liam's sister Bethany. She's wearing black block heel shoes and a glossy black vinyl bodysuit, the front of it unzipped almost to her navel to accommodate her prodigious bosom. She is studying him with a half-annoyed, half-pitying expression.

"Finally," she says. "You're up."

Doug can hardly move any part of his body beneath his neck. He peers down to discover he's bound to the armchair by a web of orange nylon straps cinched taut against him with metal ratchet buckles. He can wiggle his fingers and swish his feet to and fro on the carpet, but that's about all.

"Wh'the hell," he croaks.

"Sorry about the B&D vibe," Bethany answers while inspecting the cuticles of her right hand. "It's nothing kinky, I promise, *mon frère*." She smirks at him.

"Why… are you…"

"This is an intermission… no, not that." She closes her eyes to concentrate, then snaps them open and raises her index finger. "It's an inter*vention*. But I suppose it could be an intermission too, in a way."

Doug knows he should be alarmed by this, whatever *this* is. But his newfound extraordinary thirst has reawakened with him, eclipsing any survival instincts one would ordinarily be feeling in such a situation as this.

"I… I need a drink," he says hoarsely.

"No can do."

"Please… I need… I really need it." Sweat starts to bead on Doug's brow.

"No. You need air and food and water and…" Bethany makes a looping motion with her wrist like she's twirling a rattle. "Stuff like that. Did you know alcohol is classified as a poison? I'm sure you did. And yet for years and years you kept poisoning yourself, and poisoning the people around you."

"Just a sip… please… one sip."

"Sorry, brother dearest. You have been permanently eighty-nined—no, eighty-sixed. Is that right?"

Doug musters all the energy he can just to lift his head and glare at her. "I am *not* your brother."

Bethany's mouth quirks into a fluttery frown. "That is true. You're not the brother I grew up with. You're someone else now. Sad and sick all the time. I barely recognize you."

"Not Liam… I'm Doug."

"Doug? Who's Doug?"

"Me…" he rasps. "Inside."

"Mercy me," Bethany sighs, shaking her head. "How fucked up are you?" She slides out a slim bedazzled smartphone tucked into the bodysuit above her left breast. She autodials a number and puts the phone against her ear.

"Hi, daddy… Yes, he's awake now. You and mom wanna talk to him?… Okay, holdsies."

Bethany removes the phone from her ear, pushes a button on its screen, and faces it toward Doug. He sees Isadora and Nathaniel Fowlington sitting together on the chaise sofa in their grand hall, their expressions somber and stony.

"Oh, my poor baby," Isadora says flatly. "I hate seeing you in such a wretched state."

"We all do, Liam," Nathaniel adds.

Doug strains to train his attention on them. His mouth again has gone cottony. His breathing and heartbeat quicken. His whole head aches with a brass-knuckled throbbing. He yearns to shout at them, "GIMME A DRINK, YOU FUCKING ASSHOLES!!" Instead he mutters through gritted teeth: "I'm… not… Liam."

"He's been saying his name is Don," Bethany clarifies.

"Doug," Doug corrects her.

"Yeah. Doug. I think he's getting the DTs already."

"Whatever you want to call yourself," Isadora coos, "you're our son and we only want what's best for you."

Doug shuts his eyes tight to block out the searing brightness of the room.

"We're sorry it's come to this," Nathaniel says. "All the money we poured into the highest end rehab facilities for you, one after another. But nothing ever stuck. After a few months, or even a few weeks, it was always back to square one."

"It's not just the expense," Isadora continues. "Frankly, Liam, you have become an embarrassment to us. To your entire family. So much wasted potential. You had every advantage, every privilege. And you just squandered it."

She screws up her lips in indignation, the only hint of strong sentiment she has shown yet.

Nathaniel pats his wife's knee consolingly. "Believe us when we tell you this was our very last resort. We're compelling you to go cold turkey. You will not partake in another drop of alcohol; not another upper, downer, whichever way you favor. That facet of your life is over."

"You… can't… don't do this," Doug grunts, his head lolling side to side.

"Consider it an act of tough love," Isadora says. "And we do love you, Liam. So very much. We just cannot tolerate your bad habits any longer."

Nathaniel nods. "It's either sink or sober up, son. However it goes, we will be praying for you. And you can take comfort in the company of the Divine Ones. For they shall be at your side, bestowing their blessings and fortitude upon you in this world… and the next, if need be."

With that, Nathaniel reaches out his hand and disconnects the call.

Soon after, the nightmares begin.

Within hours, the full onslaught of withdrawal symptoms mercilessly wracks Doug's muddled mind, caged in Liam's rebelling body. He perspires profusely; his muscles spasm like they're ropes in tiny games of tug of war; his heart jackhammers his chest as if it were trying to break out. Sometimes these things all occur at once, other times they take turns. All the while he's strapped down like a death row inmate in the electric chair.

During the come-and-go moments of semi-lucidity, Doug glimpses Bethany watching him or the TV, or futzing with her phone, or napping on the sofa. Sometimes she tries to feed him some kind of lukewarm liquid, presumably a soup of some sort, a small amount of which he swallows without tasting it. Most of it drizzles down his chin.

Now and then Doug pleads and prays to anybody who may be listening: Bethany, a neighbor, God/Jesus. Whoever might help him. Though he's not sure his pleas and prayers make any sense. For all he knows, he could just be spouting gibberish that sounds like "Ploiso hulp ma." Eventually it doesn't matter, his tongue becoming a big wad of chewing gum clogging up his mouth.

Night has fallen (again?), judging from the blazing lamps and shadowy windows in the room. No longer pining for alcohol, his body just wants to sleep, but his brain's bucking and rearing.

Bethany stands in front of him, studying him with her fists on her hips. She appears irked, as if impatiently waiting for him to… to do what exactly? He can't do shit tied up like this.

Doug hears a deep-resounding bell tolling somewhere in the distance. "Buckle up, brother," Bethany says in a synthy falsetto voice. "Gonna drive out those demons of yours."

"Ohh-kaa," he answers as he watches the shiny black material of Bethany's bodysuit ooze across her cleavage, as if transformed into crude oil. It creeps onto her hands, ankles, and head, until no spot of her skin remains visible.

A series of bulbous objects of varying sizes then bubble up from the slick surface. It takes Doug a moment to identify them: bells made of bronze and silver, held together by the oleaginous sinew. They completely cover Bethany.

He's not sure she is Bethany anymore.

The bell monster's curvy body begins to jiggle. The viscous vinyl ripples and the assorted bells—there must be hundreds of them—start to peal, their clashing chimes amplifying second by second to a fevered cacophony that assails Doug's ears. He wants to mash his palms against them, but because of the restraints, he cannot. The clanging of this infernal carillon echoes in his skull louder and louder, climbing to a crescendo of agony he has never before experienced.

Doug squeezes his eyes shut. Tears stream down his cheeks. He clenches his jaw so hard his teeth crack. Then he clenches even harder. He wishes his eardrums would burst, or his head would explode. Whatever stops the goddamn NOISE.

And then, all at once, the bells cease ringing.

Doug peels open his eyelids. The Bethany/bell monster has vanished.

He wheezes a sigh of relief and basks in the welcome silence. This silence turns out to be short-lived, as he next hears a frenzied scratching sound originating from somewhere in the kitchen… maybe in the cabinets? It's nowhere near as raucous as the bells, but it unsettles him nonetheless.

The sound is joined by similar skittering noises throughout the apartment—in the ceiling, behind the walls, even within the upholstered furniture. Like swarms of tiny claws scrabbling to get out.

Or to get in.

Rough tears erupt in the plaster, wood, and fabric. From these slashes emerge what appear to be long, black needles. Doug soon realizes the "needles" are articulated, bending at the joints as each of the foot-long segments reveal themselves. They look like huge spider legs. Then the bodies of the things materialize.

Doug gulps in horror.

Each set of six legs is attached to a head/body shaped like a cherrystone clam the size of a softball, speckled with moldy marks and spiky scales.

One creature crawls out of a rip in a cushion on the sofa. It scurries toward Doug, climbs up his left shin, and perches on his knee. He stares at it wide-eyed as it studies him with two vertical columns of beady, brackish eyes. The dark trenchline of its mouth seems to span the entire circumference of its head apart from a bony hinge on the back.

The creature lifts one of its long front appendages, extends it toward Doug's face, and exploratively pricks at his cheek and lips. It then slowly opens its massive maw, baring double rows of shark-like teeth, and springs toward his face, rooting its legs onto his shoulder before sinking its ghastly jaws into the meatiest part of his cheek.

Although he cannot feel it, Doug can tell from the yo-yoing motions of its mouth that it has begun eating him.

He groans helplessly.

Dozens more of the vile creatures descend upon him, each one staking a claim on a parcel of his body. They gnash through the nylon straps and shred through his clothes, at last getting to and gorging upon Doug's flesh, making revolting slurpy sounds.

Doug thinks, with his restraints now in tatters, that he should be able to throw the creatures off him. Yet he still can't move his arms, legs, or torso. It's as though he has been glued to this damn chair.

The gluttonous things continue to feast, devouring him alive with machine-like efficiency. He still doesn't feel any pain, thank God, but his brain wants him to vomit. He doesn't actually puke though, because one of the creatures has burrowed into his belly and cleared him out of anything that could come up. Doug can't even crap himself in terror.

There is nothing he can do now but close his eyes and pray it all ends soon.

And soon, it does end. But not all of it.

When the mushy munching sounds totally fade away, Doug reopens his eyes. The good news is all the mollusk-headed creatures have disappeared, and his body appears to be miraculously unscathed. The bad news is the cargo netting's also intact, pinning him down as securely as he had been before.

Worse news is delivered to him following these realizations, presaged by a low rumbling that vibrates him as if he was seated in a classic muscle car. The rumbling quickly swells to a roar. The gaping cracks in the walls—the same ones the spidery things had created—expand in both length and width onto the ceiling and across the floors and over the doors, chaotically crisscrossing one another. As the apartment quakes more and more violently, the cracks become ruptures, exposing vistas of infinite gray sky beyond the disintegrating plaster.

The apartment crumbles all around Doug like stale bread, the pieces breaking off and whirling away in the jet stream, until it is just him falling through the firmament.

He tumbles over and over in the armchair. Sometimes he sees a churning sea of menacing thunderheads above him, punctuated by flashes of lightning. Then he is looking down at the scorched earth below him, a brown-black canvas of barren wasteland reminding him of a scene from a post-apocalyptic movie.

As he hurtles through the turbulent air, Doug visualizes his own soon-to-be mangled flesh and shattered bone and splattered blood. Then he remembers it's not him but Liam who's racing to meet the unforgiving ground.

Then he muses, *Does it matter?*

Moments before impact, Doug feels an explosion in his chest that makes the question moot.

ELEVEN

Michelle lies atop a gold silk duvet on a four-poster king-sized bed, her eyes fixed on the billowed white canopy above her. She is in a large bedroom—one of the manor's master suites—that also features a cherrywood chest of drawers, an ornate writing desk, and a lit fieldstone hearth. Yet she cannot feel the softness of the fabric beneath her, nor the warmth of the fire crackling across the room. Right now, she can't feel anything at all. Nor can she move or speak. She can't even cry.

Not unless Liam's doing these things for her.

Following the marriage ceremony (which she can recall only in disjointed fragments and flashes, resembling some Nine Inch Nails music video), Liam's spirit gradually commandeered her body, merging with it until he alone could pull, push, and pinch all her strings, making her his veritable puppet. While fully aware of what was going on, she couldn't do a damn thing about it. Not even when he made her finger herself at the Denny's just to mess with Doug. She was a silent spectator in her own body.

So fucked up.

At first, Liam talked a lot while occupying Michelle, trying to charm her, flatter her, reassure her everything was going to be fine, repeating "trust me" and "we're OK" so many times it made the words sound meaningless, even menacing. While she couldn't answer him—she wondered if he was able to read her mind, but he never responded to anything she thought at him—he must've realized she was scared.

Now he isn't speaking to her at all. She's not sure if this is a good thing.

What she does know is the Fowlingtons can do to her whatever they please, and she is powerless to fight or flee. She has no idea what they intend for her, but based on what she has experienced so far tonight, she has little doubt it's going to be bad.

Michelle remembers almost everything from the time Doug dragged her from the party—*my wedding reception*—until now. On the ride home, a phantasmal flock of Liam's ancestors rattled Doug enough to make him stop to rent a room for the night at a fleabag motel off the highway. During this time, Liam piloted her to a nearby bar to get a "celebration libation." She did not object since she knew it would be pointless; she also hoped a drink might quell her trepidation. (It didn't.) Doug found her and led her back to the motel. There Liam and Michelle were finally fully *conjoined* (as Liam put it), meaning she now has his face for a third boob.

So incredibly fucked up.

Bethany showed up soon after that and drove Michelle/Liam back to the estate, the whole trip yakking about which destination should be next on her travel itinerary. (By the end of the ride it was a toss-up between Mykonos or Ibiza, with Bora Bora being a solid runner-up.) Upon arriving at the Fowlingtons, Michelle was again whisked away to the Thinning Room to participate in yet another ritual with the family, this one involving more strange chanting while Deacon Codswell blew red, yellow, and white powders into her and Liam's faces, before wiping them off with a cloth soaked in a bowl of what looked to Michelle like pond water. A male servant then escorted her downstairs to the master suite where she is now. Halfway there, she/he began to sway and stumble; while Liam still held dominion over her body, he seemed to have worn himself out operating it. The servant had to wrap his arm around her waist and help her the rest of the way. He boosted her up onto the bed and left her lying here, all alone.

No, not *all* alone. Though Liam is not saying anything to her now, she knows he is still in there. In her.

She feels invaded. Violated. She never wanted *this*…

…but once, not so long ago, all she wanted was to spend the rest of her life with him. He was everything to her, as she was to him. She would have done anything for him. Would have gladly let him use her body if that was the only way she could keep him, the only way they could stay together.

Liam is not being cold-hearted or evil. He just doesn't want to lose her.

Though he already has.

Pangs of guilt strafe Michelle's thoughts. Because, yes, she does feel bad for him. Because she can empathize with him. And because she knows with all her heart that she no longer loves him.

I don't love you anymore! Doesn't that matter to you?

Liam still says nothing.

Michelle thinks about Doug, prays he's okay. She knows they didn't kill him. They could have done that while he was here on their property. Instead they just waited out the conjoining process, knowing that she (and Liam) would be back. Doug is lucky they did not view him as a threat, merely a nuisance, and a minor one at that. Not worth the trouble to whack or terminate or whatever the Fowlingtons call it, although they could probably make him disappear easily enough. Apparently, it's sufficient that Doug is simply gone from their lives.

A pair of prim middle-aged women, looking so much alike they could be twins, enter the room, sit Michelle up, and change her into the plain green frock she had worn earlier—her wedding dress. A short while later, the same man who escorted her to the bedroom returns with an antique rattan wheelchair. He delicately sets Michelle into the seat, offering her benign smiles and reassuring pats. He drapes a kelly-green afghan over her body, then pushes her into the hallway and toward the elevator.

Michelle presumes they're taking her to the Thinning Room again for another of their freaky rituals, but instead they bring her down to the rear patio. She makes out different voices gathering behind her: Isadora and Nathaniel, Bethany, a few others she cannot identify. They speak to each other in hushed, almost reverent tones, as if they were in a church.

After a few moments, someone rolls Michelle from the patio onto a dirt footpath, a procession of unhurried footsteps marching behind them. Nobody's speaking now. She can see the fog of her breath, hear the drum of her heartbeat. Neither reflects how truly terrified she is.

They follow the path as it arcs away from the manor house. The wheelchair trundles over small bumps and shallow ruts, joggling Michelle's body as she stares straight ahead through eyes that don't feel like her own. Like watching a movie screen during an earthquake, she imagines.

The first trace of dawn appears as a bright band of baby blue at the bottom of the dark dome of sky, silhouetting the ragged line of the treetops.

Michelle knows where they're going.

Oh god no please no no NO!

But there's nothing she can do to stop them.

Ahead the forest—and her fate—await her.

After spending a brief spell enveloped by absolute nothingness—the only way Doug could describe it, since there was nothing there whatsoever to describe—he discovers himself lying face down on a sheet of trimmed, damp lawn. He spits out a blade of grass he's inhaled, leaving a bitter, herbaceous taste in his mouth.

Achy and anxious, he raises himself onto his elbows to get a better vantage of his surroundings. It's lighter out than when he had gone aboard Bukani's ship, which is now nowhere in sight because Doug has somehow been transported to inside the walled perimeter of the Fowlingtons' estate, on the west side of the mansion. The sun peeks over the roof, casting a wide, angular shadow upon him. The chill of the morning air raises goosebumps along his arms.

Doug reflects on what has just happened to him. He'd been inserted into a replay of Liam's final hours. He reckons Aldrich wanted him to witness—no, to experience—how Liam had died. Or rather, who had caused his death.

"Before you judge a man, walk a mile in his shoes."

Or, in this case, die in them.

Seems Liam's family had permitted—if not plotted—his fatal detox. How messed up is that? It's some top-of-the-food-chain depravity.

Why did Aldrich share this with Doug? Why would it make any difference to him?

The answer is, it doesn't. Doug's motivation and mission have not changed: rescue Michelle. He knows the Fowlingtons may be orchestrating her end at this very moment, so she can join Liam wherever these batshit one-percenters believe they go after they bite the gold dust.

To hell with that. To hell with them.

Doug scampers to the nearest side of the mansion to get out of the open. Hugging his back against the cold stone, he inches along it until he reaches a curtainless casement window. He peers inside to see a small library with wall-to-wall shelves crammed with vintage books. There are no chairs, tables, or desks, but there is a cheval mirror across the room that Doug can see himself in. He looks like himself again—a minor relief, considering all he's been through.

He wedges his fingertips into the gaps of the window frame and tries to pry it open, but it's either locked or stuck fast. He eases along the building to the next sets of windows and one weather-beaten door, discovering them all to be equally inaccessible. Only when circling around to the outermost edge of the patio does he come upon an unlocked wooden door. A servants' entrance, he figures.

Doug slips inside and slinks down a narrow, wood-paneled passage, emerging into a small sitting area adjoining the grand hall. He spots one of the household helpers cleaning up after the festivities of the prior night. She's a husky middle-aged woman with a round, ruddy face and upbraided brown hair, wearing a black muumuu-style frock and a white French apron fringed with scalloped lace. She looks to be as strong as a bull and, judging by her dour mien, may have a temperament to match. Not the most approachable of people, but Doug has little choice. He needs to find Michelle before it's too late.

If it isn't already.

No, it's not! He refuses to entertain the possibility.

"Excuse me," Doug says, getting the woman's attention.

She pauses clearing wine glasses from an end table to regard Doug as if he were some obtrusive vermin.

"Sorry," Doug says. "I slept through my alarm this morning. Guess I had too much good vino last night, know what I mean?" He chuckles. She remains stoic. "Can you just point me to where everyone's at?"

"You," the woman finally responds. "You shouldn't be here."

"Right. That's why I asked—"

She backs away from him, shaking her head. "You aren't welcome here, Mr. Cunningham."

So she knows who Doug is. So much for his tardy guest ruse.

"Please, ma'am." Raising his hands in front of him, he moves gingerly toward her. "I just need to see Michelle. I think she's in danger. Do you know where she is?"

The wary woman continues to retreat, stepping into the grand hall. "Leave now or I'll call the police!"

"I can't leave, lady," Doug says, pacing her. "Not until I see Michelle. Please help me."

"No! Go away!"

"Listen, if anything bad happens to Michelle, you'll be just as guilty as them for not—"

"Anton!" the woman yells, glancing to her left. "Anton!"

Another servant appears from around a corner to the right of Doug. He recognizes him as the scrawny, black-suited valet who had been so accommodating when he and Michelle were leaving the estate, packing their bags, refueling his car.

Anton doesn't look near as obliging now.

"Anton," the woman raves. "I told him to leave, but he won't listen."

Anton then addresses Doug in his silky voice. "You must go, Mr. Cunningham."

"No," Doug answers. "Bring me to Michelle, or I swear I will tear this place apart until I find her."

"Get off the property immediately," Anton reiterates, "or we will call the authorities."

Unable to contrive any other feasible options—he'd never be able to search the entire premises himself—Doug decides to call Anton's bluff.

"Go ahead. Call the cops. Call the FBI, CIA, the goddamned National Guard. Whoever you want. I'll tell them everything I know about you lunatics, then they can turn over this place much better than I could. Who knows what messed-up family secrets they'll uncover."

Anton seems to deliberate the wisest course of action to take while the woman wrings her hands. If the police were summoned, Doug figures they would probably just arrest him and cart him off without giving the residence so much as a once-over. But if he's rattled the servants enough, then they might not want to be implicated in the Fowlingtons' villainy and maybe tell Doug what he needs to know.

"As you wish," Anton says. "We shall let the police deal with you."

Shit. Not the outcome Doug preferred, but maybe it can still work in his favor. That is, if the police aren't in league with the Fowlingtons. Maybe while they wait for the cops to arrive, he can talk some sense, even sympathy, into the servants. Or Doug can sweep as much of the place as he can himself in the hope of stumbling upon Michelle's whereabouts before the cuffs are slapped on him.

Anton fishes a cell phone from the pocket of his trousers. He dials two numbers—9 and 1, Doug presumes—then hovers his finger over the final digit in the sequence. He stands frozen there a moment without pressing it, and Doug thinks the valet has reconsidered contacting the police. Maybe because he does fear the repercussions after all, either from the law or from the Fowlingtons.

"On second thought," Anton utters in a grim, guttural voice that's no longer his own, "perhaps we should handle this matter ourselves."

When Anton raises his head from the phone, Doug sees his eyes have turned a milky white, like Michelle's had done back in the motel room in Oxboro.

When Liam had taken her. Possessed her.

Doug then realizes the housekeeper's eyes have also drained of color.

This ain't good, he thinks. He recalls how strong Michelle was when Liam was in control of her. Doug isn't sure he could beat one of him/her/them, much less two.

A younger blonde woman, hardly more than a teenager, in an identical housekeeping uniform shuffles into the parlor from a louvered side door, perhaps belonging to a pantry, and stands beside her older counterpart. She is the physical opposite in nearly every way: smaller, shorter, slenderer. Their sole matching trait at this moment is their eyes, like those of a power-washed statue.

Promptly joining this creepy crew are a grizzled man wearing a white chef's outfit (including the muffin-shaped hat), having presumably emerged from wherever the kitchen is, and a rugged-faced groundskeeper in drab green coveralls who entered through one of the rear patio doors.

All five of them share the same ocular condition, and all walk with the same halting movements, like marionettes manipulated by tangled wires. The chef clutches a large meat cleaver, and the groundskeeper grips a wicked-looking weeding sickle. The other workers each seize a potentially lethal object: the girl grasps some kind of trophy in the form of a 12" solid glass obelisk; the woman steps over to the fireplace to claim an iron poker; and Anton takes a ceremonial rapier sword off the wall.

Doug swallows hard. *I'm. So. Fucked.*

Wielding their weapons, the servants advance on him. With their clunky arm swipes and cloddish footwork, Doug dodges their attacks fairly easily, getting struck just once with the poker to his buttocks, which stings like hell. Still, they are coordinated enough to block his path every time he tries to make a break for the patio door or to another room.

Doug sees they're closing in, herding him into a far corner of the hall, giving him less and less space to evade their swings and thrusts. He backs into one of the hall's rosewood wet bars. With no other means of escape, he hops onto its gray granite countertop and slides behind it.

Doug realizes he's now trapped himself and at their mercy—that is to say, no mercy at all—should they manage to climb over the bar in unison after him. Which is exactly what they begin to do, although none too gracefully, moving like a family of sloths racing up a tree trunk.

Doug tries to shove the young housekeeper back, she being the smallest and nearest to him, with an outthrust hand palming her forehead. Taking advantage of this opening, Anton lunges at him and slashes his forearm with the rapier's razor-sharp blade, slicing through his shirt and skin.

"Sonuvabitch!" Doug yells, swiftly retracting his hand. Blood trickles from the gash, staining the sleeve of his green sweater a rich russet.

Too adrenalized to pay the wound any mind, Doug feverishly searches the meager space around him for any means of defense. Lining the three-tiered shelving behind him is an assortment of premium liquors. He grips the long neck of a bottle of absinthe and smashes it over Anton's head, spattering alcohol everywhere.

The blow doesn't faze the possessed valet.

Doug tosses aside the snapped-off neck of the bottle and next snatches a crystal whiskey decanter. He thwacks the hefty vessel into the groundskeeper's chin. The decanter doesn't break, but the groundskeeper's jaw does; it dislodges from his skull, only hanging on by whatever skin and muscles attach it to his face. Blood, spit, and shattered teeth spill down the man's coveralls.

The disfigured groundskeeper and the others keep coming at Doug, hell-bent on hurting him, killing him.

Panicked, Doug grabs at anything on the bar's prep area in front of him and pelts his attackers. He hurls a barrage of metal muddlers and jiggers and zesters, along with fistfuls of cocktail picks and candied ginger and coarse salt.

The salt hits Anton in his bleached-out eyes. Immediately the valet staggers backward several steps, blinking nonstop. Rivulets of tears rush down his cheeks. His irises have turned from ghostly white back to their normal hazel hue, surrounded by flecks of bright bloody red. He now looks at Doug mystified rather than murderous.

Salt? Really? Doug vaguely recalls reading somewhere that salt is used to trap demons or repel evil. Or maybe that was from a movie.

Hey, whatever works.

Doug again plunges his right hand into the round bamboo canister of salt, scooping up as much as he can. He loads up his left hand likewise. He flings the salt into the eyes of the grounds-keeper and the chef. Like Anton, they recoil from the bar.

Doug reloads his hands and gives the housekeepers the same treatment, with the same result.

They all regard Doug with the same bloodshot eyes and confused expressions. Anton and the housekeepers then gawk at the objects they still hold, no doubt wondering why they have them.

The chef glances all around him, baffled by how he had ended up there in the grand hall. The in-shock groundskeeper taps his trembling fingers against his ruined jaw.

"What…" Anton mutters, "happuhhh…"

Before Doug can capitalize on their disorientation, the servants' spines all stiffen at once, as though driven through by giant skewers. They drop their weapons, and their mouths, as they are levitated off the floor by some invisible force. They reach a height of twenty or so feet, their heads mere inches from the ceiling, and hover in the air, flailing their limbs ineffectually while uttering a medley of terrified shrieks and howls.

Doug freezes, gaping at the supernatural scene before him.

The older housekeeper rotates into a horizontal position and then soars headfirst toward Doug at rocket speed. He ducks behind the bar just in time. She crashes into the shelves above him, shattering multiple bottles, showering glass shards and strong liquors over him. The housekeeper then tumbles onto him like a sack of boiled potatoes, pinning him to the floor.

Using all his strength, Doug writhes out from beneath her large, limp body and scrabbles to his knees, his lungs punishing him for the exertion. Upon his head clearing the bar top, he sees Anton and the chef both flying at him at terminating velocity.

Doug again hunkers behind the bar.

The chef slams into the left side of the demolished shelving, rebounding off it and landing face down on the counter. Anton bashes into the other side of the shelves so hard Doug can hear the valet's bones fracture. Anton crumples to the floor in a flaccid heap beside him.

Christ, they're throwing people at me!

The three banged-up servants magically ascend again and rejoin their freaked-out floating allies. Readying for another blitz at him, Doug suspects. He sure as hell isn't staying behind this bar any longer so they can pile on him and smother or crush him to death.

Doug crawls beneath the flip-up countertop, rises to his feet, and quickly reorients himself. He needs to go under the servants to get to either the front door or the patio door. He figures if he makes himself a fast-moving target, zigzagging across the room, it'll be more difficult for them to hit him.

Before Doug can break into his desperate sprints, the young housekeeper sails headlong into his belly, knocking the wind out of him and propelling him back into a pink marble column. His already sore ribs bawl at him. Doubled over in agony and gasping for breath, he can only wait powerlessly for the next volley of human missiles to strike him and finish him off…

"Screw that," he tells himself, remembering Michelle is still counting on him to rescue her.

Doug raises up his head in time to see Anton, the older housekeeper, the groundskeeper, and the chef all dive bombing him at once. He side-rolls toward the fireplace. The servants smack into the same spot on the floor he'd just been. The pileup sounds like a rumble of thunder.

Doug grits his teeth and groans, the stabbing pain in his abdomen excruciating. Clawing at the fireplace's stonework, he heaves himself back onto his feet.

The servants return to their places aloft. Eyelids drooping and mouths sagging, they appear much less aware now of what's going on. Blood streaks across several of their faces. As far as Doug can tell, they're all at least seriously injured from their kamikaze-style attacks: a splintered length of bone pierces through Anton's left cheek; the young housekeeper's neck bends backward at an extreme angle; and the chef has lost his muffin-shaped hat, which may have helped contain the brain matter that's leaking out of his cracked skull. Doug is sure some of them are dead.

Yet, still controlled by whatever's possessing them, they remain fully functional as deadly projectiles.

They launch at him from different directions. Doug blunderingly bobs and weaves to avoid them. The chef's shoulder grazes his forehead, the rough material of his white coat chafing Doug's skin, and the older housekeeper clips his crotch with the heel of her shoe before skimming along the floor into a potted cactus. While they for the most part miss him, they do succeed in preventing Doug's flight, making quite a shambles of the hall in the process, overturning furniture, toppling artwork, and smashing curios.

In an unexpectedly deft maneuver, Anton trips him by bowling into his legs. Doug does a face plant onto the travertine tiles, busting open his bottom lip. He licks it, tastes his own blood.

Clambering across the floor on his hands and knees, Doug grabs the only object that is within his reach—a sofa cushion—and shields himself with it.

He knows he's slowing down, wearing himself out, while the gravity-defying servants show no hints of exhaustion.

He knows they will overcome him soon.

Knows his end is near.

I'm sorry, Mish…

"Stop these shenanigans this instant!"

Doug peeks over the cushion to see the decrepit old woman he had encountered upstairs a few hours before. Responding to her command, the servants cease their aerial assault on him and descend onto the floor as gently as butterflies alighting on a leaf (albeit butterflies looking like they've been through a hailstorm). They stand there with their heads slumped forward, their arms dangling at their sides, resembling a group of ashamed kids who were caught doing something bad.

"I don't know what riled up you lot," the old lady scolds the lined-up servants. "But you leave this boy alone. Understand?"

The servants do nothing to indicate understanding.

"Lord have mercy." The lady surveys the trashed room, shakes her shriveled head. "What a mess you've made. Nate and Dora will be mighty displeased, you can be sure of that!"

The servants display no signs of concern. Nor signs of life for that matter, other than them standing upright.

"Now off with you, before I put you in time-out."

Doug watches as translucent human forms—the word *wraiths* springs to his mind—vacate each of the bodies, eddying upward and dissipating in the air like steam from a kettle. The battered husks of the servants collapse to the floor. None of them so much as twitch.

The lady *tsk tsks*, which sounds more like *tft tft* coming from her chalky, purply lips. "Now we will have to find new help to re-place this sorry bunch." She is still wearing the same soiled light blue nightgown he'd seen her in before. This time he notices her bare feet. They resemble crudely carved pieces of driftwood.

She regards Doug with a judgmental frown, her green eyes appearing almost reptilian in the bright room.

"Why didn't you tell them to stop, boy?"

"I, uh…" Doug stammers, "didn't think they'd listen to me?"

"Of course they would! Spirits must always obey their living kin. You know that. Quit being a daft dodo, Liam! I'm not in the mood for nonsense."

The batty biddy is still mistaking him for Liam. Probably her grandson, Doug supposes. He's not sure what to do with this supposition, other than go along with it.

"Oh yeah… I forgot."

"You would forget your own bean if it wasn't bolted on." She wags her finger at him.

Doug titters in a faux show of appreciation for what the old woman probably thinks passes as a good-natured jab at him.

"Hey, do you know where Michelle is?" he asks optimistically.

Liam's grandmother sniffs the air without responding to his question. She shuffles in front of a large window overlooking the patio and gazes toward the forest in the near distance.

"Ma'am… Gram… ma? Did you hear me?"

"Smell that, Liam?" she asks him, a crooked smile crossing her face.

All Doug can smell is the potent mix of alcohols he had been doused in during the melee.

"Uhm, what?"

"The gas!" Her eyes dilate with excitement. "They're lighting the pyre."

"The pyre?"

She turns and offers him a bony hand. "Come, dear boy. We don't want to miss this!"

Doug and the old lady walk arm in arm along a flat, well maintained dirt road cut into the forest, a parody of a courting couple out for a stroll in a park. It's full daylight now, the sky cloudless and as blue as the meshwork of veins on the woman's temples. The warm rays of sunshine that penetrate the pine branch ceiling above them would feel almost pleasant on Doug's skin if not for his fraught nerves and stormy gut. While the trees obstruct most of the wind, crisp cool breezes occasionally waft up the road onto their backs, making Doug shiver in his liquor-soaked clothes. Liam's granny seems wholly unaffected by the chill, despite her gossamer-thin gown.

They have been heading to God-knows-where for more than twenty minutes now, traveling at a pace somewhere between a slog and a stroll which, while helping allay his aching ribs, also adds to his already peaking apprehension. But he suspects the lady may be protecting him from any phantoms poised to ambush him from the shadowy woodland, so he's sticking with her. In return for this possible protection, he takes responsibility for holding her up; she must only weigh as much as his Jack Russell terrier. She seems delighted to have him escort her to wherever they're going.

All the while through her dementia-addled haze, she gabs amiably at him.

"Did you enjoy your day at school, Liam?"

"Yeah," Doug answers, keeping up the charade. Mentally he says to her, *I'm not Liam, I'm not in school, but other than that, today sucks balls.*

"Will you help me pick out a summer hat at that charming little shop in South Hampton?"

"Sure." *Nope.*

"Remember when we would chase the colored children all through here?"

"Uhm. Huh?" *WTF?*

"Lovely evening for a sacrifice, isn't it?"

It can't be past noon and… wait— "Sacrifice?"

"Ah! We're here!"

Doug spots the small crowd of about a dozen people on the road ahead. Liam's family, he presumes. They stand with their backs to him in a clearing before a large, box-shaped structure made of bone-white stone. It reminds Doug of the base beneath Abe Lincoln's chair at his eponymous memorial in DC. Atop this formation is not some august statue, but rather a long mound of twigs interwoven with red and yellow flowers.

Posted between the formally dressed spectators and the hewn stone block are Nathaniel and Isadora Fowlington, their daughter Bethany, and a guy in a black suit sporting an eyepatch. They all cross their arms in an X over their chests. The four of them are facing Doug, but thankfully have their eyes closed, absorbed in their witchy pagan stuff or whatever it is they're into.

Doug doesn't see Michelle anywhere.

As he and Liam's grandmother shuffle toward the gathering, Doug can hear the one-eyed guy chanting in some strange foreign language. He also observes the red flowers in the stacked twigs are actually paper animals: birds, bears, deer, maybe a pig. Then he recognizes a face poking out of one end of the mound.

Michelle's face.

"Holy shit," Doug mutters. "Is she—"

"Yes, she is," the old woman says adoringly. "An angel."

The sulfuric odor of natural gas fills Doug's nostrils.

That's no memorial, he realizes. *It's a crematorium.*

He also surmises that, if this is a sacrifice, Michelle can't be dead.

Not yet.

The one-eyed priest switches to English. "With the blessings of our Divine Empress, we now commit you, Michelle Langley Fowlington, to the Otherworld, eternally joining Liam as husband and wife in ever enduring health and happiness…"

Jerking his arm away from the old lady's grasp—she lets out a startled squawk—Doug then bursts into a berserk dash toward Michelle. He barges through Liam's relatives, scarcely registering Nathaniel and Isadora's astonished expressions as he bounds toward the pyre with both hands outthrust.

Doug pushes Michelle, along with the immolation trappings, off the grill's top. He hears a flurry of hysterical shouting around him. A split second later, powerful yellow flames shoot upward from the iron grating.

Still bent over the pyre, Doug is enveloped in fire. He springs away from the geysers of hellish heat, reeling several steps backward. His clothes and hair, having been steeped in alcohol, act as an accelerant, instantly transforming him into a human torch. He flaps his arms and whirls around futilely. He sees nothing but unquenchable flames, hears nothing but his flesh sizzling over his screams.

The pain is so acute and all-encompassing that that part of his brain short-circuits, so all he can feel is stark panic. He drops onto the ground and rolls around in a blind effort to extinguish himself.

Within moments, it is his life that has been extinguished.

Doug passes through a thick curtain of misty golden light with bits of white fluff floating in the air like from some '80s fantasy film. His pain is gone, as has his panic. He feels weightless, bodiless. He scrutinizes his hands, arms, and torso. Everything seems fine—that is, nothing's burnt, including his clothes.

Though he is now calm, he's not carefree. Foremost, he cares about where he is, where Michelle is, and where everybody else is. He strides onward with a purpose that seems not completely his own. He wonders if the Fowlingtons have doped him again.

Doug is drawn out of the dreamy light and into a long, green hallway lined with framed pictures. He halts. Standing a short distance away in a casual blue sports jacket and beige chinos is Liam, studying a framed photo of himself on the wall.

"Hi, Doug," Liam says, not looking away from his portrait.

"Liam…" Doug responds coldly. He should be surprised to behold Michelle's dead ex appearing very much alive, but after everything he's dealt with over the past few hours, this doesn't even qualify as weird anymore. "Where the hell are we?"

"I like this pic of me," Liam says as if he did not hear Doug's question. "I look sober."

"You can do amazing things with Photoshop."

Liam grins, stifling a chuckle. "Yeah, you can. But I swear this one's legit. It was taken during one of our Christmas parties after I got out of rehab. Felt like crap, but I looked good."

Doug looks around. "What is this place?"

"I would best describe here as," Liam answers after some reflection, "my family's exclusive waiting room, situated between the mortal world and the Otherworld. Our entire property was designed and consecrated to be like our own VIP section in the astral plane. After death, most of my people come through here, moving right on to the Otherworld. But some of us stay put; those who died of unnatural causes, like from an accident, or in a war, murder, execution—"

"Overdose," Doug adds.

"Yeah. That too. Someone way down on my family tree even figured out how to bring folks here who'd bought it before this place was created. Anyways, we've all become sort of stuck here, spirits still tethered to this earth. Kind of like a big fishbowl for phantoms."

"That must suck for you."

"It hasn't been bad so far. Even in this overlapping existence, membership has its privileges. I can do crazy shit without getting hurt, mess around with the living for shits and giggles. I can even travel off realm for short periods, though it's a pain in the ass to do and not as fun as you'd think it would be. I was in your apartment once. Kind of a shithole."

After a moment, Doug nods. "So that *was* you. You watched Michelle and me have sex. That must've ticked you off. You broke my clock."

"Oh, and as you know, we can possess the living, take them out on little joy rides," Liam continues, ignoring Doug's provocative comment. "That's also a bit of a bear to do, so I don't do it often. But it has its uses."

"I get it. Ghost life is awesome," Doug sneers. "So how do I get out of here?"

Liam turns to him. "When I let you go."

Doug furrows his brow. "*You* brought me here? Why?"

"I wanted to talk to you."

"Fuck off. End of talk. Now show me the exit."

"Don't worry. You won't be here long. I just wanted to express my sympathies for your loss."

Doug yearns to punch him in the nose, craves the sound of his cartilage cracking, the sight of his blood gushing down his chin. But Doug knows he'd just be punching the air. The prick would probably laugh at him, too.

"Michelle's not dead," Doug growls. "I saved her."

Liam rolls his eyes. "You only delayed the inevitable. Anyway, I wasn't talking about the loss of her."

"Who did you mean then?"

"Why, the loss of *you*, Douglas."

"What?"

"Breaking news: you're dead, buddy."

The choppy memory of what came after he shoved Michelle off the funeral pyre rushes back to him. The roar of the flames as they cocooned him in an orbiting shroud of broiling heat. Him feeling everything, then nothing. Passing through a vestibule of ethereal light into this hallway straight out of Disney's Haunted Mansion.

"I'm not dead." Doug doubts these words even as he speaks them.

"You sure are." Liam regards him almost pityingly. "I could show you what's left of your body, but that might be traumatizing for you. You kind of look like a big burnt hot dog, charred all over with melted fat oozing out of spots. It's pretty gross."

"Shit," Doug mutters in disbelief.

"Yeah, that must suck for *you*," taunts Liam. "But hey, you tried, right? That's something to be proud of. It just wasn't meant to be. Because Michelle is meant to be with me. You can't alter destiny, Doug, no matter how hard you try." He smirks.

"Are you bragging?" asks the nettled Doug. "Is that the reason you brought me here? To rub it in?"

"That, and to distract you until the ceremony is complete."

"Don't let this happen, Liam."

"Oh, it's happening, Doug. You can't stop it now."

Doug realizes he needs to come up with a better strategy than calling Liam a dick or telling him he looks like his mom dressed him for his photo. (Doug cannot believe Liam would've chose to wear a yellow ascot.)

Doug recalls the phrase Aldrich Bukani had recited to him: *"Before you judge a man, walk a mile in his shoes."*

Doug thinks fast. He now knows—intimately—how and why Liam died. Can Doug use this knowledge to aid Michelle? While Bukani may have been helping him, he just as well could've been hindering him, or even toying with him solely for his apparitional amusement. Whatever Bukani's motive, Doug is convinced Liam is the key to diverting Michelle's fate. He's just not sure how. Nor how much time Michelle has left.

"No, I can't stop it…" Doug says, praying for a revelation. "But I bet you could."

"Why would I want to do that?" Liam replies.

"Because…" *Because why?* "Because you love her."

"Damn right I do. With my whole fucking heart. And that's why I won't stop it."

"You will if you really love her."

"Of course I do!" Liam snaps. "And I know she still loves me."

"But you'll kill her so you can be together?"

"Because it's the *only* way we can be together."

"Don't you think she's gonna be awful angry at you for this?" Doug arches his eyebrow. "Are you looking forward to spending an eternity with a permanently pissed-off wife?"

"She'll forgive me. Eventually. As you said, she will have all of eternity to get over it, and then we can live the life together we should've had."

"Live an afterlife, you mean. As ghosts who can't cuddle or kiss." Doug almost adds "or fuck" but censors himself.

"It's better than losing her forever." Liam places his palm on the empty spot of the wall beside his portrait. "Soon Michelle's picture will be here next to mine, where she belongs. It's our destiny. There's no other choice."

Choice. Doug remembers another piece of the conversation he had with Bukani. Appealing to Liam's humanity seems a long shot, but it also may be the last bullet Doug has.

"If you truly care about Michelle," Doug reasons with him, "then you'll let her choose what she wants for herself. Not drug her and have your cousins or nephews or whoever throw her on your industrial barbeque. It's crazy and barbaric and selfish."

"We are all selfish at the end." Liam says this like he is channeling Confucius. "It was nice talking to you, Doug. You can see yourself out."

Doug seethes. If Liam had ever felt genuine love for Michelle, that love has since been diluted, drained, and dissolved into this entitled sense of ownership of her. Doug still wishes he could hurt him somehow, even if it's just the asshole's feelings.

How do you insult a narcissistic ghost?

Tell him he died like a wuss.

"Not you, Liam," Doug says. "You weren't selfish at the end. You were just sad."

"How the fuck would you know?"

"I know your sister tied you to a chair, doing your parents' bidding. I know you went through DT hell until your heart exploded. I know they let you die. Your own family killed you."

Liam squinches his eyes at him. "Who told you that?"

"The captain of your cult. Al Bukkake or whatever."

"Bukani?" Liam snorts. "You're full of shit."

"Doesn't make any difference how I know. It's true, right?"

"No—"

"Yeah, it is. Bukani showed me the whole scene that played out at your place. Your forced detox. Your freaky visions. Those mutant spiders chowing down on you."

"I…" Nonplussed, Liam falters for a response. "I was really fucked up. Sick as hell. I would've been dead soon anyway."

"At least then you would have died on your terms. Or who knows, maybe you would've finally cleaned yourself up for good. Either way, it would have been your choice. Not your family's."

Liam shrugs. "Doesn't really matter now, does it?"

"Maybe not for you…" No way is Doug going to let Liam just shrug this off. "But for Michelle, she was doing great in recovery. She was healthy, and hopeful about things. I have no idea if that would have lasted. But I know the right thing to do is let her live her life her way up till the end. Doesn't she deserve to have that choice? Don't you want that for her?"

Liam clucks his tongue and squints again at Doug. "You're just trying to steal her from me."

"Why would I?" Doug retorts. "As you said, it doesn't matter anymore. I'm dead too."

Liam doesn't react, and Doug questions whether anything he said has made even a single iota of difference. Rich folks concoct their own rules that don't have to be logical or legal as long as they win. He can't expect Liam to fall far from his family tree.

After a moment, Liam relaxes his suspicious eyes and sighs. "I didn't imagine she would be mad at me. I thought she would be happy."

"Were you happy about what your folks did to you?"

"No," Liam answers glumly, as though having an epiphany about something so obvious makes him feel stupid instead of inspired. "But I understand why they did it."

"Because they were ashamed of you and fed up with you and just wanted you gone from their worth-more-than-you lives."

Liam chews on this with pursed lips.

Doug can tell he's plucked a nerve.

"Don't decide Michelle's fate for her." Doug steps closer to him. "Don't rob her the way your parents robbed you. Or are you no better than they are?"

Liam does not respond to this. He just stands there stewing pensively while evil-eyeballing Doug. Probably trying to settle on what kind of Otherworldly fury he can mete out on him.

"I am better," Liam mumbles.

"I don't think your mom and dad think that. No, they think you're just gonna die and roll over and accept it." Doug's winging it now, saying anything that might rattle Liam's cage. "What you wanted didn't matter when you were alive. Why would it matter to them when you're dead?"

"This *is* what I wanted."

"Bullshit. I don't believe you wanted *this*, being trapped here forever in limbo land, basically a prison. Your parents condemned you to this, and they made you believe you're in a better place and you thanked them for it."

"I didn't—"

"Sure you did. Your parents gave you a box of shit, and now they're tying this big bow named Michelle on it, shouting 'Happy Eternity, Son!' And then they're done with you for good."

"Shut up," Liam growls.

"You're like a dog they put down because it got rabies—"

"Shut the fuck up!" Liam barks, which causes the hallway to undulate and distort around them like a fallen raindrop ruffling oil-slicked water.

By the time the spatial wrinkles stop, Liam has vaporized and vanished, leaving Doug alone there, somewhere between heaven and earth.

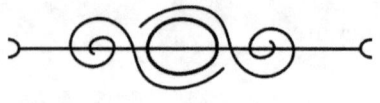

Doug wonders if he had gone too far with Liam, if he'd pushed too many of the guy's emotional baggage buttons. While Liam may have definitely decided on Michelle's fate, Doug fears he himself may have been the one who has sealed it.

Maybe it's not too late. Maybe there's still time.

Doug first tests the S-shaped iron handles belonging to a set of wooden double doors at the end of the hallway. Locked. He then attempts to go out the way he came in, now an uninviting smoky gray void. When he heads in that direction, however, the hallway magically elongates itself so there is no end to it, as if he is jogging on a treadmill.

Doug turns around and pounds on the doors with his hands and feet, accomplishing zilch. He then snatches random framed portraits from the walls, flinging them at the doors like Japanese shurikens. They each splinter and shatter upon impact, then re-materialize on the wall, in place and intact.

It appears he has run out of options. He can detect no other exit, no way to escape.

No way to save Michelle.

"You can see yourself out," he recalls Liam telling him.

Bullshit. It's a fucking funhouse.

It occurs to Doug that the laws of physics do not apply here, the Fowlingtons' so-called "VIP section in the astral plane." So a wall or door might not *actually* be solid. Neither might Doug, for that matter.

Where does that hypothesis get him?

He's already tried beating the hell out of the doors to no avail. Pummeling the walls and ceiling only result in that trippy rippling effect. He jumps a couple of times to test the gravity, which seems to mimic that of the material world, an observation that is also of no use to him.

What's he missing?

"You can see yourself out."

Is that a clue?

Could it be that simple?

Just envision himself out of there?

Doug closes his eyes like Dorothy did when she wished herself out of Oz. He takes a deep breath, then pictures himself back at the pyre. He doesn't remember every detail of it. He hopes it's enough.

When he reopens his eyes, Doug finds himself once more at the site of the Fowlingtons' outdoor crematorium, standing beside Liam's grandmother, now seated at the front of the congregation in a wood-wicker wheelchair with someone's dark tweed coat draped over her shoulders.

A long, slender shape lying nearby at the edge of the clearing catches Doug's attention. Spread over the form is an argyle blanket that is not quite large enough to cover it entirely; a pair of black shoes are sticking out. Doug quickly realizes it's someone's body. The footwear's leather is chapped, the laces charred. Above the right shoe, a band of burnt, blistered ankle flesh is visible.

It takes a moment for Doug to register that the body is his.

"Holy shit," he mutters, averting his eyes toward the sky.

The old lady swivels her head toward him and says, "There you are, lad. You nearly missed the show."

Doug looks in the direction of the pyre, its flames now shut off. A semi-conscious Michelle has been placed on it again. The twigs have been hastily re-piled on top of her, the paper animals now resembling just crumpled scraps of litter. Nathaniel, Isadora, and Bethany have resumed their positions in front of the pyre, as has the one-eyed priest. He's chanting in a foreign language again, though Doug thinks he sounds more rushed, more anxious this time around.

Doug hasn't planned this far ahead. He is pretty sure that as a ghost—*I'm a freaking ghost!*—he can't simply charge the pyre and shove Michelle off it as he did before. He recalls the servants attacking him, or rather, the spirits of Fowlington ancestors attacking him in the servants' bodies. Perhaps Doug could possess one of the funeralgoers and whisk Michelle from the pyre. Maybe the big guy beside granny. But how does he do that? Just hop inside him and wear him around like a suit of armor?

Before Doug can attempt anything, he hears a collective gasp from the gathering.

Doug returns his attention to the pyre. Michelle now sits bolt upright on it, her body rotated toward Liam's parents. Her hands part the neckline of the loose-fitting green gown she's dressed in, revealing the half-face of Liam jutting from her chest.

He looks pissed.

"Y*ou* can go fuck yourselves!" Liam snaps at his mother and father in response to them telling him, "You can't materialize now!"

"Watch your tongue, boy," Nathaniel admonishes his son.

"Why should I? Why should I do anything you tell me to do anymore?"

"What's wrong with you, Liam?" Isadora asks while the rest of their family looks on like a crowd of rubberneckers. "On today of all days, how could you treat us like this?"

"Because you hurt me. Put me through that hell."

"Nonsense," his mother replies earnestly. "We were always trying to help you."

Liam's complexion reddens, his lips crimping into a snarl. "You killed me."

Isadora glances at Nathaniel to solicit his support. He wraps his arm around her shoulders and glowers at Liam's malformed face. Neither notices their daughter Bethany slinking away, detaching herself from this conversation, from culpability.

"This is neither the time nor place to discuss this," Nathaniel tells Liam.

"I have nothing but time now, dad. And I've no place to go." A bubble of blood-speckled saliva inflates at the corner of his mouth. "So yeah… let's discuss you killing me."

"Your vices killed you," his father replies.

"My *vices* didn't strap me into a fucking chair!" The mouth-bubble pops.

"Mouth, Liam!"

"I'm *fucking* dead, mom. How much worse can you punish me now?"

"It wasn't a punishment," Isadora says.

"Yeah, right…" Liam replies. "It was 'an act of tough love.' That's what you called it, mom. You loved me to death."

"We didn't want you to die!" Isadora blurts.

"You didn't? Well, that makes me feel so much better."

"If you insist we killed you, then surely you can appreciate it was a mercy killing," Nathaniel reasons with him. "You were living for nothing but your next potable. You were miserable. Pathetic. At least now you're free of those demons."

"It was my life… my right to choose how I lived."

"And so we were just supposed to stand by and let you keep fouling it up?"

"Or you could've kept trying to help me get clean."

"How many times did we try, Liam?" his father asks. "How many stints in rehab did we pay for? At least ten, followed by the same number of relapses. You couldn't hold down a job, couldn't take care of yourself. Just how long did you expect us to continue with that cycle of self-spoliation?"

"You could have disowned me like normal parents who are disappointed in their kid."

"It was only a matter of time before you did something irreparably egregious while under the influence," Nathaniel replies. "Something so serious we couldn't easily explain it away to our friends and associates, or worse yet, the media. What if you killed someone with your car? What if it was a child? There's no way to spin that into something innocent or savory. But you'd have expected us to somehow bail you out of trouble again."

"I never expected anything from you, dad. All you ever gave me were these sky-high expectations I could never reach. You just kept pushing me all the time to do better and better and better, until all I could do was fail."

"If that was truly your fate, then you should be glad we had this contingency plan to rid you of that burden forever."

"*Glad*? You took away everything I ha—"

"You ungrateful bastard!" his mother barks.

Stunned by her outburst, Liam clams up.

"We gave you every opportunity to succeed. You had the best of everything. Attended the best schools, wore the best clothes, ate the best foods. You went anywhere you wanted, got anything you wanted. Money meant nothing to you—which was fine. Enjoying our great wealth was your birthright. But then it became nothing but a means to acquire more booze and more drugs. You squandered your life on that damned stuff, Liam. And *that* was *not* our fault."

"No, it wasn't," Liam concedes. "But my death was. Doesn't that bother you at all?"

"It bothers me…" Isadora answers, a lone teardrop pooling in the corner of her eye, "that I lost my only son long before that."

"All of this, Liam," Nathaniel adds, "is so you can finally have some peace, some happiness."

"But I don't want *this* for Michelle."

"Don't you love her?"

"With all my heart. That's why I can't do this to her."

"I'm sorry, son." His father gazes at him sympathetically. "It isn't up to you anymore."

"Why not?" Liam asks.

"The ritual needs to be effectuated. Your spiritual union has been ordained, consecrated. To not carry it through would be a violation of our sacred traditions."

"So what?"

His father regards his son as if he were an imbecile. "*So*, boy, tradition is what our family was founded on. It is the source of our longevity, our prosperity. We do not shirk our obligations to it. We do not defy the Divine Ones. That is one of our supreme commandments, as you were taught since you'd first learned to read. Or have you forgotten your scriptures?"

His father's tone dares his son to challenge him—a challenge Liam declines with a resigned frown.

"Even dead," he murmurs to himself, "I don't have a choice."

"Please Liam," his mother entreats, "let us consummate the ceremony."

Michelle's body pivots away from Liam's parents. Their son's brooding face stares off at the mansion in the distance, while Michelle's face remains gawkish, glazed.

"We'd strongly prefer not to compel you," Nathaniel continues. "But we will if necessary."

Liam moans a moment in despair, sounding like a senior cat with a bellyache. Then his countenance abruptly changes, taking on a devilish smirk and a vindictive glint in his eye.

"You should snuff out your other fires first," he says, "before you start a new one."

"What's that supposed to be?" Nathaniel asks. "Some sort of metaphor?"

"Advice."

Nathaniel, perplexed, glances at his wife. She shrugs, equally puzzled. Then Michelle's arm rises. She extends her index finger toward the dirt road they had traveled on to reach the clearing.

Everyone turns to see what she is pointing at.

Thick plumes of coal-black smoke issue from the Fowlington mansion, coalescing into a large sooty cloud in the otherwise clear sky.

"The manor is on fire!" someone shouts.

While most of the family begin racing toward the residence, Nathaniel digs his cell phone from his blazer pocket and calls the local firehouse directly.

"Kai! Send your entire brigade here at once!"

As he manically reports what's happening, Nathaniel follows his people toward the conflagration, Isadora at his side keeping up with his frenzied pace.

Only Liam's grandmother stays behind, abandoned there in just her nightgown, the man's woolen coat having fallen from her shoulders to the ground. From the wheelchair, she keenly watches the now empty pyre, waiting for its glorious flames to ignite once more.

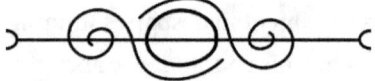

With everyone distracted by Liam's face-off with his folks, Doug managed to slip away from Liam and Michelle's botched reunion ceremony, returning to the manor house unnoticed.

Upon walking through the unlocked patio entrance, he saw the banged-up and bloodied corpses of the household help strewn across the floor. He long-stepped over the brain-oozing head of the chef as he approached the wrecked wet bar. Much of its stock had been broken and spilt, but he did uncover a half-dozen intact bottles of hard liquor. It wasn't enough.

Luckily, across the room there was an identical bar, its inventory wholly undamaged. He gathered all the high-proof spirits on the countertop, opening each one. Then, double fisting the bottles, he emptied them onto the furnishings throughout the grand hall, dousing the rugs on the floors, the curtains on the windows, and the paintings on the walls, until not another drop was left to pour on anything that looked even remotely flammable.

Doug chucked the last bottle he'd emptied into the fireplace, where it shattered satisfyingly against the stone. On the mantle he found a goose-necked log lighter. Beginning with the curtains, he then used the gadget to kindle as many of the alcohol-saturated items as he was able to, until the fire took over for him. The heat soared as the flames swiftly spread to adjacent unsaturated areas, engulfing the entire grand hall in only a few short minutes.

Burn, baby, burn.

He watched the growing inferno for a while, reveling in the incineration of this hellhole, until he heard the sizzling of eyebrows and the creaking of wooden beams above him.

Exiting the same way he'd entered, Doug now stands on the patio. He sees the congregants of the ceremony in the distance, hurrying up the dirt road toward the house. Gonna try to put out the fire, no doubt. But it'll be too late. By the time the firefighters arrive, the blaze will have already claimed much of the Fowlingtons' home. The family can sort through the rubble and remains later. They might even recover something precious or priceless that had been spared from the flames. But it would always stink like this day, the day it all went to shit.

Good.

Doug hears the clink of ice cubes in a glass. He looks around the patio and spots Aldrich Bukani, still in his smoking jacket, cargo shorts, and Crocs. He's reclined in a chaise longue, sipping a piña colada garnished with a pineapple wedge, a maraschino cherry, and a yellow paper parasol.

"Bravo, Mr. Cunningham," he says, raising his glass in toast. "Or should I call you *Miss*?"

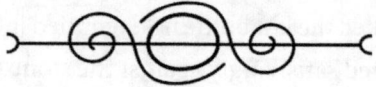

Doug discovered taking control of a living person wasn't so hard. He just had to fill the same space as Bethany Fowlington and suppress the thoughts in her mind with his own, like drowning out someone's awful music with what you would rather hear. There was some getting used to her unfamiliar and ungainly body—he needed to adjust his normal premortem posture to compensate for her top-heaviness—but the fundamental mechanics of movement were no different than if he were still commanding his own body. (He can't, however, arrest her Tourette's facial tics, which is annoying but bearable.)

"I don't care much for the pyrotechnics," Bukani continues blithely. "But your flair for the theatrical certainly brings down the house."

"You're not mad about this?" Doug asks in Bethany's voice, which he finds far less disconcerting than he should. He points Bethany's thumb toward the raging fire behind him. He hardly notices the smoke rising from the seared hem of her black A-line dress. Nor does he feel the patches of flesh on her arms and hands that have turned a deep, angry red.

"Not at all," Bukani replies. "It's simply a domicile. No more than a material thing. Means nothing to me nowadays. But you, Doug, have been a very interesting subject to observe."

Bukani takes a draw on the pink straw of his piña colada and smacks his lips.

"Pity I cannot taste this. But I do relish imagining the taste of it. Truth be told, I never drank one of these when I was alive. They are from after my time and a place I've never been. But they do look fun and refreshing, don't they?"

Through Bethany's watery eyes, Doug gazes out at the forest in the distance. "Do you know where Michelle is?"

"Not precisely. But she is no longer on the pyre, if that's any comfort to you."

"So she's not in danger anymore?"

"From the Fowlingtons? Unlikely." Bukani sets his cocktail down on the side table next to him, where it instantly disappears. "Their rituals abide by a strict set of rules, and they missed their window of opportunity for this one. Not their finest showing."

"I did it then," Doug mutters to himself. "I saved her."

"Huzzah! You're a hero, Douglas!" Bukani japes. "I must get your autograph."

Doug has another thousand questions for the ghost captain, foremost being *What now?* But that's not what he asks next.

"Why did you call me an interesting subject?"

"Because with little knowledge or faith in our beliefs," Bukani answers, "you still were able to apply the laws of our realm with some skill. It's quite impressive."

"Is that why you showed me how Liam died and all of that? It was, like, an experiment for you?"

Bukani shrugs. "Ever the inveterate scientist, even beyond the veil."

Doug again peers up the dirt footpath. The Fowlington family members have reached the halfway point between the edge of the forest and the mansion. They remind him of a gaggle of agitated geese racing to save their communal nest.

His nest now too, Doug supposes. That he just set on fire. He wonders if the Fowlington spirits will be miffed at him for that, give him the cold shoulder. Might be a lonely afterlife for him.

"Guess I'm gonna be stuck here forever like you," he laments to Bukani.

"Don't be so presumptuous," Bukani scoffs. "You're not on our team, so you're not bound by our rulebook."

Doug shoots him a quizzical look. "What does that mean?"

"You're not of our blood. Hence our curse"—Bukani's hands make air quotes when he says *curse*—"doesn't necessarily apply to you. Mind you, it is still only a theory, but I suspect you are, in a very literal sense, a free spirit."

"Free… like—"

"Like a bird," Bukani warbles.

"So then… I can just…" Doug makes a walking gesture with his fingers.

"As I said, theoretically it's possible. But then—" The old man shrugs. "You're just as likely to bump into the same invisible wall that confines me here."

"Huh? What?" Bethany says, disoriented and delirious.

"Oh… he's already gone." Bukani sighs, then rematerializes another piña colada in his hand as he stays for the rest of this unfolding family drama, a favorite diversion of his for centuries.

Bethany hears people shouting her name, among other words she cannot quite make out. She sees her relatives charging toward her a little ways up the footpath, some of them pointing at her… or maybe behind her?

She turns around and gasps.

Through the patio windows, Bethany witnesses the grand hall enveloped in billowy waves of orange-yellow flame, hell-bent on razing the only home and holy sanctum she has ever known.

Her eyes refocus, and she now perceives her sharp reflection in the glass. All her beautiful auburn hair has shriveled up, leaving bristly umber blotches marbling her hot pink scalp. The broiled skin of her face glows like a stoplight at night. One of her new triple-D breasts appears to have deflated, the intense heat perhaps causing it to burst.

Then she feels terrible, multi-barbed pain raking across her chest, head, arms, and legs all at once. She falls onto her hands and knees. Her screams echo off the expensive flagstones back at her.

TWELVE

Michelle just wants to go home.

After Liam departed her body while members of his family ran off like Tokyoites in a Godzilla movie, she slid off the stone pyre and started shambling in the opposite direction of the manor house, deeper into the bordering woods.

With no clue where she is heading, she figures she'll just keep going until she stumbles upon a public road or, better yet, a town. At one point she hears sirens not far off, but back from where she came, so they were of no help guiding her to any Fowlington-free zone. She presses on. Her bone-weary body craves to lie down on the ground, on the welcoming bed of decaying, bug-ridden forest detritus, and sleep for a few hours—or eons—but her instinct is telling her she must get the hell out of here ASAP if she wishes to survive. If she wants to live.

After several minutes of trekking through the woodland, she reaches the perimeter wall inside the estate, crowned with coiled razor wire entangled with the desiccated carcasses and skeletons of many small birds and a few squirrels. She follows the tall brick wall for a while, hoping to find a way out. Soon she discovers a solid iron door adorned with crisscrossing riveted stripes. On the left side is a large ring handle. She grips it and pulls. Predictably, it's locked, or maybe rusted shut.

As she's about to move on, she hears a crunchy metallic click. She faces the door again, tries its handle again. This time it opens easily, only its squeaky hinges conveying any further objection. She does not question what had disengaged the lock's tumblers; she just steps over the threshold into yet more deep, dense forest. But it's forest, Michelle presumes, that isn't owned by the Fowlingtons, so onward she gladly goes into this unknown territory, navigating the nature-made obstacle course of trees and thickets, hills and hollows.

She wonders if the Fowlingtons will hunt her down, whisk her back to their lair, and finish the abominable rite she's supposedly destined for.

I want to live, she tells herself again. Though she is no longer sure what she has to live for.

She knows Doug is dead. Liam had told her this when he was inside her, right before he gave her back to herself. Right before he said he was sorry.

Maybe one day she can forgive Liam. Maybe he even deserves to be forgiven.

But first she has to forgive herself, and that won't be for a long time, if ever.

Michelle's life has been a series of bad choices, most of them culminating in surrendering to her destructive desires. More than once they almost killed her. Probably would've been better if they had.

She knows for certain Doug would still be alive without her. Maybe Liam too. All the people she has ever loved wind up worse off for associating with her. It's inevitable, part of the cycle of addiction, perhaps the only thing in this world she can have faith in. She wouldn't even trust herself to take care of Doug's dog, as much as she wishes she could. It's the least she can do for him, but it's still too much for her. Her dad would keep Rocket, she thinks, but how would she explain everything to him? To everybody?

She doesn't want to go home anymore. Doesn't want to face her father, tell him she fucked up (though he would be able to tell without her saying a word). She can already hear his disappointed voice: "*Again*, Michelle?"

She feels sick with thirst, a thirst she recalls fearfully... and fondly. She retains only a faint memory of the drinks she had at the Fowlingtons, but the taste of it still lingers on her tongue, as tempting as a warm fire on a cold night.

Again, Michelle?

Yes, again, and probably again and again and again.

Because *that* is her true destiny, she concludes, where all paths lead and collide.

After trudging an hour or two through woodland that never seems to end, Michelle hears the rich-timbre tolling of bells in the near distance. She steers herself toward them.

Michelle spots the tapered white steeple first, a simple white cross planted at its peak. She emerges from the murky woods into a green pasture where a simple white church stands, the kind you encounter in those quaint rural villages you stop at to get gas and maybe a bite to eat while en route to someplace more exciting.

Right now, there's no place she'd rather be.

A rectangular letterboard sign mounted by the entrance reads *Good Seed Fellowship Church* and "ALL R WELCOME!" On one side of the building is a small cemetery populated by about three dozen graying tombstones, some laid with cut flowers of varying freshness. On the other side is a deserted playground with a metal slide, a swing set, monkey bars, and a trio of cartoonish spring rider animals.

Michelle wonders if the church holds AA meetings.

She knows she really needs one now.

With sanguine anticipation, she takes several resolute steps toward the building, as if she were on the grueling final leg of a race she never wanted to enter but has to win. She can visualize the space within: an austere meeting room with plastic folding chairs stacked in a corner, maybe a long table in the middle with pitchers of water on it, and a wooden podium where people can introduce themselves and share their successes or setbacks.

Hi, my name is Michelle, and I'm a fuck-up.

Before reaching the church's doors, her pace slows to a plod as a crushing lethargy overcomes her. Suddenly she feels terribly drained—physically, mentally, spiritually—as if she has been un-plugged. Powering down.

She's just so fucking tired of it all.

Michelle doesn't want to go in the church anymore. Doesn't want to deal with this *again*, destiny or not.

Instead, she veers right to enter the playground. She lurches toward the spring rider animals and settles down on one, a black-and-white ostrich with big brown eyes and wearing a saddle. She gently rocks on it for a while, until its metallic squeaking becomes too grating on her ears.

She quits rocking and sits there, thinking about nothing.

She hears the creak of the spring animal next to her, a smiling elephant, also wearing a saddle. She glances at it, then looks away.

"I don't think I can do this anymore," Michelle says listlessly.

"Yes, you can," a familiar voice answers her. "You've done it before."

Michelle shakes her head. "It's not that easy. Never has been for me."

"No, it hasn't. But hey, you have always chosen sobriety over surrender. Lifting yourself rather than losing yourself."

"I don't think that's true this time."

"Then why did you want to get away from the Fowlingtons so badly? Why go searching for help?"

She shrugs. "Force of habit, I guess."

"The desire to live is a good habit."

"There's a point," Michelle sighs, "when you just have to get off this merry-go-round."

"And when do you think that is?"

She snickers. "When life stops being merry."

He doesn't respond. Just when she thinks he's gone, his voice breaks the lull: "*Nothing gold can stay.*"

She glances at him. "That's right."

"But you can always bloom again, Mish. You just have to still want to feel the sunshine."

"Why should I want that?"

"Because it feels good. And if that isn't enough, it'll make me happy to see you happy."

Michelle sniffles. "I'm sorry."

"I know you are."

"I wish you were still here."

"I'll always be here," Doug replies. "For as long as you need me."

A warm tear trickles down her cheek. She tries to say something else, something she means with all her heart, something she has never told him (but wanted to), yet the words once again catch in her throat. Because those three words—the same ones she has said before to her mother and to Liam—now feel like a goodbye to her, and she doesn't want to say goodbye to Doug.

"Miss," says a different voice next to her. "Are you okay?"

Michelle turns her head. Doug no longer straddles the spring elephant. Beside her now stands a middle-aged woman with short brunette hair and plump rosy cheeks, wearing black slacks, penny loafers, and a cream-colored knit shawl draped over a charcoal gray button-down shirt. Gracing her neck is a white clerical collar, a silver crucifix pendant swooped beneath it.

"Huh?" Michelle responds.

"Are you okay?" the woman asks her again.

"Yeah. I'm fine." Michelle wipes the wet from her face with her hand. "I'm just… lost."

The woman regards her for a moment before asking, "What's your name, sweetie?"

"Michelle."

"Hi Michelle. I'm Dawn, the pastor of this church. Perhaps I can be of assistance?"

Michelle looks up at her. The pastor projects a heartfelt sincerity, unconditional compassion, righteous benevolence.

Michelle believes Dawn would be happy to help her in any way she could; Michelle's just not sure how she can. She musters a weak smile in response.

Dawn's smile is much broader and brighter. "Why don't you come inside with me?" she says, presenting a beckoning hand. "I'll fix us some tea, and then we'll figure out where you're meant to be."

Michelle nods and dismounts the spring ostrich. She walks alongside the pastor in the noonday sun toward the church doors, ready to let a higher power light her way.

"God grant me the serenity
To accept the things I cannot change,
The courage to change the things I can,
And the wisdom to know the difference."

–Serenity Prayer

If you are affected by a family member or friend's drinking or drug problem, you can get advice and find support by visiting Al-Anon at **al-anon.org** or Nar-Anon at **nar-anon.org**.

If you enjoyed this book, please support the author by posting a review on Amazon, Goodreads, your personal blog and/or social media pages.

Thanks for reading.

ACKNOWLEDGEMENTS

I would like to express my deep appreciation and gratitude to my amazing wife Emily; my amazing editor Beckie McDowell; my not-quite-as-amazing-but-still-dang-awesome beta readers Russ Colchamiro, Daniel Calvisi, and T.M. Becker; Edward Swing, Joe Gallagher, Jason Abofsky, Caroline Miller, Aaron Roth, Sydney Wedbush, Suzanne Forest, Thomas North, Lori Wilkey, and the other motley members of the Weird & Wondrous Writing group; and all the kind people, authors and readers alike, who I've met at the horror/sci-fi cons I've attended and vended at over these years. Your spirited support has made this writing journey one hell of a fun ride.

ABOUT THE AUTHOR

Sawney Hatton is an author, editor, and screenwriter who has long loved taking trips to the dark side.

Weaned on a steady diet of paranormal horror and creature features, he quickly developed an appetite for all things macabre and monstrous. With early literary influences as tonally disparate as Stephen King's *Pet Sematary*, Evelyn Waugh's *The Loved One*, and Marquis de Sade's *The 120 Days of Sodom*, he enjoys fusing the sinister with the satirical, the abominable with the absurd.

Other incarnations (reincarnations?) of Sawney have produced marketing videos, attended all-night film fests, and played the banjo and sousaphone (not at the same time).

As of this writing he is still very much alive.

Visit the author's website at
www.SawneyHatton.com

www.ingramcontent.com/pod-product-compliance
Lightning Source LLC
Chambersburg PA
CBHW070115120726
47909CB00002B/605